D1020874

TO
FILL A
YELLOW
HOUSE

TO FILL A YELLOW HOUSE

SUSSIE ANIE

MARINER BOOKS

New York   Boston

TO FILL A YELLOW HOUSE. Copyright © 2022 by Sussie Anie. All rights reserved. Printed in the United States of America. No part of this book may be used or reproduced in any manner whatsoever without written permission except in the case of brief quotations embodied in critical articles and reviews. For information, address HarperCollins Publishers, 195 Broadway, New York, NY 10007.

HarperCollins books may be purchased for educational, business, or sales promotional use. For information, please email the Special Markets Department at SPsales@harpercollins.com.

Originally published in the United Kingdom in 2022 by Phoenix Books, an imprint of The Orion Publishing Group Ltd.

FIRST U.S. EDITION

Library of Congress Cataloging-in-Publication Data has been applied for.

ISBN 978-0-06-308738-5

22 23 24 25 26   LSC   10 9 8 7 6 5 4 3 2 1

TO
FILL A
YELLOW
HOUSE

THE BOY

Summer 2008

I

The boy will live and die here: on this street that cuts the heart of town.

A quaint street by day: a corridor of boutique shops and higgledy-piggledy markets arranged over a bridge. The bridge rises, plateaus, and falls in so gentle an arc that until today, its incline was imperceivable to the boy. Here he comes, the newest boy in town, watching his shadow advance over a patchwork of paving slabs alongside his auntie's.

"Wait," the boy's auntie says.

The boy, named Kwasi, stops.

As he waits, he looks around. There, on the wall by the postbox, is a familiar poster. The poster is a recent addition to many of the shop windows on this street. It shows a cast of figures dancing and a smile of multicolored bunting hanging across a cloudless sky. The letters are too swirly to read, but their meaning is clear enough: something is going to happen here soon.

Ahead, shoppers flurry from the supermarket.

"Wait-wait," the boy's auntie says again. She is considering her shopping list, which she has written in blue ink

3

on the back of a receipt. This time, as he waits, the boy looks at his shoes. A crack has split the pavement where he stands and runs from there into the road. The road here is like the crust of a bread roll that has swollen and cracked. Traffic slows, approaching the scar of potholes, and one by one, vehicles hiccup over the fault.

The street slopes downhill ahead, where town is an array of glass fronts and awnings, from the liquor store to the chip shop: parks and churches, schools and homes, a small piece in the puzzle of London.

"Let's go," the boy's auntie says, and folds her list away. "Come."

They walk a little further before the boy's auntie stops again, this time by a sign: a blackened sign, between the newsagent's and the old cinema, that proclaims in bold letters, HIGH STREET. These words appear on several streets across the city, and more around the country; no street name is more common. Seeing these letters now, the boy understands: this busy street rests upon a bridge he cannot see, and he is standing at its highest point. Before reading these words, he assumed this place was called *Hi* Street, since everyone says hello: mums with strollers and grand-dads walking dogs.

His auntie—whom he has named Auntie Aha, for her staccato laughter—is saying hi to someone now, under the greengrocer's canopy. Kwasi stands still and listens. He is searching for a sound beneath the conversation, and beneath the noise of traffic, that might reveal what lies under the bridge on which town rests. He pictures a river of quicksand, a poisonous bog.

Auntie Aha glances his way, now her friend has gone inside. She picks up a coconut and shakes it.

"Hello," comes a familiar voice. Excitement prickles Kwasi's shoulders. Here is the Wednesday Woman, with her stroller. She comes to town by bus each week when the shop has African foods. She wears a long orange dress today that matches the ribbon in her baby's hair.

"How are you, Kwasi?" she asks. "*Ete sen?*"

"Fine, thank you," he says.

Auntie Aha returns, holding two garden eggs. Kwasi gets a gloomy feeling at the sight of those pale yellow eggs—he previously tried to hatch one, expecting a miniature garden to unfold from inside it. He kept it for some time before it rotted soft and Ma made him throw it away.

"Are you ready for school?" asks the Wednesday Woman. "I am sure you can't wait to make new friends."

"Yes, thank you," Kwasi says. He pulls his bravest smile.

"Ahaha. He will have his new uniform soon. Won't you?" Auntie Aha says. "Year two."

"Wow," the Wednesday Woman says. "Such a big boy."

The shopkeeper comes out behind them both. He asks if they want to see the yams.

"I'll come back," the Wednesday Woman says. She tells her baby to say bye, and as usual the baby says nothing, and off they go down the street.

"Let's see your plantain," Auntie Aha says. She follows the shopkeeper inside.

Kwasi slips away. He goes where his shadow, a stout, dark arrow, leads. Past the butcher's and the launderette. The ground here is speckled with pale purple gum stains. Weeds sprout between paving slabs—it is as though a forest is growing underneath, with trees covered in coarse leaves and berries big as beach balls. The crack at the top of the street could be where foliage is about to break through.

5

Kwasi backs into the felt coats that hang outside a shop. He covers his ears to mute the noise of passing cars, hoping to hear a river that runs beneath.

This much is clear to him: most settlements grow from water. On maps, capital cities balance on borders where green shading meets blue, or by fissures of turquoise. Where water gathers, life grows. He once kept a cup of water under his bed for so long that things grew, writhing, squiggly things. He had to throw that away too.

To listen better, Kwasi closes his eyes. Dadda said that losing one of the five senses sharpens the others. He holds his tongue still in the center of his mouth to untaste the lingering sweetness from the jelly beans he ate walking to town. It is tricky to forget a sweet taste. The juices of his mouth feel glittery. He bites his lip and imagines himself as one almighty ear.

Water has a language: gurgling and hissing that spreads under his skin and tickles the spaces in his throat that his voice can never fill. The sound of falling water usually means his bath is being drawn and Ma's shouts will follow. There is no sound of water here, only traffic and bicycle whistles, which, combined with muffled chitchat, melt to a gluey hush beneath his palm. Blood swishes in his ears, and there goes the *thunk*ing of his heart.

Kwasi glances down the street. Clusters of teenagers in puffed-up jackets and women in flapping scarves; joggers who huff by with music ticking from their headphones— there is no sign of Auntie Aha's tan coat, nor of the long umbrella she holds at her waist as though it is a sword. She must be paying for things inside the shop. Auntie Aha makes exploring town easy, for she takes her time talking to shopkeepers, and to cans and cartons upon shelves. "Not today, not you," she says. "But as for you, do you have lactose? You are really tempting me."

Unlike his other aunties, she won't fuss when he vanishes. When the church clock strikes five, they will meet at the bus stop to walk home.

A fence glints from the foliage. Kwasi approaches and grips a metal bar. If he can get to the other side he can climb down and see what flows beneath this bridge.

He scrambles up the railings and tips his weight over.

Should Auntie Aha ask where he went today, he might tell. But she will shake her head if he reveals that all of town lies on a bridge, and that he climbed over the fence and went below, to find a noiseless rush of river.

She will say he is telling stories; that as usual his imagination has carried him away.

★

Back home, he runs down the corridor to his room. Kicks off his trainers and slides paper from under his bed. Pencils have escaped his pouch and rolled away; he pats in the darkness and retrieves the blue, the green, the purple. Hunched on the floor, he fills a page with the river. The river he scribbles green, because the blue pencil is blunt and the sharpener is still missing. When the drawing is complete, he stands and peels the edge of his newest scene—the chestnut tree by the launderettes—from the wall and pulls some of the Blu Tack off to reuse. He takes more from behind the best picture, a self-portrait depicting his round head, the mouth set low over his chin, the mouth his aunties always pinch shut. He has drawn his nose as a circle there, and above it the eyes that stream through springtime.

7

Blu Tack in hand, Kwasi climbs onto his bed and onto the chest of drawers. Keeping steady, he stretches and presses the new drawing over the crack in the wallpaper. Then he sits on his bed and looks up at the four pictures: the river, the chestnut tree, the self-portrait, and a third drawing, of a man crayoned in tangerine and brown. Kwasi tells everyone it is Rambo, but really, it is Kwasi. It is the shadow inside him, a bright shadow crumpled up to fit.

After dinner, aunties come in for his laundry and choose from the wigs and uniforms they keep in his wardrobe. Auntie May steps in, talking on her phone: "Oh. Daabi. Oh no no. Yes. Please."

No one looks up at the wall where the secret river flows over a page.

When Kwasi has washed and put on his pajamas, Dadda hulks in and sucks the space away. He sits on the edge of Kwasi's bed and tells of a cunning spider's mischief, in his voice that shakes the walls. Ma appears in the doorway and watches with soft eyes. They tuck Kwasi into bed and instruct him to sleep well.

2

The uniform arrives in a cloudy plastic bag, announcing itself in crackles. Ma shakes the bag upside down and out tumble a white shirt and a pair of black trousers. A sweater: bright blue and soft on his fingers.

"Careful," Ma says. "Don't tear the tag."

Kwasi pulls the sweater over his face, looking through the little holes.

He zombie-runs from his room with his arms outstretched. He hops down the stairs and through the corridor, dodging and ducking aunties' hands. Outside, the sky's brilliance cuts through pores in the knitted blue. A new game: imagining how fish see.

"Let him play," Auntie May says, when Ma shouts for him to come and try on his trousers.

Auntie May gets it: these days are running out, hot blue-and-yellow days, when he has played every game twice and nothing remains but to coax an auntie to town where the people are. Something big is going to happen there, he can feel it, as clearly as he feels he will miss this newness soon, just as he misses Fridays at his best friend Tim's house, fish fingers, peas, and ketchup.

Kwasi tries to remember others from the old school, but they are orbs of light beyond his reach. Sometimes, before bed, he takes out his leaving card. Everyone drew their faces underneath their goodbyes, but none of the drawings are any good—everyone looks like ruined fruit. When Kwasi puts the card away, he prays to meet more friends like Tim. He prays that Ma will let him play outside and that schoolwork will be simpler here.

The months ahead are dense with shapes and sounds he must mimic until they are part of him. Already, he has to try. Meals may no longer be eaten on the floor, surrounded by crayons. If Kwasi perches in the wrong place to pick at his mountain of rice, he and his meal are lifted—typically by Squid, who he has named for her size, bigger than Dadda, with long arms and black and purple braids falling in ropes down her back—she carries him to the chair at the table, where the smell of polish comes up from Dadda's shoes underneath.

Tonight, when Kwasi is lifted, mouth full of velvety plantain mush, and deposited at the table, a knife and fork are thrust under his nose.

This is important, so he tries, a rehearsal for lunchtime at the new school. He tries hardest when Dadda is home, but Dadda's gaze is a spotlight, and knife and fork meet each other when they should be meeting food. The fork slips and clatters to the floor and then Ma comes and grabs his head and tells him to behave.

Tonight's meal will not end. The grilled fish watches him from the plate and its eye contains the world, towns and rivers and oceans.

"Finished?" Auntie Aha asks, though it is obvious he has not. She plants a cup of water by his plate.

He asks where a fish goes after he eats it.

Her dangly earrings chatter as she laughs.

Ma isn't amused. "Do you want to be the last person eating lunch at your new school too?"

He imagines the fish melting in his tummy and seeping into his blood, flowing into his eyes, making them stronger, so his eyes never need drops again. Strong enough to see underwater.

"Hello?" Ma says. "Why haven't you finished?"

"I don't like it. I like the fish that's crispy, the fish Tim's mum makes."

"That is not real fish. And it's not about what you like. When you do the right thing for long enough, you will enjoy it. If you want to do well at school, you need the correct fuel."

When Ma goes to put the vacuum cleaner away, Auntie Aha takes most of the fish onto her own plate. "Finish the rest," she says. "I want to hear you read before I go to work."

"Auntie." He prods a slice of carrot with his fork.

"What is it?"

"If they say I'm too slow at this school, will we have to move again?"

"Oh," Auntie Aha says. "Just try your best." She looks up at the doorway, where a patch of buttery yellow remains streaked against the white. Dadda stopped painting this morning and said this shade was too bright for a living room, although it looks fine on the front door. "It's a special place," Auntie Aha says, "isn't it? Our yellow house. Ahaha. We are all going to do our best." She moves his cup toward his bowl. "Drink up. I haven't seen you take one sip."

Drinking water, Kwasi can feel how tender his bones are

and how much he will have to eat to grow. Some sort of river waits inside him and makes his eyes give way to tears. He gulps the contents of his cup to wash the hurt out of his throat.

Another river spills at night. He goes to the toilet— twice—before curling in bed and pulling his duvet to his chin. There is no water left in him; even his mouth is dry and bright with mint. But when he wakes, in the bad hours of the night, damp has spread everywhere.

3

This yellow house—House Number Six—is barely two months theirs. On sunny mornings with the curtains in each room wide apart, it feels new and vacant. It is busier lately though; aunties keep arriving.

Five, seven, nine. They summon him as *boy,* and he calls them all Auntie. On Sundays they are happiest, spilling from sofas in perfumed dresses and slipping him toffees.

When Kwasi covers his face, they chide, "Stop this baby behavior. You don't have long before school starts. We are Black, and so we will be twice as good. Do you hear?"

Kwasi nods, though he feels trembly thinking about the new school. Everyone will know each other. The trembling is mostly in his arms, and when the washing machine runs, with his bedsheets spinning behind the clear door, the stairs tremble with him, like the house is nervous too.

Yet more aunties arrive, with glossy wigs and uniforms and new patterns of laughter. Kwasi takes care to notice how each woman sits, slouching or upright, and whether she crosses her legs. He pays attention to the motion of their hands while they talk. He is going to draw everyone before school starts. If more aunties keep coming, Dadda might even reinstate party nights, so they can play music and dance. Those nights were the best thing about the old house, apart from that one Sunday, the week after Ma made him leave school, when all the aunties got up and left and so many policemen arrived, tall and noisy with more voices speaking over radios, and after looking round the house, they talked quietly with Dadda.

After that, fewer aunties visited, only in pairs or threes. Kwasi asked if the policemen had come because of the trouble at his school.

"Don't worry," Dadda said. "It's not about your schooling."

Dadda must have fixed whatever happened, since more aunties are visiting again.

This new house has room for all. When Dadda pushed open the door of Number Six, it was clear how vast the house was. Its rooms were ripe with echoes; the ceilings bounced back Dadda's voice and the thuds of his steps. Sunlight streaked the floorboards, dripped off metal bones of chairs and door handles.

"Can we go to town with everyone," he asks Squid after dinner one Sunday, "to show the new aunties the park?" Squid, Auntie Aha, and Auntie May, who grabs him and tickles him sore if he looks at her too long, only these aunties will stay. They are Ma and Dadda's sisters. The others will move on soon, Ma says.

"We should show them everything before they go," he says.

"Another time," Squid says. "Why don't you draw something instead?"

He starts another new drawing, of aunties with the things they bring. Each auntie brings a suitcase and, soon after, a gift: a plant for the kitchen window, a photo frame, a deep saucepan. Cupboards and shelves fill with items from town. Almost every shop has contributed. Kwasi was present to witness most of the moments each item stopped belonging to town and became a part of Number Six.

Excitement bubbles inside when he thinks of it. Sometimes, it is almost enough excitement to cancel out the fear and the watery feeling he gets when he thinks of all he will have to learn. But at least there is this: if this new school is like the last, he will be asked on the first day to tell one thing he learned over summer. This summer, he has learned how homes are made.

*

There are still parts of the new house that he has hardly explored. This house has an *upstairs*, and one spare room where Dadda has set up his computer and left folders in a heap. Kwasi is not to enter that room. Another secret space is in Ma and Dadda's bedroom: a hiding place inside their wardrobe. Ma calls it a safe.

"What's inside?" Kwasi asked, on that first day.

Dadda said, "Boring grown-up papers."

When telling his classmates how this house became home, he will start from July, when they left the old house. Dadda drove the van, and the aunties rode in the back, enthroned on sofas. Kwasi sat on Ma's lap at the front. He tried to memorize the way, to notice the turns Dadda took and the buildings they passed, so that he could walk back later. He'd go to Tim's house to play.

He tried to memorize the way, but the drive went on and on. Dark buildings soared, and he could not see their tops even with his face pressed to the glass. And then the buildings gave way to a great river, a grim expanse that showed no trace of blue.

He tugged a handful of Ma's hair and, when she turned to him, asked, "What country is this now?"

Ma, prying her hair from his grip, assured him they were still in Britain, they would always be in Britain, but had crossed to North London.

He will tell his new class about the old house too, how big he felt there, with the walls close together and the rooms padded with bags. The yellow house, in the quiet after bedtime, holds its breath.

It will take a while to get used to having his own room, to the absence of snoring, of sheets tugging around him and the bed creaking. It will take more drawings to cover the walls here too, to make it feel all his.

When they first arrived, Kwasi led his aunties into almost every shop—even the ones with girls' clothes and mirrors. It is harder now that summer is running out, to get an auntie to take him to town, and although he knows the way, they won't let him go alone.

"Only bad children go out alone," they say. "They go when it is dark because they don't want people to see."

Dadda agrees that bad people operate under darkness. Ma says this town has fewer bad people than the last area they lived in, but that doesn't mean there are *no* bad people. Auntie May points out the man who sits on the corner by the church, who shouts and sometimes sings. The man looks as though he never bathes.

"Don't stare," Auntie May says. "You will provoke him if you stare."

Most people walk past that man as though he is not there. It gets easier to do each time.

There are bad places in town too: three shops no auntie will let him enter.

One: a shadowy hall where grown-ups sit or stand and drink, busiest on Sundays. Ma says bad people fill their stomachs with venom there.

The second shop is filled with pillars of colorful lights, screens that flash with shapes and words. People stand jabbing, tapping. Kwasi once wandered near, but Squid caught his arm.

The last shop is important. It does not look like trouble, even though it is the only shop of the three that does not even display that poster, with the bunting and people dancing in the street. This last shop is dainty. On windy days a breeze bubbles behind the blue banner at the front and it ripples. Too many letters crowd the banner, and it takes ages to muster the courage to try to say the word it spells.

Squid, who is with him the day he tries, snorts and laughs. "Emergency Relief," she says, and wipes her eyes. "Emergency. Say it."

He says nothing. He is in no mood to be mocked.

"You can call it the Chest. That is what people call it. The Chest of Small Wonders. There is nothing here for us. It's a very strange place."

The Chest stands shorter than its neighbors. The shop next door is shuttered. Lime-colored leaves creep up the building's seams; someone will open it one day, perhaps, and find a forest.

"Why is that shop a strange place?" he asks his aunties, but no one will explain.

"When you are older you will understand," they say.

As far as he can see through the glass front, the Chest looks huge, twice as wide as the chip shop, with vases and clocks and lamps and mirrors. Jewelry sparkles from a stand that is shaped like a wintry tree. Sunglasses watch from the shelf behind and everywhere in between are books. Books are squeezed on the ends of shelves, in boxes on the carpet, more books rest on the counter. There are clothes too, hanging limp from the walls. A spiral staircase leads down.

★

The first time Kwasi draws the Chest, it is raining outside. He sprawls on the sitting-room rug and draws the glass frontage. He scribbles lots of colors inside.

★

It is hard to know if his drawing is any good because this is a shop that rearranges itself. Collections of photo frames and scarves and vases grow and merge and disappear. Old people go in, with shocks of silver-white hair. Then well-dressed women with strollers, and teenagers holding hands.

New people staff the Chest each time he manages to see. Kwasi stands on his toes as he walks by, to see who is behind the counter, but the shopkeepers are often lost, hidden among the shelves.

The person most often behind the till is a tall, gray-haired man. The man wears a white collar under a charcoal sweater, and sharply creased trousers. He is almost as tall as Mr. Willis, who was the tallest teacher at Kwasi's old school and the reason why they had to leave. Mr. Willis argued with Ma at the school gates. Ma did not win.

"Schools here are trouble," she explained as they marched

home that day. "There is nothing wrong with you." She slowed, and her hand stroked his head. "They don't know anything. We'll move to Jericho's school. You miss Jericho, don't you?"

Kwasi could not remember Jericho. He got a bad feeling, down his back and arms. Ma went on and on about Jericho, how close they once were, and Kwasi wished she would stop. He hated to think that he could forget a boy who had once shared his bath and toys.

"Don't stare," Auntie May says now, about the shopkeeper in the Chest.

"Why?"

"Something terrible happened here. Come."

"What happened?"

Auntie May says nothing. She is watching the shop too.

The man in the shop goes down the stairs, and then all the women who work there gather by the till, talking and looking at a notepad that lies on the counter. The women keep glancing back toward the steps. Anticipation tingles in Kwasi: something is going to happen here.

"Let's go." Auntie May takes his hand. "We need tilapia."

*

There are so many new aunties now, who converse in escalating laughter and noise. Their languages are unfamiliar, but Kwasi knows the rhythms of their words. He hums the arpeggios of their sentences while he colors—his second attempt at the Chest, but on a foggy day so he doesn't have to detail what's inside.

He is finishing two portraits, as well: one of Auntie Aha wielding a sword, instead of her big umbrella, with a gem-studded hilt; another of Squid, so tall she fills the page, tapering down to tiny feet.

When Squid gets back from work, he presents her portrait to her.

"Thank you," Squid says, as she lies down on the three-person settee. She works at a restaurant and has brought plastic boxes of rice home with her. The freezer is crammed.

Auntie Aha kneads Squid's back with both fists.

"Such a nice drawing. Well done," Squid says.

Kwasi covers his face.

"Why are you hiding? You've done well, aha."

"If you want to do even better," Squid says, "see if you can walk on my back. Come on. Try and balance."

Kwasi climbs onto the sofa and from there onto Squid's back. He steadies himself against the cushions and eases his weight across his feet.

Applause fills the house.

Later, before sleeping, Kwasi studies all he has drawn this summer, the pages he keeps under his bed and others already displayed on the walls: aunties who have moved away, the prettiest shops in town, the park on sweltering afternoons.

The Chest of Small Wonders.

He gets a spooky feeling looking at it. There is no other shop in town like it, that seems to be alive, new every time he sees it, but also somehow old.

"Are you working hard for school?" comes Dadda's voice from the doorway. Dadda looks softer today. He is not wearing his shoes.

"I'm making a surprise," Kwasi says. He pushes the pages back under his bed, but Dadda is not looking.

Dadda is looking around the room, like he's forgotten how he arrived here. "Very nice," Dadda says. "Well done."

"I'm going to be really good this time," Kwasi says. "Then we won't have to move again."

"Oh Kwasi," Dadda says, in a voice that is hardly there. "You are already good. It was the school that was poor."

The house is still, waiting. There is only the faint hiss of the shower running next door.

"Not only the school, the area was bad. Now this place is better. The only problem is, we are not many at all, here. It may be just you and Jericho in your class. But if anyone tries to shame or threaten you, you make sure to stand your ground. Do you hear me?"

Kwasi wishes he had not heard. There is something new and firm in Dadda's voice, and in the hard glare of his eyes. "Yes, Dadda."

"Always fight back. You have as much right to be here as any of your peers. If not more. We worked very hard for you to be here. Fight. Understand?"

He hesitates. It could be a trick question. Dadda has never told him to fight.

"Do you understand?" Dadda asks again. "Don't take nonsense from anyone."

"Yes, Dadda."

Dadda looks suddenly sad. "Actually," he says. "Let me just." Dadda goes out to the landing and comes back with his briefcase. He rummages inside and pulls out a newspaper. "Look at this," he says, "a party for the last weekend of August. Uncle Obi will be there. Jericho's dad." Dadda presses the newspaper open. It is the poster Kwasi has seen all over town, the one with people dancing. The writing is different on this poster. There are so many tiny words, just looking at them hurts. "Let's work hard and then go and enjoy ourselves, shall we?"

Kwasi feels sunny inside, like he will never sleep.

4

THE SHOPKEEPER

No sound is so soothing as the rumble of boiling water after a long day. The volunteers' excitement has only intensified, and the shop rings with it, even now everyone has gone. It is palpable, as Rupert stands in the quiet of his basement. His fingers find the kettle's handle, which shudders with the water's gathering heat. Steam wisps from the spout. A pity that this kettle cannot sing. Jada used to whistle every time the old kettle got going, filling the basement with a horrendous discord. Never was anyone so terrible at matching pitches she heard, yet so determined to try.

More steam gushes up and he remembers too late to turn on the new fan, a steel column whose canopy reaches over the sink and stove. He has to squint to read the buttons, but still their labels make no sense.

The volunteers were excited about installing this fan. He tried to say it would be wasted here. He told them, "I don't see the need for it. I'm the only one who comes down here."

"It's just that the vents have done their time," Lizzie, self-appointed volunteer representative, said. "Things fall apart, don't they?"

The volunteers were already set on painting the back wall and replacing the washing machine, so he let them have their way, although every purchase, every additional cost, tilts the Chest toward bankruptcy. They had heard the Chest used to be spectacular, in a past era, with a reputation for unveiling astonishing and humorous displays, and that people used to come in not only for cheap paperbacks and budget clothing and pieces for their homes, but to stay a while, to read the guestbook and leave their own comments, to write about what was new in town. With sunshine in their voices, the volunteers promised improvement, put forth ideas imbued with optimism that had once been abundant here to the landlord, without consulting Rupert, negotiating more time to catch up on rent. They spoke of the future as though it was more than guaranteed. Lizzie even bought him this new kettle as a gift, a celebration.

Rupert climbs the stairs, taking care not to spill his tea, and settles in the armchair by the window display. There is a small crack in the bottom corner of the glass; he ought to fix it before winter. There is this feeling again, that he has missed out on so many small faults, before the volunteers joined him, that all the effort will be for nothing. Soon summer will end, and business will slow again. He will miss these long afternoons, when the street outside is heaving. There go the builders, to the liquor store no doubt. There goes the vicar's wife—Rupert starts to wave but she does not look up. It is dark in the shop and bright outside; perhaps she can't see him. Teenagers surge against the flow. Heading for the estate, most likely, where parties have raged all summer.

He sips. Sweet heat tingles down his throat, works down his chest like a gulp of light.

Mothers and children pass by, eating ice cream. Here comes that African woman again, in her long trench coat, and her sturdy umbrella. This time her son is at her side, not skipping all over the street. Still, the child stares as he passes.

Years ago, when Jada was here, a little girl came in and threw a tantrum, kicking and wailing and rolling, convinced the dollhouse in the window had been taken from her. Sometimes parents do that, quietly donate toys their children have outgrown. In this case, the mother was not guilty; the dollhouse had never belonged to the child. Nevertheless, Jada went and lifted it from the window display.

"It's been waiting here for you," she told the child, placing it on the counter before her. "And look, Mr. Rupert's given it a clean."

He takes another sip. He can't be giving things away for nothing anymore, and word of generosity spreads. This boy has gone by many times.

Here he is again, peering into the shop.

The child's eyes twinkle. Bright eyes in a cheerful round face. Rupert feels sorry then, for the sourness in him. Regret is a bruise in his chest. He tries to smile, but his mouth is full of tea.

5

The volunteers are definitely plotting something. Their ebullience has altered. They whisper among themselves all day, and keep glancing to check on where he is. He has too many helpers this summer. He doesn't remember taking most of them on.

September is coming, and some volunteers will return to work at the secondary school; others won't feel up to coming in when the weather deteriorates. They have helped more than enough; business could have stopped in June if not for their efforts, and when Councillor Obi comes by on his walks, with his little boy in tow, the volunteers are there to catch him in a web of chatter.

But now they loiter, gossiping, by the doors today, back early from lunch.

"I hope you ladies remember," Rupert says, "I am not a fan of surprises."

Lizzie removes her sunglasses. She has the same quietly gleeful look she had when she caught him mixing powders in the basement, in July.

"I thought this was just a wild rumor," she confessed,

when she found him. "I didn't think you actually used this stuff. Wow. So you add it to your tea?"

She wanted to know where he ordered his herbs from, how they made him feel, and did the landlord know? To which he replied: "Legal highs are just that—legal. Don't you have a pint now and again? If you don't like that I like them, write to your MP to raise it in Parliament."

"All right. I was just asking."

"Stress-alleviating, that's your answer. If you have more questions, go to the library and ask Jeeves."

He should have sent Lizzie away that day, for sneaking up on him in the basement. The basement is special. It contains the plans he drew with Jada, in the trunk her friends from America left. He will open that trunk some-day, once he gets a moment, when the volunteers let him be. Small jobs patching up the building are not what will save the Chest. One of these days he will do justice to the work Jada began.

"Let's hear it then. What's going on?" Rupert asks the volunteers now.

Lizzie clasps her hands over her dress. A decision is made between the women, without words. Their quiet gains a gravity. It will be further trouble that needs fixing. Perhaps the issue of the rent has not been resolved after all. The Chest could be wrenched away, and Lizzie will be the one to tell him, in her teaching-assistant voice.

"Okay, here it is," she says at last. "We've been invited to host a tea party. It's an exclusive late-afternoon tea for raffle winners at the Street Party."

A grim feeling passes over him. "The Street Party?"

"Friends of the High Street. We're designing tablecloths and napkins, and we could use the tea set in the basement. Marie is baking cupcakes and pastries."

The Street Party was a fine idea, until Councillor Obi got involved. First the article in the paper, where the councillor went on about how parties bring communities together, how every high street deserves a celebration. Now the party will be a rally for Obi's ideas for the borough. He will go on with that smile, which makes it hard for anyone to imagine that he could ever say no.

Regret moves through Rupert. He rubs his elbows. The shop feels hollow around him, all the spaces on the shelves, the deafening silence from below, where customers might have been enjoying cocktails, had Councillor Obi granted him the license to serve drinks.

"The last Saturday in August? I have plans for that day," he says.

"We know it falls on your wife's birthday, Rupert," Lizzie says. "We thought we could do a theme that celebrates her life. Our own celebration, separate from the Street Party." Lizzie looks to the other volunteers. "I've been told Jada would have loved a party here, and that she was involved with the Friends of the High Street."

"That was years ago. She stopped wasting her time with them quickly."

"We were going to tell you once it was arranged, we didn't want you to worry about the details. Here. Have a seat. I know it's a surprise."

He sinks onto the chair.

The volunteers stand around him. One goes to the window and flips the open sign over.

Rupert folds his arms, as if that could stop the regret

from seeping down through him, and stop the spreading sense that everything that matters has escaped his hold. It seems to be downhill wherever he turns. He is either giving ground or losing it, and it is impossible to know, for the contrition in their smiles, that these volunteers mean well. The underlying feeling persists, a sense that volunteers come hoping to simplify the Chest, reduce it to the kind of business that Jada would have hated.

"It would be nice. There are so many stories about how busy this place used to be," Lizzie says.

"And it would be separate from the Street Party?" Rupert asks. "Because it's an important day for me. And if the Street Party is going to turn into a veritable rally . . ."

"It's separate. Friends of the High Street specifically said Jada would have liked to do something here, alongside the festivities outside. We would like to celebrate Jada with you this year, Rupert." A hand alights on his shoulder.

"That's thoughtful, but really," he begins, but his throat closes.

"You were together for a long time, weren't you?"

He coughs. "She would have been sixty this year. Fifteen years since she passed."

"I've heard so much about Jada since I moved here," Lizzie says. "From some of the parents. She had a workshop she did at schools, didn't she?"

"Oh, she was full of ideas. I was always content to take things slowly, but Jada, she had so many dreams she wanted to share. She'd traveled, she was exploring Europe when we met. I always used to tell her, the world won't go away, we'll get to it in time."

"Think about it," Lizzie says.

He doesn't want to think about it, but it eats at him all

29

afternoon. It would be a change, to celebrate her life here with a full shop. Before Jada fell ill, birthdays were simpler to mark. She loved birthdays: as soon as the day was light, she crept about decorating the sitting room and eventually returned to bed to disturb him with a song on the boom box—Michael Jackson, Bee Gees, cheerful stuff he loathed. The smell of pancakes softened him, coaxed him out.

"Another year closer," he would say. Every year, twenty-five years. Each hangover settling heavier.

"I'll sleep on it," he says when evening comes. "I'm not impressed at all that you planned to keep this a surprise."

"Well, now you know," Lizzie says. She is by the door, bus pass in hand. "It could be special."

"We usually do something quiet. I do, I mean. Jada liked to spoil others but never wanted fuss herself." He looks back over the shop. Irritating as it is, he can't help but picture it, how they might arrange tables, what they might do to set the mood to host such a party. "We'd have to make room up here, move the trunks downstairs. And I suppose we could bring the benches up. Or we could find chairs. I'd have to tinker with the stereo. I don't know."

"We'll take care of everything," Lizzie says, with a small smile. "It'll be fun, bring more life to this place."

6

THE BOY

"It is a wonderful—and increasingly rare—privilege," Dadda says, looking up from his magazine, "to die within the vicinity of one's birth."

"What now? What do you mean?" Squid asks.

"Well. Am I wrong?" Dadda says.

The aunties erupt in disagreement.

Kwasi pushes his beans, with their eerie black eyes, to the edge of his plate. Something has changed over these past few days. Arguments last forever. He has no chance to say a thing when their discussions get noisy.

"That is the way it should be," Dadda says, the light reflecting bright blue off his glasses. "If a place is working properly, people should never need to move away."

"Ho. It is not true."

Ma hums agreement. "Some places, if you stay too long your mind will unravel from boredom."

"It's true," Auntie May says. "And if people don't leave their corner to go and find trouble, eventually trouble will find them. There is no single place where a person can live and die well."

"So many countries with different foods and you want

to live in one village." Ma gets up. "Ignore him." She gathers empty glasses and goes to the kitchen.

"All this movement," Dadda says. "You look at how so many Jamaicans have suffered in this country, because they have been scattered, removed from their land again and again."

The aunties respond with a chorus of dismay, shaking their heads.

"Oh no."

"That is not true."

Auntie May claps her hands. "Goodness."

"Honestly."

"Anyway," Dadda says. "You look. People who are fortunate enough to be settled are content; there is no need to be restless, no need to get up and wander."

"Get up and wander. Is that what you think happens?"

Kwasi presses the beans into mush with his spoon.

Dadda eases into quiet, now and again clearing his throat or turning the pages of his magazine.

"Are you still eating there, Kwasi?" Squid asks, without even looking his way. "Make sure you finish all the beans."

Kwasi finishes his mouthful hurriedly. "When we go to the Street Party," he asks, "can we get fish and chips?"

"We will have to see," Dadda says. Work is busy-busy, he explains; they may have to do something fun on another day.

"Another day? You mean, we can't go to the party?"

Dadda looks up sharply. "Did I say that?" he asks. "I said wait and see."

Kwasi has the feeling, as he eats the last of his beans, that he does not want to see. Something awful is unfolding in Dadda's magazines and newspapers that makes him gloomier each time he reads. Ma says the banks are collapsing, all over the country. It is hard to imagine a whole bank collapsing; the big Barclays on the high street is still standing okay. Ma says lots of people will soon have to find new jobs.

"Do you have a new job, Dadda?" Kwasi asks.

"A new old job for me," Dadda says. He puts his magazine on the table. "I am the Connector. We will help people find work. A recession is just a prolonged spell of poor weather. We keep moving, regardless."

"How do I draw a Connector?" Kwasi asks.

Dadda looks confused.

"If I want to draw a picture of you doing your job."

"What do you need to draw it for? You want to show your friends? Not everything is for showing. Not everything has to be shared; some things are just to stay inside this house."

Ma is back from the kitchen, in the doorway watching.

"Tell me," Dadda carries on, "are you excited for school? Not long before you start."

He is trying not to think about school. Thinking about the Street Party is nicer. It is only three days away.

After dinner, sprawled on the living-room floor, Kwasi presses his pencil to the page and draws a square. He draws a horizontal line that cuts that square in half, and more lines down and across, slicing it into rectangle tiles, then into a jigsaw of triangles and squares. He puts his pencil down and shuts his eyes, but the old house remains beyond reach.

Frowning, he turns the page and starts again. He draws round-edged rectangles of sofas and then stops. This sofa—whose warm leather skin he was looking forward to shading—was actually at an uncle's house.

33

"Kwasi," Squid calls from the corridor outside. "Are you still drawing? Come and help us get the beds ready. We need a strong young man to help."

Kwasi gets to his feet.

Each night, Squid drags mats from behind the wardrobe and he helps to unfold the bedding. Squid and Auntie Aha still sleep in his bedroom sometimes. They roll out a thin mat and lie together, with an empty duvet cover draped over the bolderous curves of their shoulders and hips. Kwasi holds himself awake, pinching his thigh under the sheets and biting his lip when drowsiness threatens, until their breathing falls into sync and their snores tear the darkness.

Just two sleeps before the Street Party, while he is looking through a comic in bed, a new auntie comes in. She is half as wide as the others, and her steps make no sound. Narrow feet poke out beneath the hem of her pink nightie. She rolls out her mat, which seems vast as a sea about her. Kneeling, she ties her braids into a bun, over which she knots a black cloth.

This auntie does not wish him a good night's sleep. Does not turn off the light. She folds into bed and pulls the sheets over her ears.

Kwasi gets up. He goes to the switch, stretches, and clicks it.

By day, the new auntie keeps to the kitchen, vanishing among thorny scents. Kwasi can't get near the kitchen without his eyes weeping. She sees him, looks away, and smiles.

"Does she speak?" Kwasi asks Ma.

"She doesn't speak English. She is from the village."

"How old is she?"

"Kwasi. We don't ask such questions."

He glances around to make sure she is not near.

"What should I call her?"

"Auntie Baby. She won't stay long," Ma says, and strokes his head. "Dadda is working hard. We are all doing our best, okay?"

"Is this for Dadda's new job?"

"Don't worry, Kwasi."

A car comes after dinner to take Auntie Baby to her job. Kwasi feels lucky to see her before she goes, for silver jewelry glitters on her collarbone and at her ears, her curly wig transforming her into a fairy queen.

In the morning, the day before the Street Party, Kwasi braves the kitchen again. Sizzling and roaring come from the stove, and Auntie Baby is leaning against the worktop, watching the pan's contents.

"I'm making this for school." He offers her his drawing and points to each scene in turn. There is Dadda, at work with his computer. There is Squid, stirring a pot in her restaurant. There is Auntie Aha, mopping in a big empty hall. There is Kwasi, standing beside a building labeled SCHOOL. He has drawn Auntie Baby last, in a box with nothing else. He offers her the page along with a pencil.

Auntie Baby puts her wooden spoon aside. She wipes her hands on her wrapper and looks closely at the page. She puts it, with the pencil, in her pocket.

Later, when everyone is getting ready, but no one will tell him why, Auntie Baby is nowhere to be found.

"I gave her my drawing. Is she coming back?" Kwasi asks.

"I don't know where she went," Ma says. "Maybe for a walk."

Aunties fill the bathroom, painting their faces with brushes and pencils. Black ink for their eyes; crimson, pink, violet for lips; and for their faces, powder that looks like Ovaltine, that smudges the walls and doors. Traces of their preparation will remain for days after. Aunties line their eyes and draw eyebrows where they really have none— Kwasi finds his sharpener here, repurposed for eye pencils. They spray floral mists that make his eyes tear up. The scent clings to the towels, to all that is soft.

"Auntie Baby has my drawing," Kwasi says, but no one is listening.

He goes to the front door and pulls it ajar. Cool air gushes over his hands and nips his chin and ears. He glances back, but his aunties remain huddled in the bathroom. Highlife music erupts from down the corridor. The walls ease. The house sways with sound.

Kwasi steps over the threshold. Cold seeps through his Scooby-Doo socks. Probably Auntie Baby has gone to town, to see how it looks at night. He could go after her. He could go and see if that shopkeeper is in the Chest, drinking tea and watching.

He peers into the night. Far ahead down the road, a tree detaches from the thicket. It stretches tall, and two branches unfold and hang at its sides like sinewy arms.

Kwasi glances back inside. The aunties are dancing silhouettes, hands flashing from the living-room doorway, shadows cast by skirts and hair.

The ground is plasticine-soft, and the door is heavy in his grip. The air is a second skin. He has read in books about trees coming to life, enchanted people emerging from trees they were trapped in.

Kwasi starts toward the street. His heel has just touched the pavement when the wind picks up. The door thuds shut behind.

Ahead, the tree rises, teetering closer. A second tree hobbles beside it. And then both are changed: they are not trees, but two figures, people heading his way.

Terror burns under his skin. He backs against the door. Knocks and beats until it swings open and he falls into Ma's skirt. A cloud of ginger and pepper and vanilla surrounds him. Shouts descend. From beyond comes the gravel of Dadda's voice.

"What is this?" Ma's palms clamp over Kwasi's ears. "What have you done?"

Words dry in his mouth. His eyes run and his shoulders shake.

Ma lets him go. "This child. Lord have mercy."

Squid takes him in her strong arms and lifts him. He is trembling, and tears stream down his cheeks.

"Sorry, sorry," Squid says. "Oh. Don't cry. It was supposed to be a surprise. That's why we didn't tell you. We are not going out this time—we have visitors."

"Jericho is coming," Auntie May says. "Jericho and his daddy. Open the door. Let's see if they are coming."

Soon, two guests sit on the three-man settee: one very tall man and his unsmiling son. Their scents—shoe polish and smoke—color the room.

Only when prompted by Squid does the son speak, to announce he is seven.

Kwasi sinks against Dadda's belly and says, "I'm seven and a quarter."

Dadda shakes with laughter.

"Big boys," Squid says. "Especially you, Jeri. Look at how you have grown."

The aunties are generous with such observations, but this time the boy before Kwasi really is colossal: chunky, inflated, like an uncle—only squat and compact. If Kwasi drew this boy he would do lots of circles: a snowman shaded deep brown. The boy is very dark but not as dark as he seemed outside.

"Big Jericho," says Auntie May.

"Jeri-Jeri."

"Jeri-co-co."

Jericho inclines his head as though deciding whether they are worth his time.

Aunties bring trays loaded with plantain chips, plump round doughnuts, and slices of cake. Fizzing malt is poured into glasses, and clinks sound as grown-ups touch glass to glass. Kwasi gets his own cup of malt—it's only half-filled and most of it is foam, which spits at his nose. As the foam dissolves, his reflection wavers on the drink's surface.

Dadda's leg jigs under him again and Kwasi looks up. All the room is watching. He was not listening and now they want something.

"Go on," Ma says. She has hesitated in the doorway. "Kwasi, speak up."

Dadda's knee bounces, bobs him up and down, up, down, up. He tastes spices from dinner.

"Tell us. What do you want to be?" Dadda asks.

Kwasi shrinks against Dadda's chest. It is hard to speak

38

with everyone looking. He covers his face. Jericho's dad is laughing: a deep rumble.

After the visitors leave, Kwasi is glad. He sits by Auntie Aha and pulls the excess of her patterned blanket over his lap.

"Kwasi-Kwasi." Auntie Aha meets his gaze with shining eyes. "All these weeks you have been saying, 'Take me to town, take me to town.' Today, town visited us." Jericho's dad is important, she explains. "Big King Obi. He has lived here longer than anyone. If anyone needs help, he is the one we call. Next time he talks to you, speak up."

Kwasi can't think of what to say. The sound of splattering water from upstairs spreads in the quiet. "I didn't know the answer, and everyone was looking."

"But this is the easiest question of all." She takes his hands in hers. "If someone asks what you want to be, say whatever you want. Anything. Even me, when I was growing up in Ghana, I could talk all day about what I aspired to do with my life. How much more so you, here, where you can really do anything? What do you want to be?"

Still, he can't put it in words. Dadda already explained that drawing pictures isn't a real job, that he will have to do something more.

"Anyway. It's time for your bath."

Dadda comes into his room after bath time, holding out his mobile phone.

"King Obi wants to talk. Here, take it. He will be at the party tomorrow. You will go with Jericho."

"Can't you come?"

"Kwasi, I have to work. Here, take the phone."

A thick sob is squeezing up inside his throat.

"Take it," Dadda says again.

The phone is lighter than it looks. Kwasi grips it with both hands. "Hello," he says.

"Young K. How are you doing?"

He wants to cover his face again, but it is impossible to hide with only a phone to speak into, and only his voice to give. Dadda turns away. He is looking at the drawing of the river under the bridge.

"Fine, thank you," he says. "Should I call you Uncle, or King?"

"Brilliant question. My title is Councillor."

"Okay."

"I'm also Lead Member for Community, so it's my job to make sure everyone feels welcome. How are you liking your new home? I heard you've been exploring the neighborhood."

He can see it now. Even though Dadda can't come to the party, tomorrow, with King Obi, is still going to be the best. King Obi will be able to take him to the Chest. He can make sure his drawing is just right, and then he can finish that piece and put it up on his wall.

"Are you there?"

"I'm here."

"Well, Jericho's excited to see you again tomorrow. And if you like, you can stay for a sleepover."

Kwasi looks across the room at Dadda, wondering if Jericho is hovering nearby too, with King Obi, listening to the other half of their conversation.

★

Auntie Baby returns at bedtime, and then takes forever in the bathroom.

When she emerges, and joins him in his room, she looks ready to go out again.

"Where did you go?" Kwasi asks. "Did you go to town?"

"Come," Auntie Baby says, sitting on the chair in front of the long mirror on his wardrobe. She's adjusting her wig, his favorite: a short mane of lustrous black coils.

He hops down from bed and joins her by the wardrobe.

"Hold." She gives him a little box of pretend nails, all colored in like strange petals.

"Hold." She gestures, and he presses the fake nail over her real nail. They wait as the glue dries. The house is quiet. Somewhere, in the toilet or sink, water gurgles.

"Hold." She produces another fake nail, for her thumb. He presses it firmly into place.

When all her nails are set, Auntie Baby faces the mirror. "Oh." She looks like she might cry.

"What happened?" he asks.

She gestures to the cases and makeup brushes on the cabinet behind her. Wiggles her fingers, dismayed. She has forgotten to powder her face.

"I can do it," Kwasi says, picking up the brush. "I'm good at coloring in." The brush is lighter than it looks. He dabs it in the tray of powder and glances at Auntie Baby.

"Kwasi." He thinks she's going to tell him off, but instead she smiles. She closes her eyes and tips her face up toward him.

7

THE SHOPKEEPER

It happens on the Friday, after he locks up at three. The volunteers have decorated the front door with a wreath of fresh flowers, and the smell is so intoxicating, it's hard to step away. It really brightens the shop. Since Jada passed, he usually only changes the front banner every six months or so, the morning after counting the votes, all the preferences people have marked for which charity the Chest will support next. Only then does he go out and hang a new name up. It could be another big charity next— the Poppy Appeal is always popular, they've supported Diabetes UK, Amnesty International, Samaritans; a local organization could also do well this time: the hospice, the children's disability center, the food bank. It is nice to discover what people choose to endorse, and jot it in his Black Book of Giving. It's interesting to see what the community cares for.

He could stay and speculate, breathing the perfume from these flowers, but there is work to tackle. The volunteers will help set up, see whether they still need more chairs, and settle what lighting to go with.

The Street Party will go on all day tomorrow, everyone

will be out enjoying the sun. Later, winners of the lucky draw will arrive for the tea party. The brass band will play in the car park outside, where a small gazebo will be raised early tomorrow, followed by speeches and photographs and food.

"I've had another thought," he says, back inside the Chest. Faces turn to him. New volunteers, lads who brought tables over from the school, someone's brother and someone's partner, here to help with heavy lifting. "We'll need a sign to show the loo is downstairs. Do we need a sign to say it's unisex? We might get someone in a chair. Might need to talk to Jack, see if we can direct people to use his toilets. Winners can bring three guests, so we're working with parties of four, maximum, but we want people to talk to each other. If we lay out larger tables—ah, but then we could only get five or six. How much room will the band need?"

"How about," Lizzie says, and leans her elbows on the counter, "you go out and take a walk. Just go out and enjoy the sun and don't think about the Street Party. Go home and put your feet up and come back tomorrow and see how you like what we've done? We can move things around in the morning."

"You know how I feel about surprises."

"It's not a surprise if we've told you to expect it. Please?"

"You're not sending me home to rest. I'm not yet sixty, you know. Plenty of years of work left in me."

"Rupert. We've got this. Go."

★

Kicked out of his own shop. He can't help but laugh. Stepping into the shade, he loosens his collar. It must be twenty-five degrees. If Jada were here, they would have enjoyed a walk, up through the park to the wilderness by the brook. It's been too long since he walked up this way, and now he wonders: How many of the other shopkeepers have moved on? Are there new regulars at the pub? Best to head for the park. The ice cream van might be around.

Music pours from passing cars, a golden retriever pants from the window of a Mini, its sunny mane tousled by wind.

The park stretches ahead, heaving with sunbathers, little ones splashing by the pond. The pond is no compensation for the lost river, but it glitters, and the ducks look pleased with themselves. He finds a quiet patch in the shadow of a chestnut tree and settles among the dandelions.

Now and again a dog trots close, sniffs about, and rushes off. He would do well to get a dog. He could keep one easily if he carries on like this. Keeping busy this summer has kept him sober and grounded. These past weeks planning for the party have been wonderful. A dog would give him an excuse to get out and about more. Perhaps he could get back into longer hikes.

There goes Jack-Not-Daniels from the pub, who waves and shouts hello. Rupert waves back. He loosens another button, sits back, and closes his eyes. This is it, the feeling he wakes up looking for, of feeling rooted at the center of a mighty flow, watching the world stream around him, the fleeting harmony that comes from brief alignments of so many shifting parts. Gratitude swells in him: the Chest is still afloat.

Underneath the chatter, the ice cream van chimes. With the delight of a schoolboy, he gets to his feet.

★

It is still busy when he heads back with ice cream and lollies for the volunteers in a plastic bag with ice from the corner shop. He walks down the avenues to sneak in through the back door; hopefully they've left it open, on a day like this.

It sounds as though they have. Laughter carries over the empty car park. A baritone voice emerges as he gets closer. He stops behind the bins and peers into the shop. It's Councillor Obi.

". . . mixes it at home and brings it here in sachets or tea bags."

A woman he cannot see replies, her words just out of earshot. He edges closer.

All are laughing now.

He reaches down and takes an ice cube from the bag. Closes his hand around it.

". . . can be useful, in a sober, sensible way. It really looks fantastic. You should be proud. It's going to be a wonderful day. As long as there are no extra ingredients in the teas."

"It's a shame. I thought he might have sought help. I know Drew spoke to him, Drew's had trouble with drink for years. It's not the same, but . . ."

"He's a functioning addict, that's the trouble. It's never quite bad enough."

"I will stay away, for the greater good," Councillor Obi says. "Maybe he'll thank us, when he's sobered up, and when this place is doing better. You're a godsend, ladies."

There it is at last: the end of summertime. He should have expected this. It shouldn't hurt this much, shouldn't press in his throat like this. People are what they are, he should not have tried to forget this; their impressions of him will never shift.

*

He goes into the post office. It is staffed by strangers. No one looks up. Which is fine, he only needs a sheet of paper, a pen, and an envelope. Once he has these, he walks back and sits on the brick wall by the pub.

His volunteers signed no contracts. He suggested drafting one back in May and they told him not to be silly.

He writes:

Dear Lizzie and friends,
It has been quite a summer with so many hands on deck. However, I have decided that the Chest of Small Wonders will move in a different direction this autumn. As such, volunteers will no longer be needed. Thank you for your service. Please rearrange the tables, return all items of furniture to their places, and leave the shop as you found it. I am sure you will enjoy the Street Party, and the rest of summer. Thank you for your work, and I wish you all the best.
Rupert

*

Walking back home, he presses the bag. Sure enough, the ice cream has melted. He could put it in the freezer when he gets home. He could eat it all, slowly, through these last days of sunshine.

But the bag is dribbling onto the street. He lifts the lid on a stranger's bin and throws the watery mess away.

8

THE BOY

"We are going to have a party, a *party*," Auntie May sings. "A *street* party."

The house is electric. Kwasi cannot stay still. With everyone coming to town at once, someone will be willing to buy cookies, Ribena, or even McDonald's. Pride flushes from Kwasi's shoulders to his toes: he will look back from the queue where he waits with an auntie to place their order and see the rest of the group, their bright dresses, all of them talking with fluttering hands and smiles, all of them his.

"Party-party-party," Squid sings.

"Let's go," Auntie May says. She grabs his hand.

The sun is white light high in the sky. Kwasi gallops ahead, over cracked paving slabs, until Squid bellows for him to wait. He stops, looks back at them. The Wednesday Woman has joined them, with some of her friends from out of town. Her baby won't stop laughing, waving its tiny hands.

Kwasi pats his pockets, which are stiff with two of his best drawings: one of the Emergency Relief shop front and another of how it might look inside. It helps to compare a drawing with the real thing up close, to get the colors right. So far, that's been the trickiest part. Even when he holds the pencil gently and shades in tentative strokes, the colors still seem too heavy.

The street has never been busier. Girls and boys run in bright T-shirts and shorts, sandals, in swimsuits. Mothers follow with sun hats and bags stuffed with towels. There are daddies wearing sunglasses and puppies straining on leads. None of the other groups are dressed in as much color as his aunties. He can feel other families watching, and perhaps they are looking for a grown-up man. If Dadda was here, their group would be perfect. Kwasi slows down as the street thickens with strangers. He reaches up and slips his hand into Squid's.

People step aside as the aunties advance. Something cold unfolds in Kwasi's chest but Squid does not seem to notice; she proceeds with purpose as the crowd streams around them. Kwasi squeezes Squid's hand and, without breaking stride, she squeezes back.

He used to believe his weightiest thoughts were bound to theirs, that they sensed his hunger before it arrived, that they knew when he was ready to cry and lifted him before he wailed. He felt their rhythms too, knew when they would sit all evening laughing, could guess what they were going to cook before smells rose from the kitchen. He knew the songs stirring within them before they opened their mouths and joined the chorus. Always one auntie tapped a beat or hummed some strip of melody and in the old house it spread. Without realizing, song worked through them all, made instruments of their palms and feet and voices, one hummed, another whistled, most sang, and their voices folded the refrain in harmony. Song filled the house, then faded. Kwasi always knew, in some way, which melody flowed beneath chatter and quiet.

Now, he must speak to be heard and reach to be felt. He squeezes Squid's fingertips again. She stops walking and hooks her hands under his shoulders and at last she lifts him up and perches him on her hip. He breathes the coconut fragrance of her hair. She made it shiny with coconut oil—this, she insists, is different from both coconut milk and coconut water, so Kwasi may not drink from the bottle she leaves by the bathroom mirror. Nor may he run his fingers through her braids and lick the flavor from his fingers.

"Here we are," Auntie May says. They have reached the highest point in town. Blue and green balloons are everywhere, and little triangular paper flags are strung on white ribbon from the lamppost to the bus stop. Bubbles are drifting closer, a flock of them, filmy and rainbow-colored. Kwasi reaches up and one bubble bursts on his fingertips. Squid jigs him higher.

Sunlight slants over tables spread with cups of hot sugared nuts. Auntie Aha is already ahead, negotiating with the vendor. She is always convincing shopkeepers that their prices are wrong.

There, by a candy-floss stall, surrounded by smartly dressed children, is King Obi. Everyone around him is illuminated. He rises, and his voice booms from deep below. Kwasi finds himself waiting to be seen, to be recognized. There is no sign of Jericho.

Squid lowers him until his shoes find hard ground.

"Here you go." Auntie Aha stoops and hands him a cup of nuts. "Don't eat it all."

"We can sit here," he says. "It's the best view from here."

They are at the highest point in town, in the middle of the street, and the view over the park will make a good drawing. "Look. Everyone else is stopping here."

The aunties spread blankets. The road has vanished beneath crowds, beneath mats and blankets and coats and deck chairs and families, opening into the park where the main stage is. King Obi stands surrounded by boys and girls; crowds approach from the bus stop. The bus itself turns and heads the wrong way.

Kwasi drinks the last nuts from his cup. He leans back on his hands, then turns over and lies on his stomach, peels back the blanket edge. Here it is: the long scar in the middle of the road, the point that shocks trucks and cars and slows cyclists down. He presses his fingers inside the buckled earth. He saw on the TV that there's fire inside the earth, far underneath.

Applause bursts from the crowd and Kwasi sits up to see. There are too many grown-ups walking, settling in clusters, like flowers dispersed over a field. And then Jericho appears. His face is painted yellow and purple and green, a butterfly or a clown.

Jericho skips down by the stalls and stops on the makeshift stage.

The aunties cheer. A bearded man rises beside Jericho, waving for quiet.

"Here it is: our first Street Party!" the bearded man says, and applause rises again. "When I started Friends of the High Street, this is what I said we needed. Young Jericho has done a great job designing some of our posters. Isn't he gifted? He's going to announce the raffle winners. You have about a minute to enter, if you haven't yet."

The aunties fuss. They rifle through their bags and call

over the teenager with the bucket. He accepts their change and tears off tickets with numbers printed on them.

"Hello, everyone." Jericho's voice carries through the speakers.

A cheer sweeps through the crowd. Kwasi gets that watery feeling, even though he is not sad. Something about Jericho's smile, which is on the big screen now as well, makes him feel silly. Everyone is watching Jericho. Even worse, it is becoming obvious now that King Obi is not going to join them, like Dadda suggested. They will have to share him with everyone, and listen to and watch him from afar.

More cheering startles him. Jericho is reading something, and some people are getting to their feet, clapping.

In the applause, nobody notices Kwasi stand and slink away.

Down the street he goes, ducking into shadows of shop canopies. At the Chest, he looks back. No one has followed him. He takes the first page from his pocket. Unfolds it and unfolds it again. He holds it up alongside the real shop. Way up in the sky, something mighty shifts. The colors are still too loud but the drawing is almost right. His skin tingles.

Shielding a section of the glass, Kwasi peers inside. Bookcases and mannequins obscure the shop. It's silent, without cars rumbling by. The doorbell is too high and the sign definitely says, in slanting, joined-up letters: *Closed*.

A wreath of flowers engulfs the sign, pink and yellow and white petals. If he knew their names, he would whisper them for luck. Tim's mum, who insisted he call her Grace and not auntie, would know their names. Grace had a chart on her big kitchen fridge that showed flowers and birds with their names.

"Every flower has two names," Grace said, when she found him staring at the fridge. Magnets covered it, and photos—Tim as a baby with inky eyes and no teeth—and a dark picture that Tim said was his brother or sister, who was getting ready to be born.

Kwasi pushes the door. To his delight and horror too, it opens.

It smells like house Number Six on day one: paint, pale colors, and space. Lemon and vanilla. He closes the door behind him and waits as his eyes adjust.

Arranged over the nearest shelves: a battalion of Russian dolls whose painted faces watch with biblical concern. Stuffed animals stare with beady eyes alongside little cars and trucks and a dollhouse: a mansion. He turns and finds a wall of books, colors and sizes messily arranged. There is a globe, and he goes to spin it.

Mannequin arms reach up from the shop's corners, as though frozen mid-dance by a witch. Their white hands sparkle with jewelry. The faces have no eyes drawn in.

This corner feels like standing in one of Ma's black-and-white films. Everything looks as though it arrived by accident, and the bracelets are all tangled. He reaches out for the scarves: some feel fluffy, and others slip between his fingers like water turned to cloth. There are cushions and candles and trays and bowls and, crowding the back window, a cluster of potted plants, surrounded by empty vases.

The counter is lower than it looked from outside. He climbs onto the chair. It has two cushions, one to sit on and another to lean back on. It spins like Dadda's office chair.

Kwasi grips the counter and pulls himself forward. He

gets the second drawing out from his pocket and opens it, smooths it on the counter. He drew the shop's insides as a blur of things, guessing. But the shelves fall in roughly the right places. Only the spiral stairs are missing, the twisty banister at the back right corner that leads down. Stairs are tricky.

Light wavers up from below. Kwasi pushes back and tumbles off the chair. His drawing falls. Books slide off the counter and crash down; pens rain after them. A big box falls, coins spilling, flashing like so many wet eyes.

Torchlight blinds him. "Hey!" The voice is like the bark of a dog. The man comes from the staircase, keys jangling and glinting at his waist.

Kwasi squeezes past the chair. He falls through the door and lands palms-first on the pavement. Scrambles up and runs.

Only at the second bus stop does he slow. Panting, behind the shelter, he feels the weight of damp that's soaked his shorts. He puts his fingers in his mouth to stop himself from crying. The drawings. They are inside the shop.

A shadow falls over him.

"Kwasi." Firm hands squeeze under his armpits and swing him up high.

Kwasi shuts his eyes against the swooping view. The King holds him tighter. He moves in long strides, and Kwasi feels each footfall in his jaw.

"I know you like adventure. But you don't have to go on your own."

The dip-and-rise of King Obi's strides reminds Kwasi he is too far aboveground. He grips tighter, but his palms are slippery. Mums and boys and girls are everywhere, all Jericho's friends. If he could only disappear and have a second try at this. If only the scar in the high street would open wide and he could fall into the river below and disappear.

Everyone he will spend the next decade studying alongside, failing to befriend, hiding in toilets from, now meet him like this: carried by Jericho's dad, hiding his face.

9

THE SHOPKEEPER

Rupert backs against the bookstand. Gifts slide and clatter from shelves.

The kid has gone. The shop is his once more.

He goes to the door and lifts the sign. It definitely says closed. He lets it go and it knocks the glass. Outside, stragglers are meandering toward the noise of the Street Party, likely to catch the speeches and see the raffle draw.

Back at the till, the tin of pens and the suggestion box are fine. He'll have to bend and pick up the change from the donations box. Much is disturbed but nothing is missing.

He walks out between the bookcase and the mannequin, back down the steps. Takes a second for his eyes to adjust. At last, here is the kettle, the bottles and vials around it, ruby, jade, violet. He selects one, weighs its potential in his hand.

He fills his cup with steaming water. Adds a splash of color.

"Here we are." He sets his mug down. Selects another vial, dark green, his newest. "Happy birthday, Jada. Time's racing," he tells the empty chair. "And not because I'm having fun. Not at all." He fills her mug with hot water and syrups. "Our health," he says. He clinks their mugs.

Holds hers over the table's edge and tips a trickle onto the floor. The liquid glints between the dusty boards and seeps away. He imagines all the drinks he has poured her over the years, a river deep below.

★

Time does not fly, it falls, and Rupert plunges with it, through autumn and into Christmas. Spring. New aches bloom each time he wakes; his body conspires against him. Occasionally, he glimpses his reflection in surfaces, in the glass fronts of shut-up shops. How lean he has become. Some days his blood flows thick as glue and it's all he can do to heave himself upright and sip from his bedside flask.

On better days, he goes up to town and back, up the incline of the street and down once more, up from the basement and down again. A new underground station—something road or this-that hill—opens less than a mile away, and even the morning bus is upgraded to a double-decker beast that rattles up and down the street. A good thing; growth. Growth in spite of recession is nothing short of a wonder. But his strength and focus are waning. He is behind on paperwork again.

He opens and shuts the shop on a whim. Some days he stays behind the till barely two hours before his head clouds and he calls it a day. Outside, he finds boxes sodden with rain, bags pulled open by the homeless or torn by foxes. He finds his shutters sprayed with tags he cannot read, shapes in lime and pink.

Late one damp Friday in April, after Woolworths shuts for good, on his way to retrieve a box of books, Rupert misses a step, overbalances, and tumbles face-first down the stairs. Pain wracks his joints and slices his tendons.

A memory of Jada flares, a humid night downstairs, dreaming of what this shop could become. This little unit on the corner, facing the direction she swore town would grow in, a place for a bus stop, where people would be tempted in from waiting. Jada made it sound like all the world would come; they had only to get up, get ready, and open each day.

He grits his teeth, a sob swells in his throat, and he coughs. If he had not sent Lizzie and the others away last year, they might be around to help him now. He can see the look of startled concern that blanched Lizzie's face, from the last time she came to the Chest, after he turned the sign to *Closed* and refused to let her inside. She wanted to make her case for weeks after he sent her away; kept coming back asking to talk. And now at last she has moved on.

He presses the splintered step below, levers himself up onto his elbows. He feels along the wall, holds the ledge, and pulls himself up.

Time falls faster after the slip. In three months he is back, limping through the shop. He accepts a volunteer, Tulip: a precocious dark-haired teenager who apparently has nowhere better to spend the summer. She declines the allowance he offers.

They open regularly that summer, and Rupert tries to stay present, taking no more than one cup of ordinary green tea a day, for this is Tulip's first job. She's smart; he ought to show her what good work can be. Besides, it is only for a summer.

But Christmas arrives and gaudy lights cover everything in town and Tulip is still here. During the school term she works weekends.

"I appreciate your help," he tells her one night as they

lock up. "But your grades are important. Don't get stuck here and blame me."

"There are worse places to get stuck," she says.

He shakes his head. "Might not even be here next Christmas." This admission pinches something at his core. He is behind on tax payments. Dull work, maintenance, hassle upon which the shop relies.

How calm Tulip looks behind the till. Some days she draws the objects on display as still-life exercises, in a green schoolbook. "For art," she says, and tucks her black hair behind her ears.

She won't let him see.

Winter brings snow, the lowest temperatures since '82, and through the cold, Tulip comes faithfully in. Pipes burst in February, and damp bruises the walls. The neighboring shop, a narrow unit that was once a travel agent's, has been empty for months now; it is hemorrhaging water.

Tulip helps him strip the shop and repaint the walls with polka dots, lilac and green, carry white bookcases from below and paint them sunset yellow. Books wait in stacks as the paint dries. He shows Tulip Jada's plans in hardback notebooks, plans to make the Chest an emporium of affordable delights, to serve cocktails and teas in the basement.

At the start they were foolishly certain. "People fear anything new," Jada told him then. "We need to show them it's safe. We open our shop, get our license, and serve cocktails, but we don't say what our magical ingredients are. We can call them syrups—it's all the rage in Amsterdam. And when it takes off here, we'll be ready with recipes."

They might have got the license to serve Jada's beverages had Councillor Obi not interfered. He sensed crisis looming even before the recession; he took his role at the

Council far too seriously, scrutinizing businesses' trajectory. Psychoactive cocktails and teas were not part of his vision.

"It's basically alcohol," Rupert tried to explain to him. "Jada is a nutritionist. She studied chemistry. She knows how it all works, and it's perfectly safe."

"Rupert," Councillor Obi said. "Let's not open Pandora's box. The Chest is lovely as it is."

"Councillor Obi wouldn't have it," he tells Tulip now. "Legal highs are a gray area, not prohibited but not to be promoted, at least not for what they are. We still have a few drinks below. Spirits."

"Spirits?" The poor girl pales. "Oh, like alcohol. All I could think about was ghosts."

Inside, he wilts. She must have heard the stories then, the stories about him. About Jada's death. He had allowed himself to imagine that, given enough time, those who remembered would move away or forget, but Tulip's face makes it clear: his story has been told, again and again over dinner tables and school gates, at barbecues and over the telephone. He has become a strange and lonely man, a weirdo who may have drugged his wife to death; and worse, a mangled version of Jada suffers on in rumors people tell.

★

The year Tulip leaves for university, women from the church pour in. Chatty women, with Churchillian silhouettes, who accost shoppers and usher them in, trading treasures for news. They buy Rupert a teapot for his birthday, along with loose green leaves he will never use. They have misunderstood his attempt to explain that he likes his tea green; he prefers more potent herbs.

His new assistants seem, in a comforting way, oblivious

of Jada's interest in alternative highs, and her vision for the Chest, the cocktails she never got to serve. Instead, they have concerns about the state and trajectory of the shop.

"A dump," Elaine, a recent grandmother, laments. Her hair is a graying plume about her mousy face. "A fire hazard. All that clutter downstairs."

Laughter fills the shop again. And sure, some of it is at his expense, but it is better than silence for now. He spends Christmas with his new staff at their Anglican church, his company the only payment they will accept.

"You run a charity shop, Rupe," Elaine says. "No matter what you try to call it, that's what the Chest is, for now. You take donations and cast-offs, make them look wonderful, and give the bulk of what you raise to charity. Am I right or am I right? We'll not take from the needy."

He does not object. It is sweet that Elaine sees the charities they serve as one. The causes they have donated to are equal in her eyes.

That Christmas, Elaine gifts him a cane for his limp, a birch staff that parted the Red Sea in a Sunday School production of Moses. It is heavy beyond time.

He returns home after Christmas dinner full and silly and rather drunk. Twenty-ten is almost done. A full decade into the new century on his own. Sixteen years since Jada last held his hand. His reflection grimaces back from the mirror in his hallway, weathered and lined.

★

Elaine and her friends do not waste time. To reassure the landlord, they get to cleaning, reaching parts of the shop no one has touched in years. Behind the counter, he finds a folded page, a drawing that carries him back to the day after the summer party two years before, when someone left it in the Chest. One of the volunteers he had just dismissed, he thought at the time, although now he is not so sure. He remembers putting the drawing away, something to deal with later. The drawing is tender in a way that can't be looked at for too long. He presses it into a hardback poetry collection, to help smooth the creases away.

It hurts more than it should, knowing that someone took the time to sketch the shopfront, to capture it in the sunshine, under the old Emergency Relief banner. It takes him back further still, to '84, when he and Jada opened shop, the delicate optimism that once warmed this place.

A dash of purple and two droplets of emerald and time trickles backward. Moods are as much science as they are art. So Rupert recalibrates; he telephones the rakish Dr. Hyde to amend his prescription. He doubles his dosage. He has all extracts brought dried in unlabeled sachets.

In this way he retains a little of the peace from '84, and the optimism from autumn '91, when the Camden crowd visited, late nights after hours in the Chest. The Camden consciousness explorers. Adding color to his tea now, alone as he may be, opens the terrifying joy of the unknown, of diving backward and up, with Jada's warmth against him.

"*We* made it," Jada would whisper. Theirs: one second-hand bookshop, bar and café, charity shop, with a basement of armchairs and stools, beer mugs, glasses, candleholders, cupboards, cases and twenty-five years in each other's sight.

Cleaning is just the start. More maintenance is needed, but it is hard to stay present. Few things anchor him: small tragedies, departures, and losses. Deaths of people from before, people who stopped visiting after Jada passed. Warnings from the council, highlighting missed payments, ground him for a while. There is a screen that keeps him from the place where life unfolds.

He brews stronger highs to balance the lows. Two types of happiness: stimulants and depressants; the thrill of acceleration and the mellow bliss of unwinding. He has mastered mixtures to compress summers; muted, he leans at the counter watching strangers move between bookcases. Winters take more. He adds syrups to black coffee.

More deaths: Alice from the jeweler's passes, and her shop closes soon after. The twins from Manchester die. Marie, the French baker, dies. A death every other month in the new care home brings grieving relatives and friends to local pubs. Always someone there recommends donating to the Chest, and unwanted things come to rest with him.

Buildings, too, expire. Somewhere between 2012 and 2014 the Anglican church wilts and is sold over the bowed heads of its shrinking congregation. Chairs, piano, sofa, and stools arrive by van, though he clearly said no furniture. The nursery by the park closes, becomes a block of flats. Stuffed toys and dolls arrive in boxes, despite his attempts to explain: no one buys secondhand gifts—no matter how good their condition—for children anymore.

When the Old Tavern closes, he takes in glasses to add to his collection below the Chest. Jack-Not-Daniels joins him for a beer. "You should come to Cornwall," Jack says. He insists sea air is good for the heart. "You can still say hello to folk, without worrying they don't speak English. Are you still brewing your old 'perfectly legal' teas?"

"As long as they're legal. Kinder on my liver. I'd say you missed a trick, only serving alcohol all these years."

"I don't know, Rupert. At least with alcohol you know

exactly what you're getting. What about Cornwall? You must be getting on for retirement."

"There's more I want to do with this place."

"Is there now? Well. Let's drink to that."

It isn't a lie. Something binds him here, clearer by evening, the work he and Jada began, the space they could not name. He wonders how long potential can remain just that.

He gets so foggy-headed some days that he looks over the shop and can't comprehend what it wants to be, or who Elaine is, and how long she has been coming in and where the other churchwomen went and what people think when they walk in. He could be living the same eight minutes over and over. Each time the bus passes, it begins again.

And then time hesitates.

It is autumn 2015, and Ms. Reilly-Duffell has passed away, and the Chest gets its biggest replenishment yet. Rupert is exhausted just hearing about what's coming, over the phone in the morning. His toes are rubbed sore in his sturdy shoes, his trousers too loose about his waist and his collar too tight against his throat.

He visited her once or twice, many years ago. She was the iceberg sort, who kept her head down. A steady churchgoer and quiet charity enthusiast, who brought Quality Streets to pass around every council meeting; who lived, for thirty years, in the two-bedroom flat over the bookshop, whose hanging baskets poured vines and petals all year round. A woman so tentatively present that no one felt her absence until forty-nine days after she expired—in the bathtub, Elaine tells him, when she nudges the first box of Ms. Reilly-Duffell's possessions over the Chest's threshold. He leans his elbows on the counter.

"Imagine the smell." Elaine makes a face. Her cheeks

are rosy from the morning chill. She's left the door ajar. "Roger told me the council forced their way in—poor woman was months in arrears—housing officers found her. Place was a dump, a real hoarder." Elaine's silver mane bounces as she shakes her head and tuts.

He should have worn his walking boots. Cold air stings his shins and claws up his thighs. "Busy week ahead then," he says.

They share a smile, solidarity, then get to work, unpacking and sorting Ms. Reilly-Duffell's possessions, which trickle in all morning. By eleven, Rupert gives up on reminding Elaine to close the door. He takes his coat from the hook, works his arms through the sleeves, and buttons it to his chin, knots his scarf under his throat. At the door, he takes a nub of chalk from the bookshelf, raises his arm, and writes, in bold letters, on the hanging chalkboard sign: CLOSED UNTIL FURTHER NOTICE.

The influx of boxes culminates with a van-load of crates. Two men come in, carrying a black trunk between them. "To the back," one shouts.

"Should have brought the trolley."

They set boxes by the stairs and pass by again. "Easy, breakables," one worker tells the other, as they carry a crate in.

Rupert rubs his shoulder, sore just from watching. "We don't take furniture," he says.

They stack chairs and push them between the back bookcases. "We spoke to Elaine, she said it's not a problem."

A lamp, a set of mirrors, an electric fan, a rocking chair. Most of it is odd bits and pieces that look vaguely foreign—from travels, perhaps—whose value is gone with Ms. Reilly-Duffell, with the stories she lifted them from.

Outside, the sudden activity has drawn a small gathering.

Or perhaps it is Elaine who is creating something of a buzz, trying to make it seem as though something new is in the works.

Rupert walks away. He gets his pocketknife from the drawer beneath the counter and starts to cut the thick cardboard boxes open.

The day's light ebbs. He works in darkness for some time, and then lights a candle, another, three. He breathes cinnamon and ginger, like Christmas has come early, as he unboxes the gifts of Ms. Reilly-Duffell's passing. Shoes, barely worn, black, low-heeled, padded.

"It's a good haul," he says, when Elaine returns, for she looks like she needs to hear it. "Look at this." He holds up an ornate photo frame. He has seen it before, vaguely remembers Ms. Reilly-Duffell's living room, the smell of mothballs and Rich Tea biscuits.

"Look at that indeed. Must be worth a bit."

"Right you are," he says. "Plenty more. All empty."

"We can hang some of them up. It's been a while since we decorated."

He places the frame back into the box.

Elaine takes her leave, to pick evening discounts from Tesco and return to her grandchildren. He turns the light off when she goes. That will save a little money at least. The candles are burning low and shadows jump up the shop walls.

He could work through the night. There is plenty in these boxes. Halloween is close, so as well as arranging these new items, he ought to think about putting together a display. He'll need to walk around, ascertain where each item should sit. He might have to put up new shelves, move the bookcases, arrange the shoes around the mannequins. Inwardly, he smiles. Jada would have stayed up with him. With the shutters down they would have worked until sunrise.

Nocturnal transformations of the Chest once fascinated customers. People visited early to see the shop's new look—friends, and then friends of friends and more, amazed by how new a familiar space could become in mere hours. And what fun it was to go all out; how he loved the themed nights they planned, in order to shift specific goods: the pink giveaway in '91, to raise money for breast cancer research, the cozy-house giveaway in '94 raising money for the homeless: rugs and curtains and cushions and blankets and lampshades, the Chest pounding with house music until the council arrived.

Elaine will have a go at him if he stays. "It's not safe," she will say. She will remind him of the stabbing that happened five minutes away, outside the Chicken Palace. Not like he'll be a target; the kids are killing each other. This will not convince Elaine, who believes good people are fated to suffer in this life, as sure as water is to fall. Still, he stops unpacking.

The eight-o'clock bus stops outside and spills commuters.

A shadow falls outside: a rough sleeper, bedding down, or perhaps trying to get inside the unit next door. Next door seems to be their latest Shangri-la; voices echo from the other side of the wall some nights when Rupert sits in the basement, laughter and steady thumps. Sure enough, there is a barrage of pounding now, and then a brisk click from next door.

Books fall from the corner shelf. Startled, he reaches for

the knife. Tensed now, he looks around. The noise from next door is the only disturbance.

He straightens and steps around the mess.

One of the books, a second-edition hardback, is damaged—the block of pages inside are disconnected from the spine. He lifts it to study. Careful stitching might repair it. Pages have slid out from other books, yellowed pages fallen loose. Annoyance is heating up his blood. He gathers them and slots them back inside, pushes the book firmly onto the shelf. There from the pages of one coverless poetry collection has slipped a faintly creased page. Rupert takes it carefully.

The image: a picture. A pencil drawing, a colored-pencil—or even crayon—rendering of the Chest.

It's startling, how easily he can feel restored. The simmering inside has eased away, leaving something like serenity. He places the drawing on the countertop, underneath the edge of the guestbook, hopeful that when morning comes, this feeling will meet him here.

IO

THE BOY

It is silly to be so nervous about tomorrow night. He can't stop thinking about how much more experienced everyone else will be though, while this will be his first time out at Halloween, at the age of fourteen.

Thoughts spark off other thoughts. There is no way he can start tonight's homework. So he is sitting on his bed, ready when Da calls. The phone's screen flashes with a Ghanaian number, and inside, Kwasi backs away from the hurricane of excitement, from the feeling of being chosen for something important. It is obvious why Da is calling: Ma told him about Halloween and asked him to call; she is hanging around outside by the stairs.

"Hello?" The line is kind of bad, but it might be this phone, the spare mobile that has no internet or anything, the one he will be entrusted with tomorrow night. "Hello?" he says again. "Can you hear me?"

"Yes, yes. I'm here," comes Da's voice.

Kwasi shuffles back to his pillows and slouches back. Old Blu Tack marks are high up on the walls, like eyes on many blank faces blurred into one, watching him back.

"How is school?" Da asks.

Heaviness sinks inside him. Here is the same script they go through every month. He recites the answers, trying to vary his pitch to sound grateful, fine, good. Yes, thank you.

"Keep working hard, then," Da says. "I heard you went swimming today. Well done."

"Yeah." When he closes his eyes, he could be in the water even now. It will get more vivid at night, when he is actually tired, it is like his muscles miss being in the water, like they are dreaming of swimming again. Ma insisted on going swimming today. He swam extra fast, even swam backstroke, watching the ceiling, water lapping at his ears. Hopefully it let Ma see how strong he actually is, that she doesn't need to worry about him going out when it is dark. He remembers diving, watching others under the water, that kid Ismael, who he sometimes races and underwater-handstand-battles against, their somersault routine, another life that happens only through motion.

"Some day, you will be ready for the sea," Da says now.

"Yeah."

He probably could swim in the sea already; it can't be that difficult. Ma will never let him go near the sea unless he takes more swimming classes, so still he goes back and forth and back and forth, wondering how she will measure when he is good enough.

"You know," Da says, "I'm thinking about putting a pool in the house."

"Yeah." Ma mentioned it one evening, but only so Squid could laugh at it. Everyone seems to think this house Da is building in Ghana is a big joke, that he will give up on it soon, like he did with so many of his other business ideas. "A pool will be nice."

"The property market here is really coming up. It's very

exciting, you can feel it. And property is the best business to be in, Kwasi. It's a matter of legacy. You will understand it more as you grow."

"Yeah."

"For now, enjoy yourself and study hard."

"I will." For a second, worry pinches him, that Da will ask if he is in the top set for math yet. Thankfully though, Da goes on about sport instead.

"Swimming is fine, but you should try other sports, games that let you play as part of a team, you know?"

"Yeah."

"And I hear you are still drawing pictures? Why not spend that time playing with your peers? You should live in the real world."

"I know. I'll try for the football team again maybe."

"Good."

In the background of the call he can hear children's voices. Speaking Ga, maybe. The sound of it twists something in his chest, like a tap there is being tightened, so not even a drop will escape.

"Anyway. Have fun with your friends tomorrow. And don't do anything foolish."

"I won't."

"I will be back soon, for a visit."

Inside, his shadow-self threatens to rise. He catches it in time and keeps it from soaring. Da has been saying he will visit for years. It's dumb to get excited. "I know. Can't wait."

"We have almost finished with the house. If I am not here to watch everyone, people will just help themselves to the materials, you understand?"

"I know."

"Anyway. Make sure you have finished your homework. You do your work, and I will do mine. We will enjoy ourselves soon, okay?"

After the call, Ma's footsteps creak away, down the stairs. Maybe she has some reason to be nervous. He feels sick thinking of it, where he might be at this time tomorrow.

He gets up to pack his bag for the morning. There is the homework sheet for English, but now it's too late to try to finish it. He folds the sheet up and puts it away. And here is a letter from Mrs. Nibley that he was supposed to give to Ma. It lists all the homework he still owes and says it would be good for her to make sure that he is on top of things. He listens. All is quiet on the top floor. The only noise is from the TV downstairs, and one of the new aunties on the phone in the kitchen.

He goes out to the bathroom, leaving the door ajar for light, because the big light turns on the fan, which makes him nervous since it's so loud. He tears Mrs. Nibley's letter to tiny pieces, over the toilet bowl. He puts the lid down quietly, so that when he flushes, the noise is muffled.

Back in his room, he is not sure whether it is too early to text, since Ma gave him Jericho's number at dinnertime, to say something like, this is my number by the way, in case Jericho doesn't have it. Jericho will want to see his phone, and everyone will laugh at how old it is.

If he asks for Ma's other phone, which can go on the internet, she will remind him of the time when another student's mum called her, said he was harassing other kids. And then she found someone had made an account with his picture, his own name taken, that someone, one of Jericho's friends—they never found out who—was pretending to be him, saying stupid and hurtful things. He plugs the phone in to charge and goes to his door and listens. Sounds like an auntie is in the bathroom now. He sits on his bed. He will have to wait before taking his shower. The phone buzzes, and he feels it in his teeth. A message comes through from Jericho.

"Hey. It's Jericho. Get loads of sleep tonight yeah because tomorrow is going to be sick."

Smiling, he puts the phone under his pillow.

II

THE SHOPKEEPER

When he remembers this strange day it will be in terms of interruptions.

The first of which arrives at eight.

Rupert is reading back through the guestbook when she comes by. Her eyes meet his as she passes by the shopfront and she smiles, then in she comes, wearing a jogging suit and pristine white trainers. Her dark hair is gone, all of it, but it's her all right.

Tulip.

Every move makes a stranger of her, her poise: tall and lean. He has seen but not recognized her, the young woman running sporadically these past weeks. She was a teenager last time they spoke, when they worked together here.

"How are you?" she asks. Her eyes are heavy with concern. "I haven't seen you in ages. Wow, it's so different here. And downstairs? Can I look?"

He folds his arms. All the shop's warmth has gone since she opened the door. "What does the sign say? Or do they let you forget how to read once you make it to university?"

"Okay. I guess you're busy. When will you open?"

"When the sign says we are open."

She crosses her arms. "What if I have stuff to bring?"

"Bring it when we open."

"You haven't changed, Rupert," she says, the slope of her shoulders softening.

"Makes one of us." It sounds more bitter than he intended.

"I'll see you later."

There she goes, jogging away. If she's back from university for good, she should be looking for work, at some office in the city. That haircut will not help her.

He goes carefully down the stairs, running his hand along the brick wall.

The basement. Cobwebs and dust drift in the light like sparks, a fur of dust coats the furniture. Floor tiles have crumbled at their edges. From the lulls in traffic and between the clanking noise of trains comes a dripping sound of steady plops. He drags a shelving unit away from the wall. A good one, baroque, chipped mahogany varnished to the warm reddish hue of a chestnut. One of the shop's earliest pieces, from when he and Jada toyed with the idea of making a bookshop of it. He considers a narrow shelving case, which will fit neatly between mannequins.

Upstairs, he turns on the stereo. Frosty piano notes of John Lennon's "Jealous Guy" tinkle through the shop.

He unpacks paperbacks: an eclectic mix that will be hard to shift. He works them between thrillers and crime books. He goes back down to the basement, comes up cradling a mug of emerald tea. "Dancing Queen" jangles from the stereo. He can't help but hum along.

His second interruption is in the doorway.

"Jesus on a bike." He steadies himself against the brickwork. It's Councillor Obi, in a tremendous gray cloak.

78

"Rupert," he says. "Sorry to scare you."

Tea has splashed over the floor. Rupert puts his mug on the counter. Fumbles under the till for the remote control and jabs until the stereo's lights are extinguished.

"Really didn't mean to make you jump, although while I'm at it, Happy Halloween," Councillor Obi says. "How are you doing?" He is a bear of a man, despite his almost daily walks, out in all weathers, parading up and down, as if there's no work to do at the town hall. The shop seems too small with him here.

"Very busy." Rupert clears his throat. "We're closed today."

"I saw the sign. Good sign. Vintage."

"You're welcome to look around when we open." He turns back to Ms. Reilly-Duffell's books. "All our proceeds go to charity—to Shelter, until January."

"Wonderful. So is your vision for the Chest to be more like a straightforward charity shop?"

"That's not what I said."

"Ah. Still going down the business route?"

"Well, I have to eat."

"Indeed. And drink, and everything else."

"Can I help with anything, Councillor?"

Councillor Obi looks at the mug on the counter. "What's that you're having? Is that fruit tea? Mango, is that? I enjoy a nice infusion now and again."

"All teas are infusions," Rupert says. "Everyone is partial to an infusion of some kind."

"I tried hibiscus tea the other day. Very calming. Lowers blood pressure. We should have a cuppa. Lots to catch up on, big changes coming after Christmas."

"Is that so?"

"The consultation wrap-up is tomorrow night. Time to decide as a community what we want to see on our high street."

"Will the community be deciding on what to do about the empty unit next door? It's either the homeless or kids that get inside."

"Ah." Councillor Obi stretches his arms. He is almost two decades younger than Rupert, with the presence of someone who reached his full height very young. "That's a matter for Community Safety. I'll mention it at our next meeting.

"In the meantime . . . ," Councillor Obi takes a leaflet from his bundle and places it on the counter. "We've not officially launched just yet, but you might want to consider applying."

"A leaflet for a scheme before it's launched, in a shop before it's open. Great. I'll take a look. You have a good day."

At last, the man wishes him well and leaves. Rupert stands by the door.

The leaflet is about a shopfront improvement fund. Elaine will want to try. Councillor Obi is out of sight now, but there is no guessing how many other shopkeepers he has spoken to, making them believe they are the first.

The stillness of the Chest feels oppressive. Rupert puts on his jacket and goes outside.

The new café across the street is doing all right, judging from the bicycles chained at the front. People are out on early lunch breaks. Sun emerges from concrete-gray clouds and lights the frost on the path. Their steps have left glittering prints clustered at the bus stop. All the paths people take down the road are stamped in silver, to vanish as the day warms or be erased by nightfall.

A thump sounds behind him. A woman wearing a black headscarf has dropped a bulky plastic bag by the door. Her eyes flash an apology. She backs away toward the car park.

"Oi," Rupert calls. He has reported these visitors to the council for littering, for illegal dumping and he will do it again. They come from the large houses on the avenues, most of which are sublet. Newcomers make up those homes every few months; mattresses and broken chairs appear in the park and get dumped here.

The woman gestures toward the bags. She spreads her arms, and her palms open and close in exasperation. She turns and goes.

"Bloody hell," he mutters.

Halloween. Elaine wasn't keen on decorating last year; it is apparently satanic, American and compounding the obesity crisis. But there are plenty of horrors he could bring up from the basement for a display.

When Elaine arrives after lunch, she brings boxes of tea bags, washing powder, and detergent in her shopping trolley. "It's coming together. What do you reckon?" She explains that she bumped into Councillor Obi at the bus stop. "Here." She roots through her handbag and produces a leaflet. "We could do up the front."

He takes the leaflet and smoothens it on the counter. The same as the one he already has, titled: Funding for Business Innovation and Improvements.

"It's free money," Elaine says. "There'll be more information at the consultation. Down at the town hall. I'm not working tomorrow. I'll have time."

"It's a free world."

"We need to be there. I don't know what today's takings are, but last I saw we're not going to make Christmas rent."

He sits back down behind the till. "It's not great. I'll have to have a word with the landlord again."

"We need to do better. It's been like this for years, Rupe. With all the change coming, I wouldn't count on the landlord's pity this time. From what I've heard, plenty of developers are looking at this corner. I'm sure they will be at the town hall."

"They can look at our corner all they like. As long as we sort out rent, it is still ours. We can only focus on what we can control. More than enough to keep us busy."

"I know you have ideas for the place. We ought to speak to the councillors, see if we can get help. This could be our last chance to get back on course."

"You're welcome to go along and share your ideas. The Chest is run by the people, for the people, after all."

"I will. But if you come along, they'll know you're serious, that you're interested in making this work."

"I'm still here. I'd say that's proof enough."

"Right." She knots her scarf in a series of jerky tugs.

Regardless of Elaine's negativity, this is a night for celebration, so Rupert splashes violet into his coffee, a dash of whisky, and a capful of turquoise voltage. Vanilla from his silver flask too, natural and clean for balance. Its aromatic heat carries him back to '72, Camden before it fell, crashing at a squat and finding home in strangers' laughter, in shared drinks and smoke. He raises the cup to his lips.

Upstairs he puts the stereo on.

Out pours a blizzard of his adolescence: of rock and punk that carried him through Thatcher's years, a haze he emerged from with no plans or qualifications. Enter Jada. At a gig—a dreadful punk group in a cramped pub—they bonded over outrage at bad vocals, pressed together in a sea of jostling strangers, and spilled into the night knotted at the fingers.

Jada of San Diego, who brandished her background as an explanation, an excuse, a license. Never here to stay, she and her ephemeral friends existed in a realm of livid joy, wringing the flavor from their youth, before they were called back to wealthy families and to lives that had awaited them since their conception.

He closes his eyes, tips his head back, and twists. Music pries him open. His arms reach wide apart.

The sound of banging yanks him back.

A third interruption: a boy in a black mask is outside, smacking the door.

Rupert's heart plunges.

Thub thub thub. The boy's palms drum the door. His breath spreads as smoke around him. A dragon boy, whose eyes gleam black through the holes of his wool mask. Rupert looks more closely. The intensity of the boy's stare is not an attempt to scare—he is terrified.

Rupert wipes his hands on his trousers and unlocks the door and the boy tumbles in. Rupert shuts the door and backs against it. The boy peeks out from behind the bookcase, eyes wide in the mask's holes. His gaze flicks over Rupert, to the door behind. "Please," he says, an octave higher than expected. A masked quiver of a boy cocooned in a black puffer jacket.

Shaking now, Rupert goes to the door. Outside is empty darkness, cut by red and yellow lights that pulse across the street from the Chicken Palace.

Shouts carry up the street, and the boy flinches. More shouts and hooting: kids out having too much fun.

"All right." Rupert turns the key. "They can't be real monsters," he says. "No matter how good their costumes are." He stretches, and bolts the lock at the top of the door.

The boy does not appear amused. He stays still, shoulders hunched: a small boy—anywhere between ten and fourteen.

"Should I call someone? You want me to call your mu—'

The boy gives a severe look.

"Well." Heaviness seeps through Rupert's muscles again. He plods toward the staircase. "What will you be having, tea or coffee?"

12

THE BOY AND THE SHOPKEEPER

It's hot underneath the Chest. A low-ceilinged hideout. Smells like cinnamon and dirt. It is surreal that he is in here, like a nightmare has swallowed him. Inside the Chest, after all these years. It was the only place that looked open. A place his memory pressed smaller, thinned to a façade, so many times walking past, quickening his pace.

The shopkeeper goes to the sink and takes mugs and teaspoons from a cupboard beneath it. "Coffee, was it?"

"Yeah, please." He has never tried coffee, but it seems appropriate, possibly his only sensible choice tonight. His gums ache from the cold. His legs ache from boots and fists and falling on concrete.

"Thank you," he says, when the man puts the mug before him.

He lifts his face. The ceiling is darkness giving way to more darkness. He raises the mug. It is too hot, so he puts it down again.

"You'll want water," the man says, and fills a new mug from the tap.

Kwasi takes the mug of water in both hands and gulps.

"Is there someone I should call?" the man asks again.

"You don't know them? The people after you? They're not your friends?"

"No," he says. "And no." It was silly to think they could be his friends. He has avoided them for too long to expect better.

"You live around here then, do you?" The man is still at the sink, brewing more coffee.

"Maybe."

"Maybe." He adds to his coffee from a little silver flask. Inclines his head: Want to try?

The syrup makes the coffee taste like vanilla. The man pulls a chair up and they clink their mugs. This might be the strangest night ever.

The ground shudders and he jumps. "The Underground," the man says. "Carrying people to better places."

There is banging upstairs. The man puts his cup on the floor.

"No," Kwasi wants to say, but no sound will come.

"Better see what's going on," the man says, getting up.

Kwasi looks about, noting cupboards, shadows he could vanish into. But instead, when he gets up, he finds himself following the man. They creak up the stairs.

It is impossible to tell who is outside. They are one beast with many eyes and arms. They are all still wearing balaclavas, engulfed in the night's darkness. Shouting, waving. He can't even see if Jericho is with them. The man goes toward the glass.

"Don't," Kwasi says.

But the man walks on. Kwasi steps behind a bookcase. He doesn't see what happens next, but one minute they are jeering, clamoring, the next they scatter, melting into the night.

The man turns round and goes back to the stereo. "There I was thinking I'll have a quiet night, enjoy some music."

Kwasi wants to smile but can't. Pressure is sliding inside him. "Is there a toilet here?"

In the toilet, he washes his face. Tears have reddened his eyes. He splashes more water at them, puts the toilet lid down, and sits. There is the trembling again, another train going. If those trains ran through the night, he could run to the station and hide there. He is supposed to be staying at Selim's tonight. He can't go home yet.

"Everything all right?" the man calls.

He gets up and washes his face once more, then pulls the balaclava back on. The floor shudders again, but this time the sound is coming from upstairs.

Back above, he finds the man looking through a basket of cassettes.

"There's something special about these mixes, the sequencing," he says, without lifting his face. "My brothers put some of these together. A comprehensive collection from the seventies. It was just noise to me then, yowling vocals and drums. And then—and I remember this so clearly—on my thirteenth birthday I woke to David Bowie playing through the house, and it was like discovering a new sense."

Kwasi sits on the top step, the man by the stereo. The man won't stop talking, like maybe he is nervous or doesn't know what else to do. He explains about the first time he heard each song. Kwasi closes his eyes.

"You don't want me to call you a taxi?" is the first sentence that really hits.

Kwasi shakes his head.

"Right. I'm getting more water."

It's getting light outside. A pristine stillness has fallen over this place. Exhaustion is a spreading fog inside his head. "Can I have another coffee too?" he calls. "Please?"

A familiar song plays as the man goes down the stairs. Kwasi takes a book from the nearest shelf. It's super old, with a hard blank cover. An inscription is written on the inside page, something too slanted to decipher, the letters falling into each other. He turns the pages for a while, staring at the blocks of text, waiting for meaning to emerge.

The man returns with two coffees. "I don't have anything for you to eat."

"Not really hungry," he says. His stomach is a cold pit. "Thank you."

"Thank you too," the man says. "I haven't listened to this mix in a while. Those were good times. Now, where was I?"

The man tells about a show he snuck into with his brothers. The way he talks is kind of sad; it's like he has loads of stories he never got to tell anyone, so he can hardly stop speaking. But now exhaustion has caught up with Kwasi.

"You're falling asleep there," the man says.

Outside, it is bright. Ma will have left for work by now. "I think I'm good to go."

"Get out of here then, go on home," the man says.

Kwasi tumbles into the new day: a bat.

He flies home.

13

There was a time when he could nap in the basement, with no disturbances. This time, Tube trains startle him, and voices climb in the unit next door. Rupert comes up from the basement with a very strong coffee at ten. Outside, the street is erased by fog, a haze swallowing chimneys and streetlights. Cars emerge from the gloom and figures pass like apparitions.

Out from the fog rolls a shopping trolley. It comes squeaking and clanking over the white gasp of traffic's noise, loaded with cardboard boxes stacked high, pushed by gloved hands curled over the bar and a figure that is—from the dipping gait and stubbornly pointed chin—Tulip.

Rupert grabs his coat, puts it on, wincing from the aches in his limbs. He goes out to meet her.

"I have more," she calls. "Uni stuff." She is pushing the trolley as though it is a pram, with a plum-colored beanie pulled down to her eyebrows; from the nose down she is all scarves. Even her coat seems to be one thick scarf, pale gray folds winding around her. Her boots are beetle-black, working quick steps and counter balancing the cart's momentum.

"How much more? Why don't you get the car and drive everything up? Wait a minute and I'll come along."

She stops at the crossing and the boxes teeter forward. "I don't drive."

"I thought you had learned."

"I learned. Just not well enough to pass."

He pushes the door wide. The trolley squeaks in, the top box brushing the *Closed* sign.

"Everyone fails first time."

"By the time I'm ready and can afford insurance"—she unwinds her scarves and coat and bundles them—"driverless cars will be here."

He steps back and shuts the door. Leans his arms on the trolley.

"If you keep working for free you won't even be able to afford a trip down the street in a driverless car."

She turns the lights on and the shop blurs. It must be in his head, because she goes on talking. New aches knot down his back. He has not fallen asleep here in years. He pads back to the till and sinks onto his chair. Hopefully, he does not smell.

"Would that be okay?" says Tulip.

"Of course," he says, although he did not hear what she asked. Something about an art event.

"Eek. Okay. Wow. Thanks." She unloads the trolley, then swings it round and disappears.

He looks out. Teenagers are hanging out by the chicken shop across the road, a group of boys in tracksuits, their trainers snow-bright. They keep glancing back toward the Chest. He sits out of sight, looking toward the back doors, thinking, with some relief, whatever happened last night may not have been too serious; if those boys had really wanted to cause trouble, they could have tried the single-glazed window. He ought to get that replaced, should have sorted it years ago.

He is nudging a bookcase toward the door when Tulip returns. He leaves it to help her inside. She has brought a new trolley-load of boxes.

"You really had a ball at uni, then."

She gives a cryptic smile.

"How's your family? They don't want you keeping this?"

Her parents retired, she tells him. "They moved. They wanted sunshine. And to escape London."

"Sunshine. It was only a matter of time until your mother missed the Portuguese weather."

"Wow, Rupert. I guess so. Okay, maybe."

"So, you have to manage the house alone?"

She nods in a way that suggests she hardly believes it.

"Will you be sticking around? Commute from here every day? Or are you going to divvy the house up and rent it out?"

She slides away and goes winding scarves around mannequins and adjusting hats. He'll have to take it all down later, to run it through the washing machine.

"And then where would I live if I just rented the house out?" comes her voice from behind the piano. "Here? You know, they're going to put flats around here, luxury new-builds. Council plans leaked." Her voice trills up an octave and she says, "Prime location in the center of a vibrant community."

"Where did you see that?" It is a ridiculous idea. But at the same time it seems inevitable, another tilting that he has missed, more of this place sliding.

"Internet," she says.

"Luxury flats, what nonsense. Not with the mess next door."

"Who are they?" Tulip calls, coming out from her corner. "Next door? Is it actually a mess or is it just that they're living communally, so we have to call it a mess?" She approaches the counter, her gaze fixed on something there. "Oh whoa." She takes the pencil drawing of the shop in both hands, to look at it closely.

"I forgot about that," Rupert says. "I need to find a frame for it or put it somewhere safe before it disappears again. I lost it for a long time."

"Is this from the woman who passed away? Elaine said she had loads of frames."

"No, it's not. Here, let's have it." How odd, that he should feel so nervous, seeing her holding that drawing. "If you just leave it there. Thank you."

"Where is it from then?" There is tenderness in Tulip's gaze. He imagines in this moment, she sees what he sees in that picture. "Where's it from?" she asks again.

"I am afraid I don't know. Let's find a frame for it though, before I lose it again."

★

By six, exhaustion overtakes him. It's hard to keep his eyes open. He has managed to put most of the new things away and found a small wooden frame that now holds the drawing of the Chest. He places it on display by the till. And this is when Elaine arrives. "Are we going then?" she asks. She has had her hair permed and is wearing her Sunday coat, cream felt stitched with soft pink.

"Going where?"

"To the consultation thing," Tulip blurts. "Just to see."

"If we don't take part," Elaine says, "we'll have no right to complain about anything the council does next year."

A horn blares outside. Sirens wail and red-blue-red flashes over the bookcases and mannequins as a police car whizzes by. Rupert grips the counter. The sirens' cries shift key as the car races away. The sound rings on through his head. His whole body has been quietly braced for this, a consequence from last night. Something serious must have happened. All those rowdy boys.

"You don't have to stay all evening." Tulip's face is a plea.

"They always have tea and coffee," Elaine adds.

Too tired to argue, he takes his coat from the hook. Perhaps the councillors will say something about last night's trouble.

"Christmas lights will be up soon," Tulip says, as they start down the high street. "It will get busier, everyone will be out looking for gifts. I went to this market last year that was so adorable, they had these tiny . . ."

Wind and traffic drown the rest. Rupert feels adrift, floating past the bus stop and the crossing where commuters wait. People brush by, leaving snippets of conversation. They pass the empty unit where the Barclays was, toward the town hall's stern silhouette. A monument to brutalism repainted after a protest; now it is caked in determined white.

Today, colorful banners billow over the windows: "High Street Consultation," followed by instructions—in bubbles and wavy letters—"Have your say" and "Tell us what you think" and "You make it, so make it you."

Inside, wallpaper collages of photos display town as it used to be: black-and-white markets and terraced housing on the road over the bridge; here are old maps tacked with Post-its, sketches showing new housing blocks rising beside the Sainsbury's, new frontage for the market, pop-up stalls, and outdoor seating.

"Imagine curating all this." Tulip gestures at the displays. "Fun."

"At the taxpayer's expense," Rupert says. "I bet it's some consultant they've parachuted in to pay by the day."

"Let's not do this," Elaine says. "This isn't about your disagreements with the council. Let's be open-minded."

"A pity Councillor Obi wasn't open-minded enough to take Jada's ideas seriously."

"New chapter, Rupert," Elaine says.

They slow in the reception hall. Tables around the room's edges are covered in cups of tea and coffee and piled with leaflets.

"Employment is up ten percent," Tulip reads.

He can't help himself. "You would hope, since they're hiring everyone. What was it they wanted us to do?" He tries to remember Councillor Obi's proposal two, no, three years earlier, a particularly rough winter, when Jada's family were on his case again. He was behaving, sober and present. Councillor Obi shouldered in one afternoon and complimented him on his tie, the fragrances of his shop, then concluded with an employment proposition.

"Part-time Enterprise and Innovation Advisor." Elaine dabs the edges of her eyes with her handkerchief. "They tried to recruit us. Oh. Look. They're still going for it." She takes a leaflet. "'Over one in three council officers is a local resident.'"

"Is that why you hate coming here?" Tulip asks.

"Where to start," he says.

"I'm sure they meant no offence, they probably—"

"Thought they were doing me a favor, yes. I don't know how much economics you've studied, but it should be simple: people want, *need* things—to use, to make their lives interesting, easier, and so on. Businesses work when they meet people's needs. End of."

"He'll start going on about the invisible hand again," Elaine says to Tulip.

"I was not going to mention that, but since you already have, and I'm glad you remember it is a hand, not a fist this time, Elaine—what I will say is that a good, healthy market, whether a town center or a national economy, works on mutually beneficial exchanges." Sadness swells in him, with alarming velocity. He feels small again, a boy in the little house in Peckham, nursing fish and chips while listening to his father's Friday lecture. The most important thing, his father said, was to be useful, watch for what makes people happy, what people are willing to pay for: "And do it with a smile," he'd say. "Never cling to a particular job. Only arrogant people set themselves up with baked-in plans, they must be this or that. Useful jobs matter more. But what people want changes. Trick is to always stay ahead."

The way his father said it all those years ago made it sound easy, natural to stay ahead. It seemed that he and Jada had a good shot, with a shop as fluid as the Chest.

"Tea?" Tulip asks. "Rupert?"

He comes back to himself to hear the roar of the room's chatter. Businesspeople mill around, smiles in suits. There are mothers and campaigners, workers from the care home, bearded youths from the new café. There is Tulip, heading for the teas, talking to a woman whose face is stapled with piercings.

He goes to the corner, to the blown-up photograph of the view up the high street, looking toward the park. Shop signs jut out like flags; how well the colors match. Town is new yet old, and here is the last pub standing, with her owner, Mick, outside, looking contemplative. These photographs must have been taken in summertime, for there are children everywhere and the Chinese buffet was still open.

How it has deteriorated since. It's rough and unkind even in daylight now.

"If you'd like to go into the auditorium, please," a woman says, and ushers him toward a set of oak doors.

★

"These past weeks," Councillor Obi says from the stage, "you have shared fantastic ideas about what you want from your high street." Light glares off his oversize white shirt, which he wears untucked. "Your responses have blown us away." He shifts, to address the far side of the room. Behind him, the image on the screen changes, displaying a view up the high street, there is the Chest, with a gathering outside it. At the heart of that gathering, although he cannot see her, is Jada. This scene is seared in his memory: he was inside the Chest, exhausted after putting together a display for the Royal Society for the Protection of Birds, because he found a fallen bird's nest in the car park, a rare species—he has forgotten its name. Yes, he was inside, exhausted after combing through everything inside and reorienting it around a nature theme. The image flashes and then is gone, replaced by the council logo.

"We are wired to notice what is wrong," Councillor Obi continues. "We all see that homelessness has risen, that vulnerable people sleep in doorways."

Rupert looks to Elaine, but she appears unaffected. That photo only showed for a moment, and it was taken before her time.

"We are all shopping in new ways, and our fantastic Tube station makes it easier to simply shop elsewhere." Councillor Obi pivots again and continues in a gentler tone. "Our young people, youths who could have started businesses, hang out with nothing to do. We have tough challenges, but we have imagination, we have determination, and, thanks to the mayor, we have funding."

A cheer fills the hall. Councillor Obi raises his hand and the noise trails into applause. For a moment, it is as though he is looking directly at Rupert.

A leaden feeling grips Rupert. He may have gone too far last night. Paranoia always follows a heavy session and makes questions of everything. He had vanilla and cinnamon out on the counter that night, but also his voltage syrup. Whisky, as well. Surely he didn't give the boy anything extra.

Heat burns his cheeks. Last night seems like a dream. Still, he can't remember how or when or if the lad left, if the boy might have run out into danger, if those other boys waited up for him.

Carefully, he shifts. The chair, though hard, feels like it might give way. Councillor Obi's voice buzzes through the speakers. Rows of people around him listen, rapt, as though they hear something he cannot; something he has lost the ability to notice. He leans forward and peers down the row, but no one meets his gaze. Beside him, Tulip raises a hand and rests her chin on it.

His mouth is dry. There must be at least a hundred and fifty people here. Of all the trick-or-treaters out last night, someone must have seen the kid run into his shop. And how many here knew Jada? How many refused to accept that she was terminally ill, preferring instead the rumors that his teas were too much for her? He closes his eyes, but the relief of shutting out the crowd is quickly tempered by awareness that dozing in public is not an appropriate thing to do. He jolts awake. Something has changed: shouts go up, questions are hurled from the back.

"But what will you do?"

". . . a concrete plan . . ."

". . . another year of dithering . . ."

"When are you going to do something about the dealers in the car park?"

He sits forward and rubs his tired arms. "What's this?" he asks Tulip. "What's happening now?"

"The new flats." A wicked glint lights her eyes. "Remember, I told you the council papers leaked?"

"Here we go," Rupert says. His exhaustion deepens, like he might never leave his seat. "There I was hoping tonight might be straightforward. Typical. Trust the council to mess up their own plans."

On the stage, Councillor Obi waves for order. "If you just let me finish. If you just let me finish."

A woman near the front gets up and climbs onto her seat. "This is a sham—you have already decided what you're going to do!"

Jeers go up. People rise, adding their voices to the clamor.

"If you just—" The microphone screeches and drowns Councillor Obi's words. Groans fill the hall. People cover their ears.

Rupert gets up. He goes out into the corridor. At the lifts he looks at a map of the building. The council is a labyrinth: there is an office for parks, leisure, loneliness, safety, community cohesion, education, special education, adult social care, registration, and nationality. There is no sign, in all of it, for a place to piss.

Dizzy, he follows the luminous green exit signs, until he pushes open the doors and steps into the street. Cold envelops him, scalds his face. He walks down two units, then four, but there is no sign of the Old Boar, the pub with the pool table and dire sticky seats. His bladder is heavy. He curses. A whole pub—toilets and all—vanished.

Up toward the Chest, kids loiter everywhere. Music jangles from mobile phones. He hurries up the road.

14

He's dead. Finished.

But no. Focus.

Still breathing, cradling his pounding head. He looks up. Da's office never seemed smaller. All the books rammed on the shelves like accusations. Look at everything we cover, they say, look at everything we have given you. He didn't even finish the physics test today, because he was still thinking about Halloween, thinking about what Jericho and the others will do as soon as they catch him alone. He will get in trouble for math too, since he still can't find his calculator. Worse, Mrs. Nibley might call the house any day. Other teachers will get their opportunity to complain at parents' evening before Christmas break, when the extent of his shortcomings will be laid out clearly. It's obvious how it will go. Squid will accompany Ma, and the two will argue on the walk back. Their voices will rise inside the house.

He grinds his teeth. His math notebook lies open in his lap. He has every book he could need for school, this office too, designated as his study as long as Da is in Ghana. Floor-to-ceiling shelves are stuffed with books, hand-me-downs from family friends, textbooks, and encyclopedias with tissue-paper pages. The top shelves overspill with Da's documents. The computer on the desk is silent, the computer he wished for years to use, could only play on during those special Sundays when Jericho and King Obi visited with red cylinders of Pringles and cans of ginger beer. Those evenings put Da in a brilliant mood and culminated with the four of them huddled around the screen, taking turns setting high scores, racing cars down winding mountain lanes, swerving and gripping their seats.

He is distracted again. Mrs. Nibley is going to tell Ma he is always distracted, that he does not follow instructions. She said to type up his homework, especially essays. She will remind him, come parents' evening, she has no time to decipher his handwriting, no time for his messing about. Her fine brows will arch higher and her eyelids will flutter behind her thick glasses as she reminds him he will be starting his GCSEs soon.

Mrs. Nibley says typing will help him work faster, but typing makes the letters seem scattered and distant. He has to work harder to call them together, to push each one into being. He would sooner grip a pencil and imagine it as a tap, where he is a water tank and the tap pours ink. He has drawn it, black ink from a well deep in the earth, feeding up through the house's foundations through the pipes and cables and up through where he sits, pouring answers through his clenched fist. He has drawn it across many sheets in his big orange folder.

A catalog of procrastination, Squid calls it.

"So," she says, whenever she catches him working on a new scene. "You can't finish your homework or tidy your bedroom. You cannot prepare for tests, yet you find time to doodle." She gestures over his pencils, his crayons and chalk. "When you lift this head of yours and look around and see your classmates have left for universities, you will have these doodles, receipts for your wasted time. Well done. At least you have kept them in one place."

He keeps them in one place because if there is a fire, this is all he will save. Da used to test the fire alarm some mornings to annoy Ma, but the aunties never do. They cook so much there is bound to be a fire someday.

He folds the corner of his math book down. The other side is ruined with doodles.

Shifting his leg from under him, he pushes his trousers up. He has never seen anything like the bruise. Black, tarmac black in places, like a handprint wrapped around his shin, violet at the edges, like a universe. He presses gingerly at the edges, presses harder, working down to his ankle. The anatomy textbook said pain is an alarm, a signal that something is wrong. He presses nearer and imagines the pain as a sound, a wailing. Fire. He pushes his trouser leg down. Hopefully it will heal before PE. It could have been worse. It would have been worse if he hadn't run into the Chest. If the man had not locked the door once he was in. Then Ma would know he'd been beaten up. She would never let him out again.

Fight, Da would say if he found out, *always* fight back. Or they will walk all over you. Da warned that people would tease him, because his skin is so dark. This was before he knew how short Kwasi would turn out to be, how he would stammer and lisp and be the worst at football.

Anger thistles his throat. Da failed to mention that boys almost as Black as him could also turn on him—almost, but not quite as Black, they remind him; he is a new category of Black, and they find new things to compare him to. Blick. Boot black, blue-black, Velcro black, stickman black, so Black he doesn't need a balaclava; so Black, they say, the real reason his ma won't let him out at night must be because she is scared he will disappear.

This bruise proves they are wrong: he could descend deeper into blackness. The ink smudged on his hands and arms also reminds him he is not Black, but Brown. Lighter than he seems at school, when he catches his reflection in mirrors.

Come parents' evening, teachers will say: Kwasi is too quiet, unfriendly, and he upsets other children. He has a naughty look about him.

It will be on a Friday, so he will have to stay at home for days after. The aunties might haul him to church. Or more aunties might visit after, and pile in with their opinions.

"Why do they have to come here?" he asked Ma years ago, in the weeks after Da left. "Why do so many people have to stay with us?"

Ma put aside the bowl of peas she was shelling and beckoned for him to come close. He sat on her lap, like he was small again, like he had not just started secondary school. "People helped us," Ma said, "your dad and I, when we came here."

Ma told the story again. How she and Da arrived from Accra separately, how they might never have met if not for King Obi, who gave them work cleaning and cooking in his restaurant in Tottenham. They met over a vat of curry goat and began an endless discussion of small dismays, firstly concerning how different Caribbean cuisine was from food Back Home.

"Why do they call it rice and peas?" they would say. "These are beans. Rice and beans."

English people were not ready, they agreed, for serious African foods.

"We were lucky," Ma said, stroking Kwasi's head. "Remember I told you about the first woman prime minister? Yes. Even with the bad there is goodness. It was she who allowed people to buy council houses. Thatcher let us buy homes and King Obi had many. Together, we had homes all over. It was a blessing. And a very great relief." She told him sometimes they shared work: aunties covered each other's shifts, and English bosses and customers could not tell. "Some went to Coventry, Liverpool, and Bristol. Even to Scotland. Everywhere, working hard. Wherever you want to travel, someone will be there to welcome you. We do the same for all who come to us. Because others helped us, we also help others."

A stone hardens in his throat when he thinks about this now. For all the aunties he has said hello and goodbye to, no one really helps with how doomed he feels. He would trade them all to have Da back. Everything felt much firmer with Da around.

After parents' evening, Ma and the aunties will argue. They will take over the office and call Da on his laptop, and tell him to look at his son.

They never acknowledge that detaining him on weeknights so that he can study doesn't help. It was lucky that Jericho even invited him to come out, and persuading Ma to let him join Jericho's Halloween night took weeks. All he got for his efforts is this bruise, this bruise and a memory that hurts like a bruise, with violet edges inside his head.

★

At first the aunties had a million reasons why he shouldn't go out:

Halloween is of the Devil.

It's too much sugar.

Did you hear about the children who harassed that poor woman last year and she suffered a heart attack?

In her own home. They threw eggs at her windows. Imagine.

This Halloween. It's not a good thing, it teaches that you can just threaten to trick someone and they should give.

Ma sucked her teeth.

Anyway. It is not our culture.

A murmur of agreement.

It's about witches and darkness. We don't believe in witches.

"Actually you *do* believe in witches," Kwasi said then, and he rarely said anything, aware of how wrong his voice sounded, so pale and flat, confined to English. "You said Auntie Baby was one."

A look passed between them. Auntie Baby, who stayed almost a year but barely ever spoke, apart from through her cooking, flavors so compelling that Da insisted the others clear out of the kitchen and leave food preparation to her. Her ingredients arrived in brown packages, and when Kwasi trailed after her on shopping trips, she rode buses to distant markets. She chose curling leaves, paper sachets of bright red powder, smells that were almost-ginger, almost-mint, almost-pepper but too bristly, too harsh.

She never spoke but always knew. Small things: she always left the house before King Obi arrived for one of his surprise visits, and she took the washing in minutes before it rained.

He remembers how after she left, the other aunties said she had enchanted a man into loving her, a white man. It had seemed a cool idea to Kwasi at the time, that she might actually know how to cast spells. Sometimes he would leave drawings and she would add things in, and she liked to color in his black-and-white drawings. But then she disappeared, taking her food and spices and conspiratorial smiles with her, leaving him on his own.

Ma ignored his comment about Auntie Baby that night as they discussed Halloween. "Listen, Kwasi," she said. "Everyone knows there are witches, practitioners of crooked things, people who have traded goodness for influence, who labor for wickedness. But we do not encourage them; we do not celebrate their holidays, disturbing people at night to pester for toffees. Do you hear?"

But when Jericho and his dad visited after church that weekend, their first visit in years, King Obi went on and on about Jericho's Halloween costume, which was inspired by a Nigerian god, Shango, how long it had taken them to make the outfit together. Knocking on neighbors' doors, King Obi said, got people to talk to each other.

"Kwasi," Squid said. "Why don't you go and take part?"

And just like that, everyone was encouraging him to go, all the aunties leaning forward in their seats, their eyes glittering, their voices competing.

"You can dress as a superhero, it does not have to be satanic."

"You can dress as an animal."

"Yes, you should go. Collect plenty of chocolates. Bring some back for us!"

And so he went for his first Halloween, dressed—after

negotiation—as a skeleton, white bones painted over his black top and trousers. It was not evil, he argued, since everyone has one. It's like being really, really naked. That made Squid laugh. She told him to take his nonsense outside, and to give her love to Jericho.

Jericho was waiting at the roundabout where their roads met, wrapped in his green anorak.

"We're going to Selim's," he said.

Selim's: a tight flat in the block behind the Asda that was supposed to be condemned. Some of the aunties who had once slept here in Da's office had progressed to flats of their own in Selim's block, about which they complained when they visited on Sundays: the council takes months to send plumbers, the council does nothing about noisy neighbors, the council refuses to enforce its rules. You will find music blasting at all hours, people smoking weed, injecting themselves, dogs running loose inside the property, children playing on the lawn.

Inside, Selim's place was a concentration of aunties' complaints, cluttered with boxes of clothes and perfumes Selim's mum sold. Music throbbed from the back rooms, which were filled with Selim's brother's friends, who stood clutching plastic cups. Everyone padded around in socks or tights, drawn toward a Twister mat on the sitting-room floor. Girls with devil horns and wings squealed, falling over each other, contorted and tangled up. "Spin it! Spin it!" they shrieked.

"Let's go, funny-bones." Jericho grabbed Kwasi's hood and tugged him back. "Fanny-bones."

Kwasi elbowed Jericho. "At least I'm not dressed as the Green Giant guy. What happened to your costume?"

Jericho looked down at his coat as though he had never seen it before. "Allow it. It's a solid waterproof."

Back down the corridor they went, into the stinking humidity of Selim's room, a tomb piled with clothes and old Domino's boxes. Music boomed, and vocals raced over it, words that made his cheeks burn. Guys from the year above were by the window, leaning into the night, breathing smoke. Four, six, nine. Kwasi straightened, held his shoulders back so they wouldn't call him Kwasi-modo again.

"Here." A bundle of clothes hit him in the gut. As he bent to pick them up, the older boys laughed.

He unfolded black jeans, a black top, and a mask. A clown mask, with scarlet lips curved in a deranged grin, rosy cheeks, and sharp eyebrows.

Jericho gave him a balaclava. "Put this on."

He swallowed his questions. Tugged each item on. To his relief, Wade and Kaseem, who had arrived dressed as pirates, got the same treatment. A glow swept inside him; he was—at least for that night—like them. In costume, no one would know how different he was.

"Oi." Jericho thrust a cup under his chin. "Drink. Holy Communion."

This communion burned. It clawed his throat and singed his stomach. He gritted his teeth.

He went with them, following, feeling a buzzing expansion, becoming bigger than his body. Max punched his arm and told him he was a noob. Wade said he was a lightweight idiot.

"Hey." Jericho elbowed him. "Get it together."

It was then that Kwasi realized they were to do more—worse—than fill backpacks with sweets that night.

In the end, he didn't do most of it though. He didn't wriggle through the crack at the back of the empty shop unit with the others or retrieve the backpack. He didn't even hold the backpack until they were riding the bus. But when Selim slapped his back and said, "Arms out," Kwasi obeyed.

"When we get off . . ." Selim slipped the bag's straps over Kwasi's arms, to rest on his shoulders. "When we get off, go to the roundabout and give this to the guys in the Nissan."

Kwasi rubbed his eyes. A headache had commenced: gravelly weight dragged back inside his skull. The ache is still scraping in his head now. It should have been simple. Take the bag off and pass it to some guys in a car. Then they could go back to Selim's. He could drink more and feel looser inside.

At town's edge, they got off the bus, in the realm of warehouses and green spaces that weren't quite parks, nauseatingly vast in the darkness.

Kwasi looked over the junction. Traffic swept in from every direction, circling the roundabout, a carousel of headlights. Jericho and Selim were explaining something, but traffic erased the sounds they made. Water gurgled beneath: a brook, or puddles flushed with rain. A burst pipe. He looked down. The paving slabs were raised and cracked, bordered by weeds.

"There." Jericho pointed. Sure enough, across the roundabout, a car was parked with lights blinking, three—four figures standing around it. Jericho slapped his back. "Go."

He started forward, but Selim yanked him back by the bag's strap. "The lights, dickhead."

They waited. When the green man flashed, beeping, Kwasi bit the soft walls of his mouth and hurried across the street. He stopped by the hedges, on his way toward the car: the last point where he was invisible to both the boys behind and the guys ahead. He felt, in those moments, that he could disappear. He could melt into the trees—find a hollow and crouch there, and the bark would close around him.

He rubbed his neck. He wriggled out of the backpack and crouched, a palm to the slabs for balance.

Gingerly, he pressed the bag, feeling. It seemed stuffed with foam. He checked no one was looking and then unzipped the top.

Fear knocked him backward. No way was it real.

He peered inside again and touched his fingertip to the black muzzle of the weapon, then zipped the bag shut.

He doesn't remember rising, walking the rest of the way to the car. He doesn't remember handing the bag over. Doesn't remember what music spilled from the car's open doors, or the strange smell of the smoke that poured from the windows. He doesn't remember the bus ride back and how plain the high street looked, how comforting and simple.

"Do you know what that was?" Jericho asked him as they waited outside the liquor store. Selim's brother was coming to buy more drinks.

"I think so."

"You think so."

"I don't know. Was it real?"

Jericho's face soured.

"What?" Selim asked.

"Why would you open it?"

After that it is blurry, like his memory doesn't want to keep this part. It must have been Wade or Selim who kicked him. Someone else shoved him and he fell. Boots struck his back. He curled and shut his eyes. Blow followed blow. It stopped at once when a car drew up, screeching with dubstep. Kwasi lifted his head. Selim's brother climbed out.

"Guys, let's move," he said. "Oi. Anyone need snacks?"

"Hey." Jericho helped Kwasi to his feet.

He wiped his nose. The pain had yet to hit. All his muscles were too stunned.

Jericho squeezed his arm. "We'll get pizza."

As the boys piled into the car, Kwasi backed away and ran.

To the lights of the high street. Toward his secret place, under the bridge, where the hidden river flowed. He was going to climb over for real this time.

Shouts echoed up the street, footfalls and hoots.

Light winked a little way up, from the Chest. Wade's shouts were so close, there was no way he could outrun them. His legs ached and he had not eaten and he was going to vomit nothing. He stumbled up to the Chest, banged on the door.

Just because he got away that night does not mean everything will be okay. Things will probably get worse. He takes the mobile phone out. Jericho has sent messages that he can't even bring himself to open. Best to give the phone back to Ma.

He will have to face the guys at school tomorrow though. Tuesdays are the worst; everyone messes around in Art, and because they have to sit in a big rectangle around the mess of things they are to draw, Jericho and Wade and the others will pick on him. Plus there is Enhancement Class, where they are watching that documentary about the British Empire, and Mrs. Nibley is going to be on his case. If she gets really upset with him, she might call the house to complain and ask about the letters Kwasi has been destroying. And then there is parents' evening. The thought turns his stomach. Every teacher will be there to pick him apart, and the aunties are going to learn the truth, the truth marked on reports stowed in his locker, how hopelessly behind he is.

Laughter rumbles from the living room below.

He needs a plan. Some kind of distraction, to take the aunties' minds off his grades.

Kwasi looks around at the papers Da left. Plans for new companies he may or may not have started by now in Ghana. Some are written purely in numbers. For all his ideas, Da wrote none of his advice down, and the conversations they shared are a mess inside Kwasi's head.

15

He knows them, but does not. It is as though the couple smiling from across the till are a mix of many faces of acquaintances from a past life. Their names won't come to him.

"Good to see this place so busy," the woman says. "We were starting to think you had closed."

"Still here," Rupert says.

"It looked so quiet every time we went by," the man says. His accent has a familiar lilt.

And at once he sees them, with darker, fuller hair, showing off cat's cradle tricks from their childhoods on yarn one afternoon, shortly after Jada fell ill.

"Meera," he says, and the woman's face lights up. "I thought you had moved."

A look flits between the two. The man, whose name Rupert can't recall, leans closer and says, "We saw the photo on the council website, the one of your nature display? After you rescued those birds? Made us think to come in, to see how things have changed. What a wonderful time that was."

"The photo is on the website?"

"Yes. There are some lovely photos up, it's so nice to see old memories there. It's a shame about the flats though."

Meera shakes her head. "It's very sad."

"But maybe they will just want to develop the car park," her husband says. "It's a dodgy space, back there. A little investment could be healthy. Just as long as we don't lose the character of this place. Did you know about those plans, Rupert?"

He tells them he did not think the plans were serious. "I'm busy enough with this place."

It is exceptionally busy this week. Every transaction adds color to Ms. Reilly-Duffell's life. Elaine tells a story for each trinket she sells: how Ms. Reilly-Duffell traveled—eloped, in fact—to India in her late teens with a young communist chap, this little elephant statue here was a gift he gave her. And the mugs? She made them—her grandmother was a potter and left her equipment—she made these mugs because she loved tea, she would have loved there to be a local tearoom.

Elaine looks pointedly at him.

Everyone she asks agrees a tearoom would be lovely here. Too many cafés are popping up, Craig from the locksmith's says, soulless spaces where music crushes any possibility of conversation and people purchase nasty over-priced coffee and abscond toward the Underground.

The mugs sell quickly—they will make lovely gifts.

As much as it stings to admit it, the boost in business is due in part to Obi. First-time visitors come because Councillor Obi issued a challenge after the disastrous consultation event: this year, everyone ought to try to do all their Christmas shopping on the high street. Some of the Chest's new patrons told Rupert to his face they would not have come had Councillor Obi not encouraged them to. They looked thrilled, unabashed to be following Obi's suggestions. All this despite the leaked plans. Rupert kept his lips sealed.

He has been trying to appear more cheerful than he feels, since Elaine took him aside on Monday. This week is important, she told him, so he should lighten up. New shoppers will come, and first impressions matter.

"Yes, ma'am," he said.

He leans forward and his foggy reflection surfaces on the counter. His beard has withered. Behind him, fairy lights overhead twinkle, and shadows are thrown by scented candles at the back around the photo of Ms. Reilly-Duffell smiling in a fantastic hat, participating in some stall at the primary school fair, surrounded by children.

Christmas music fills the shop. Jingle bells with no lyrics, so people take it upon themselves to hum. Three shoppers are at it now. Rupert grinds his teeth. It feels like a lifetime since he sat down with a good brew, something to calm his thoughts, to stop him noticing so much, to stop the churn of regret that has been building since the council event on Monday. He has a wearisome feeling that Elaine is right: they will not make Christmas rent, no matter how much they sell. And if the council plans go ahead, the landlord will have better options for this unit next year.

In all the business, people are bringing more than they are buying. The woman with the headscarf is back, this time holding a box. She stands waving outside the front.

"What have you got for us?" Elaine calls, opening the door.

The woman shakes her head. Waves, gestures, drops the box, and then is gone, as suddenly as she appeared.

"What's going on there?" Rupert asks.

"They're from Brook Street," Elaine says. "The semi-detached house where the Morrisons lived? You know the Morrisons! Rita? Terrible lisp. It's sublet now. Plenty of kids. They have a little boy in Ronnie's class." Elaine pulls a face. She goes and drags the box inside.

"Well. At least they're taking an interest," he says. "Generous of them to give to us."

"More like offloading junk."

"You haven't even opened it yet."

"One of them makes scarves or tablecloths or something." Elaine tears open the box and pulls out a sunny square of linen. "What are we going to do with this?"

He can't help but feel annoyed at Elaine. Helpful as she is, her approach to work, and to the Chest, does not quite align with his. It's not about knowing what something will become; it's about helping a customer to imagine a purpose for it. "I'll put it below, run it through the wash."

"There's so much. Oh, that's a lovely pink. But there must be something wrong with it. Why else would they leave it here?" Elaine sets the box aside. "I meant to ask. Any updates about the fund? Have you signed up online?"

"What?"

"You looked at the leaflets, didn't you? Rupert. It's been a week."

"I'll get to it." He adjusts the framed drawing, leaning it against the jar of pens.

"What about our takings? How is Christmas rent looking?"

"We're all right," he says.

"I spoke to Councillor Klade, and he suggested a space like a living room, for people to come in, sit down, have a chat. They want more spaces where people can come together, that's the sort of business they are likely to fund."

"More cafés, then? Pubs?"

She glares at him. "Quite a few people have said they remember the Chest used to be really special, that they always could rely on it for something new. Tulip said the last time she volunteered here, years ago, you had plans for a sort of tea experience. We could do something with that. Just . . . We needn't complicate it with your herbs."

He flattens an empty box. "Those herbal teas were Jada's idea."

"Rupe, we can't go into the new year like this."

"I'll take care of the rent. I have furniture at home to shift."

"This isn't working, scrabbling around at the last minute, trying to get just enough to keep this place open. Honestly, do you want this shop to work?"

He rests his boot on the cardboard, flattening it, and looks at his hands, how hot they are from a little exertion, from this growing annoyance.

"We're riding off our reputation from years ago. Don't you think Jada would have wanted to try something new? I spend as much time here as you—more, since half the time you're not really here. People aren't buying things."

He presses his hands together. "Look. Whatever you want to do for Councillor Obi and all the little rules he's setting out is up to you. But I'm not turning this into a playground or a substitute for the libraries and youth clubs his council shut."

"Right," Elaine says.

★

They have argued before, in silences that last for weeks. He thinks, at times like these, he could dismiss Elaine, but he cannot run this place without her. Elaine, after decades cleaning schools, hospitals, offices in the city, has mastered the art of making things new. If she takes a week off—if her grandchildren miss her or her husband is poorly or her hip is playing up—dust gathers; maintenance becomes his life.

"Rupert."

He did not hear Tulip come in.

She removes her beanie and runs her hand over her head. "Everything okay?"

"Fine. Busy day."

She gathers the last of the empty boxes. With ease she pulls their edges apart and presses them into sheets. She works twice as quickly as he could and stacks the waste by the back doors. She says she has been tidying her parents' loft all day, looking to see if they can convert it into a study or a guest bedroom. That she has been thinking about sharing space, reading about squats and communal living.

"Unfortunately, that age has come and gone," Rupert says, and opens the Black Book of Giving. "What a time it was."

"I think we'll have a resurgence," Tulip says. She joins him at the counter and opens the jar of pens. "Seems like everything is going backward anyway, so."

"Well. The laws were different then," he says. "The law never goes backward. And the music was better then too."

"Did you work out where this came from?" she asks. She puts the jar of pens aside and lifts the framed pencil drawing of the shop. "It looks so good here."

"Still a mystery. Our first piece of fan art."

She looks like she has a joke and is contemplating including him in it.

"What's funny?"

"Years ago I tried to paint the Chest, the view from the back, when you come up the stairs. It's out of date. It's how the shop was when I volunteered—no, it's how I *remembered* the shop to be when I volunteered."

"Oh? And it's changed?"

"It has."

"Tell that to Elaine."

"It was such a special time. I think that's what I was trying to draw, I knew this place would always feel like home."

Something gives way inside him, and the quiet between them deepens.

"I will never forget when you walked up to the till with your CV in a plastic wallet, 'I'm here to volunteer.' What a thing." He remembers her gaze wandered beyond him, appraising the shop with cool assuredness. "We've had some wonderful times here, haven't we?"

"We'll have more." Tulip places the drawing back onto the counter. "Tea?"

★

Over lemon and ginger tea, Tulip apologizes for discussing Jada's plans with Elaine.

"I shouldn't have brought them up. I should have known she wouldn't like the sound of herbal teas. I think I sort of did know, but. Anyway, I didn't say a word about your recent order," she says. "Elaine definitely wouldn't be cool about that."

"Elaine is particular."

119

"She was recommending wigs for me." She puts her cup down and reaches up, smooths her hand over her head. "Apparently I'd look good with a bob."

"I didn't know you saw my delivery come in. It was late."

"I heard a motorbike in the car park—I was going up the back way to the park for a run. So I waited by the bins and there you were. You're not very subtle."

"I don't need to be," he says. "It's all legal. What were you doing out running after dark?"

Tulip doesn't answer, instead looks around the basement. "How do you keep track of them? Do you give your mixes names?"

"Used to," he says.

"We could try new herbs together."

He laughs.

"Genuinely. I'm curious about what you find so nice about them."

"I don't think that's a good idea."

"There was this shop outside Durham. A headshop. They sold stuff online too. I was talking to this woman, a poet who came in the other day, and she was saying that you used to have these afternoon socials down here."

"Oh." Warmth flushes his cheeks. How strange, to think of people who hold these memories too, scattered elsewhere now. "Years ago."

"She was super cool. I didn't know we had poets here."

They sit in the quiet for a while.

"Can you believe how Councillor Obi tried to justify the whole thing about the leaked plans? Like we just need a load of new residents to bring life to this place, probably people who just want to be near a Tube station. I bet they would never come into a charity shop. They probably order most of their stuff online."

Something shadowy falls over her. A new edge has sharpened her voice and hardened her gaze.

"Better to focus on what we can do, rather than get lost in whatever the council is doing," Rupert says, doing his best to keep bitterness from his tone.

"What the council is undoing, more like."

"Well. What about this art event you were talking about? I wasn't listening properly when you said it. I'm happy for you to use this space, although I know it could be tidier. Did you want to put it on the noticeboard?"

"Oh. It's just me and a few friends," she says. She looks like she has only just remembered asking to use the Chest. She smiles, grateful and a bit sheepish. "We used to meet at this bookshop near King's Cross, but they closed. That whole area is weirdly privatized."

"If you put it on the noticeboard, maybe other people will see it and want to join?"

"I just want to see how it goes first. It's been ages since we did anything creative together. Everyone's always traveling or working."

Voices burst from upstairs. Cackles and shouts. "What's happening?" Tulip asks.

He edges forward on his chair. "Wait."

The din of voices is louder. It seems to be coming from the back.

"Should I go see?" Tulip asks.

Something thuds upstairs. He feels it land inside his gut.

"I'm going to see. Might be people from next door."

"Wait just a minute," Rupert says, but Tulip is already on her feet.

*

Joining her upstairs, all is still. Only egg is in motion, three dull yellow cores, stretching, a slow explosion of slime, sliding down the glass.

16

The library is filled with everyone who does not belong. Kwasi places his backpack on the table. Miss has dragged the tables together, so all the smaller desks that were hidden behind bookcases, where he could have drawn without being disturbed, are slotted together in four islands. Two tables are already full.

"Quietly," Mrs. Nibley says.

Five boys push through the doors and race to the computers.

"No reading silly things on Wikipedia," she says. "No random googling. No memes. Homework only."

It is a pointless announcement: One, everything besides homework brings up an error page on these computers. And two, everyone has a phone. Jason Murray has his out already, under the table.

"Listen," Mrs. Nibley says. "Kwasi, pay attention."

He looks at her. It's dumb when teachers do this, act like he can't hear them unless he is looking right at them, as though he listens through his eyes. The girl settling at his table is the one who should get told off—she is wearing headphones under her long hair.

"Right. I have marking. If you need help, put your hand up. No shouting. This is a library."

It's not really though, not now. Even the librarian has taken her tall steel thermos and gone. In a matter of seconds everyone's whispering.

The girl opposite him looks up and scowls.

Hugging his bag, he retreats lightly toward the corner where the big hardback atlases are.

Mrs. Nibley glances up and then back to her books.

He crouches by the atlases, like he's reading the spines. He drags his bag into the corner, the spot behind the pillar where he is out of sight. Might as well try, so he unfolds the worksheet from his blazer pocket. The page is crowded with French words and spaces waiting to be filled. He turns it over and it's blank, not even a bank of words to choose from. He is apparently supposed to just have all these missing words in his head.

The whispering from beyond his alcove is one grating hiss, and underneath that is the computers' wheeze, and underneath that the pecking of the clock. He folds his worksheet and puts it into his blazer pocket, instead pulls a thick book from the shelf and opens it. Its pages are filled with scenes of fiery rivers of molten rock and photographs from on high, of crowded cities: Rio de Janeiro, Kingston, Mumbai. The pages are cool to touch, but their fragrance is sweet and warm, alive with vivid colors of places that look like alien planets. Caves with icy spikes of teeth.

He closes the book. Heavy, but it will just about fit in his bag. He's got the beginnings of an idea about a new comic, about an explorer.

"Kwasi."

He jumps. Mrs. Nibley towers over him.

"Why don't you work at a table? We have snacks out, and you should drink some water. Up you get."

Now everyone is listening. "I like sitting here."

"Kwasi." She still can't say his name. Sounds like she's calling him crazy and can't pronounce her *r*'s. "Come and sit properly, where I can see you."

"You can see me. I'm right here."

"Right. First warning."

His throat feels thick. Two classrooms away, Selim and Wade are in detention for forgetting their workbooks. Mrs. Nibley might send him there, if he pushes it. Shakily he gets up, returns to his table. The girl who was sitting with him is now using the computer by the photocopier; Gemma has taken her place. She doesn't look up when he sits. Now and again, she turns a page. Maybe this is how she gets so smart, by reading until nothing else exists. Even so, she is only good at history; she did even worse than him in math.

"The juice is under the table," Gemma says, without a glance at him. "Have it if you want."

He looks under the table. A stout bottle of orange juice. But he'll need the toilet if he drinks. And he might run into Selim if he steps out of the library.

He straightens. Mrs. Nibley glares at him from the desk.

"There's nothing wrong with it," Gemma says. "I just don't want it because it gives me zits. And I don't want it on the table."

Her eyes meet his. Quick, darting eyes. He opens his book and stands it upright to shield his face. The clock ticks and ticks. All that noise and yet, each time he checks, its hands have hardly moved.

★

"How was it?" Squid asks, when he gets home.

"Okay."

"Good. Dadda is on the phone."

"I need to go to the toilet first."

He hurries up the stairs, but someone is in the bathroom. And another auntie is in his room, talking on the phone. He sits on the landing. Smells like tuna cooking, which is the worst. He should have eaten at homework club or bought chips.

"Sorry," Auntie Aha says, when she comes out of the bathroom. "You are home so early. I hope you were not misbehaving."

He shakes his head.

"You finished your work? That's good. Sometimes you need to study with your peers, to encourage each other. You are learning about the world."

Auntie May is coming up the stairs. "Your father called. He's at Cape Coast now. Come. It was just now, so maybe we can quickly call him back."

His shadow inside starts to uncurl, but he stops it, remembering: Da will just run through his usual script. Maybe he will ask about Halloween, or if Kwasi has tried out for the football team again yet.

"He said he tried to call you, on your mobile."

"The spare one, you mean? I told Ma, I don't need it. I left it in the living room." He gave that phone up because of Jericho, who sent messages he dared not read. "I'll talk to him next time."

17

The landlord has sent a letter. They would like to remind him that Christmas rent is shortly due, and they encourage him to notify them as soon as possible if he is going to have any difficulties this time. "Moreover," he reads aloud to himself, "it would be good to catch up in the new year to discuss your long-term plans for the Chest of Small Wonders, in light of the Council's new strategy."

He looks up to the window, where a faint smear remains from last night's egging. It is quiet out today, not least because there is yellow tape at the crossing near the station. Rumors of a knife attack. He is trying not to think about it, that a serious incident took place close by shortly after he and Tulip headed home. That perhaps the eggers—schoolboys, most likely—were involved.

Councillor Obi, undeterred, is out marching, leaving apple-shaped stickers on shopfronts, a trail of green and yellow that reads LOVE LOCAL and EVERYONE'S BUSINESS. He is coming toward the Chest with his teenager in tow.

"Here we go," Rupert says.

"What's this?" Elaine leans out from between bookcases. "Be nice," she says as Councillor Obi approaches the door.

Councillor and son step inside. As well as stickers and posters, they bring a box, from which they unpack maps and council-branded paraphernalia.

"Thought you might want these, while you're decorating," Councillor Obi says.

"We only advertise our cause," Rupert says. "If you have a charity in mind for us to support, pop it in the book and we'll let the people decide. For now, we're fundraising for Shelter. We'll not distract from their work."

Councillor Obi smiles. "Ah, Rupert, Rupert."

Since they have already brought the papers though, he finds himself looking. He slides a stack of postcard-size photographs of the town hall aside. Beneath are other images of views around town, of the park and the old church. "We would rather not have your crest here making people think this is a verified waste center. We get enough rubbish as it is."

He looks up, in time to see the teenager smirk.

"I thought you might have an idea of what to do with these," Councillor Obi continues. "Stunning photos and maps from our consultation events. It would be a shame to throw them away."

"You could recycle them. There's about forty different recycling bins outside every house."

Elaine coughs. Without looking at her, Rupert can feel the warning in her gaze.

"Recycling is important—it restores purpose." Councillor Obi flashes his teeth. "That's why the Chest is so wonderful. Rehousing. New homes for so many quiet treasures."

He can't believe how smug the councillor looks. A typical politician, pleased by the sound of his own voice.

"*Local* homes. You won't catch me sending treasures to be rehoused in Stoke."

The door opens and a small crowd bustles in, their coats slick with rain. The umbrella stand is already crammed, so they carry their brollies with them between the aisles, dripping all over the floor. A young crowd—they might be Tulip's friends. Perhaps they've come to see the place, ahead of Tulip's still-life drawing session here tonight.

"Something happened near the station?" he makes himself ask.

"Nothing to worry about. It does look dramatic, but the police are just doing what they do." Obi puts his pamphlets onto the counter. "Just thought I'd see how you were doing. Now. I'm actually looking to get a little something for my sister before the Christmas rush."

"It's the *post*-Christmas rush you'll want to catch," Rupert says. "That's when everyone offloads the gifts they don't want. Perhaps your sister will come in to return something then."

Councillor Obi laughs without smiling. Behind him, his lad is wearing an inscrutable expression.

Elaine joins them. She looks through the pamphlets Councillor Obi has placed on the counter and takes out a postcard photograph. It depicts the scene outside the Chest, the nature display. "This is the one," she says. "Saw it on the website."

"It's a great photo. Before the consultation we asked residents to share photos from happy moments on the high street over the years."

"I remember that day well. Jada was somewhere there," Rupert says. "At the heart of it, as usual."

"Always. You know," Obi says, "if Jada had ever run for

election, she would have stolen my seat. Erica used to joke about it."

The young shoppers fall quiet.

"I think what I'm trying to say is this . . ." The councillor has aged after all, and in his stillness he withers. Lines bracket his mouth. "I know how it— Well. I know how it can feel when you lose someone you love."

The boy coughs and fidgets with his zipper.

"But they're both smiling over us. At least they have each other up there, hey?" Councillor Obi says.

The shoppers trickle out after Councillor Obi goes. Elaine follows soon after, off to get groceries. Rupert locks the door shut and stands watching traffic pass. There, bundled up in a dark blue coat, across the street, stands a boy, a round face blurred by distance. There he is—the boy from Halloween.

Rupert drops his keys, trembling with relief.

Across the street, the boy squirms his bulky rucksack off, balances it against the rail by the road, and unzips it at the top. He freezes, looks about, and then in a flurry of motion pulls a carrier bag out from under his coat. Inside is a little box, in the fiery orange and yellow colors of the Chicken Palace, which he pushes into his backpack. Relief stretches Rupert's smile. The soles of his feet feel aglow. He takes his coat from the hook and struggles into it. The door puts up a lot of resistance, until he remembers he's locked it. He finds the keys from the floor and lets himself out.

Shouts go up as he rushes out, and a woman falls against the shopfront. Her shopping trolley skids down the pavement. In a flurry of bright jackets, construction workers rush to help her.

"Sorry," Rupert says, raising both hands. "Didn't see you. I'm sorry."

The men step in his way. "Be a bit more careful, won't you."

He backs away, to the crossing. His arms are shaking. It's still busy, but he doesn't recognize a single face. It is as if everyone he knew has moved on, slipped away around him.

Across the street, men and women go up and down, to the bus stop, toward the Tube, toward homes and to the shops. He waits, watching for the schoolboy and his backpack.

"Hello? Rupert? What are you doing out here? I thought you'd gone home." Elaine has returned with her shopping. "It's freezing. What are you waiting out here for?"

"I've forgotten something," Rupert says.

Elaine holds the door open. "Oh, I should say . . . I got an email from the landlord's team, they'd like a meeting in the new year."

Back inside, he goes into the basement. Pours water and gulps. It is possible to overwhelm the mind, to unravel oneself. To see things that are not real.

"I'm heading off," Elaine calls. "Are you coming?"

"Soon," he says.

"What on earth are you waiting for?" she says, and moments later: "Anyway. As long as you're all right. Take care."

He is waiting for Tulip and her drawing session. That is all. Senseless, since she has her own key. Probably they are waiting for him to shove off, if they are still interested in coming here at all. Why they would be is beyond him. This street is for the dying, or the dead, the edges of the economy: pound shops and chicken shops, betting shops and charity.

★

He might have stayed if he had known that on the walk home he would almost get hit by a car. His fault, for watching the pavement. It is asphalt here, which seems new. He remembers Elaine mentioning the slabs were to be removed for their risk of tripping people. It happens like this: when he lifts his face the streetlights are a haze of gold, suspended from obscurity. A forest of youths huddles close by, smoke rising from their company. Rupert is in the street when his boot slides on a patch of frost and his leg gives.

A car skids, blares its horn. His hands scrabble; the road is a cold scab and he pushes himself up, palms finding the car bonnet.

"Shit." A brown face leans from the car window. "Oh God. Are you hurt?"

Yes and no. He shakes his head.

"Are you sure?"

Yes, yes. Steady again, he hobbles across the street.

He is still trembling when he gets home. He flicks switches and the pipes groan to life. He sheds his coat and scarf, then goes up and runs a bath. Cold is in his bones.

In the bedroom, he opens the wardrobe. When he and Jada moved in, they were thrilled with the safe back here. All the stories they swapped, of what might have been hidden over decades past. Now he has been into neighbors' homes, and their layouts are similar. Row after row: a town raised to house workers drawn by the city, whose work drove a revolution, drove a nation to imagine that it could rule the world. A town of houses around a lost well, all with a secret safe in their closets. Homes older than high street banks.

In the bathroom, he stops the taps. The room is steamy, and the water burns his fingertips.

Every cell of her—the freckles on her arms, the blank spaces of her eyebrows, drawn in again daily, her mouth of too many teeth, all on display with her fantastic smile, the holes in her ears where she'd hang new arrangements of silver and gold and colored stones. Chestnut curls about her shoulders, curls they would not wait for chemo to take, and her head, which he had cradled so often, lying together in the bath, which he'd kissed through winter nights, all fireworks inside, webs and nets of dreams, impossibilities gone to smoke.

Councillor Obi will never know what it is to have nothing of her, who held half his life. Councillor Obi has his woman's son.

Shivers wrack him. Noise seeps from next door, voices, new people again. He'll have to introduce himself eventually and tell them to keep it down.

He mixes poppy tea—his strongest. Undresses, remembering his father's words, that two kinds of men struggle to sleep: sinners and the idle. The over- and underspent. Before, he would have walked. Long walks to the edge of town, where wilderness began. A picnic among bluebells, and the gurgling of the brook lost in the nettles. Dandelions. He can't think about that now. And it would be senseless to walk tonight, while police tape is still up.

"We're part of the city now, whether or not we take the Tube," Elaine said. "Mind, it's not too late to get out."

Everyone sensible is moving to Essex, Kent, Surrey. Feels

like he is not moving at all, apart from this sinking. The London he loved is gone and he has failed to keep his small part of it beating in the Chest. It is all going to come to a head after Christmas, even if he makes rent. The landlord will want a reason to keep him, with the change that's coming. Wavering between purpose and absence has left him nowhere.

18

Two men are injured and a teenage girl is said to be in a critical condition.

The story repeats, and the banner races across the bottom of the screen BREAKING NEWS BREAKING NEWS BREAKING NEWS. The aunties won't change the channel. They want to see the moment their own Tube station appears, want to see the truth of what happened there, what warranted so much yellow tape and complicated their routes to work. It's not going to happen. The news is covering bigger problems, incidents elsewhere. Kwasi slides forward on his seat and gets up. The doorway is clear, empty.

Squid's head lifts.

"Finish your food," Auntie Aha says. She is sitting on the edge of the sofa with her palms held out, waiting for her nail polish to dry. "Sit down and eat." She points with her chin.

On his plate, three roasted potatoes are melting to yellow mush, into grease and oily stew; the peppers, curled and shiny, make him think of cockroaches, of beetles. Potatoes are miraculous, how quickly they fill him, their rounded taste and bland sweetness. The aunties are treating him, rewarding him for behaving, for how focused he has been on finishing homework and the extra worksheets Ma got. It will not be enough. And this is assuming that no one will find out that he delivered a gun. It could be anywhere now.

A shooting in Enfield.

Kwasi shuts his eyes. Prayer has to be a scam; the aunties are always praying for things that never happen, and even if it worked, Kwasi would be at the back of the line.

BREAKING NEWS BREAKING NEWS BREAKING NEWS.

He could pray for Da to return. All this trouble really started when Da left. The house lost its magnetism; aunties came and stayed for mere weeks, aunties who hardly looked at him. Aunties who spoke unfathomable languages, from Burkina Faso, Nigeria, and Liberia. Some nights they stayed up telling, in a kind of mixed-up English, lies about Da, stories about men.

Da is all the warm notes missing from the house—now there is just a flurry of voices and nothing binds it together.

But even if Da returns, Selim and Wade and Jericho are still waiting. His teachers still think he is not trying.

Squid says he would have been caned to his senses, had he grown up Back Home; he would never waste a grain of rice. They bring up life Back Home more and more lately. He's seen videos of Africa in geography, always the places that are really bad. When Comic Relief comes around he shrinks in his blazer, cheeks simmering, grits his teeth through the videos Mrs. Margaret plays of impoverished kids in Africa, tense until they explain this is Kenya or Nigeria or Congo or anywhere he can argue has nothing to do with him.

"Boy. Are you still eating?" Squid says.

He nods.

"If you don't finish your food," Squid says, "tomorrow it will be waiting for you."

Kwasi lifts his fork and stabs the biggest potato.

Squid sucks her teeth and goes, leaving him and Auntie Aha with the TV.

Da used to talk over the news. He would say, "If these boys had grown up in Africa," and "If these boys focused on their studies," and "If these boys stayed home and behaved . . ."

Now no one says anything. They let the news tell itself. Kwasi presses his hand over his chest. His heart is doing that thing again. A heart is as big as a fist, but his heart might be as big as two, two grown-up fists boxing to get out.

He could pray for the bag he delivered to disappear, to fall somewhere its contents will never be recovered or used. It's hard to remember if he was wearing gloves when he handed it to the people in the car, or if he only dreamed about wearing gloves. Here is a prayer then: that if the police find what he did or did not touch, it will be in a different bag, and that it will have been through so many hands that no mark he left will be detected.

19

When Rupert pushes the door, it opens with a plaintive cry.

The Chest looks redeemable in the slanting light. He will go downstairs and gather his sachets and empty the lot into the toilet. Best to quit while there is business to keep his mind busy. Best to quit while the sun is out. His aching head taunts: Last night you went too far. But yet not far enough.

On the other side of the counter, two picture frames stand where there was one. Small wooden frames whose glass fronts throw a white glare. Someone has put the drawing of the Chest into a new frame, and opposite is a new work. He squints: it displays a pencil sketch of the basement. Tentative, gentle, a scene spun from cobweb-strokes. The rendering is heavier at the edges: heads, necks, shoulders coalesce. Silhouettes sit like ghosts around the scene's edges, with raised teacups. More figures emerge from the scribbles: figures caught in whorls of color, dancing.

He straightens and hurries to the stairs. Down, carefully, into shadows. All is as he left it here, only tidier. There is no further evidence that Tulip and her friends were here.

*

Of course the sunshine does not last. It is going to get worse toward Christmas. This is the first of many days when the air and ground are chilled enough to welcome snow, but the sky retains its water. Walking-through-a-freezer days, when clouds have clotted and at last break under the weight of their gathering, but only rain falls. Icicle rain, needles of it caught in bluster, hit his skin like electric shocks. Small enough to be flakes of snow, but not. No miraculous geometry, no incandescence coating the grass. Only water, seeping through earth. Here it comes now: rain roars all afternoon, as Rupert watches through the glass.

Sales fall sixty percent on the average rainy day. On a day like this in November they plummet by over eighty percent. The few who venture in come for shelter. Jada would have served them fruit tea in polystyrene cups. They might have purchased something out of gratitude or to remember her kindness.

Two vagabonds from next door wander in, bearded men who smell of tobacco. Rupert winces as they finger through paperbacks, turns on the stereo to cover the sound of dragging feet. He suffers through endless crooning about feeding the world, followed by an awful rendition of "The Little Drummer Boy," thinking how much brighter his mood might be after just one cup of something strong. He went down earlier to throw the lot away. But the fragrance in that cupboard.

At last the rain abates and the rough sleepers go. Moments later the smell of smoke wafts in from outside. He goes to the door and shuts it properly.

And then the urge to go downstairs and brew something

wicked is overwhelming. He stills, his hand curled around the door handle, trying to recall why he is here.

He mentions it to Tulip, when she arrives at five, that things will get tough soon, with the weather turning.

"It's pretty grim," she says, struggling out of her boots, gripping the door handle. "And this is only the beginning." She bends and rubs her feet, her mismatched socks: one plain black and one yellow with pink stripes.

He rests his arms on the counter. "Beginning of what?"

"Of the end. A storm is coming. It's flooding up north. Don't you watch the news?"

"Occasionally. It's nice, now and again, to be surprised."

"To be surprised," Tulip repeats doubtfully.

"I was surprised by this, earlier." He touches the frame that holds the basement scene, then nods at the original drawing, which sits alongside in its new frame. "It looks like the work of our mystery impressionist."

"I tried to work in the same style." She comes and takes the second frame in her hands. "It's not even close."

"Was your art night any good? I thought you might not want to go ahead with it, with the police tape near the station."

"It was fine. It went well. Everyone loved the Chest, it's the perfect space. And it was special for me, you know, to show them my part of town, to show them we have interesting spaces out here. I didn't see the tape, I guess it was gone by then. Wonder what happened."

"Best not to worry too much. As long as you were all right in here."

"Yeah. I was talking to the poet I mentioned before. About making the most of spaces we have, showing how we want these spaces to be used, rather than just talking about it."

"Oh yeah?"

"We were talking about art and resistance."

"Speaking of resistance, did you hear any trouble from next door last night?"

"No. Dead quiet. No more eggs either."

They share a smile.

"Who do you think threw those eggs?" she asks. She goes and sits by the piano.

Rain patters outside. The fresh scent calls him to the door.

"Kids with nothing better to do," he says. "I had better lock up."

It's cruelly cold outside. Spitting. Quickly as he can, he pulls the shutters down.

He looks back and almost jumps from his skin. A boy stands by the alleyway. A shadow of a boy with bright eyes and a curious open face. Motion hangs about him even as he waits; his presence is a great springy question mark. The boy retreats into the alleyway, out of sight. Rupert's chest is skittering, with both terror and concern. He is almost certain, although he can't be sure, it was the boy from Halloween, or a different kid, perhaps one of those who threw eggs at the front. But no, he tells himself. It must be the boy from Halloween; there was something so quiet, and tentative, about him.

Rupert pokes his head back inside the Chest. Tulip is looking through the guestbook now.

"What's up?" she asks, lifting her face.

He looks back. It's definitely the same boy, standing by

the wall, looking ready to disappear. Rupert beckons him, but the boy tenses and backs out of sight again.

"Is something happening?" comes Tulip's voice from inside. She closes the book, pressing her hand over the cover. "Oh God. Are we going to get egged again?"

"Not at all," Rupert says. "Only we shouldn't stay out too late. It really isn't safe. Come back earlier tomorrow, if you can. All right?"

"Huh? Oh okay." She comes nearer and reaches for her coat. "I meant to say." She hesitates, one arm in the sleeve. "I'm thinking of having more makers' events here. It's so nice in the evenings. Would that be okay?"

"We can chat about that another time."

"Sure." She pulls her coat on and struggles back into her boots. "Don't get caught in the storm."

He watches her go out and away down the high street. Pushes his hands into his pockets and looks back toward the alley. "Hello?" he calls.

Silence.

"Are you in trouble again? Or just hanging about?"

Silence.

"If you're just hanging about, you might as well come inside. I won't have you catching a cold outside my shop."

The boy materializes from the alleyway, from the space overgrown with weeds. The whites of his eyes glisten.

"Don't you have a scarf? Gloves? It's far too cold to be walking about like that." Rupert ushers the boy in, closes the door. "What's happening. Are we in trouble again?"

"Is this shop even open?"

"Well. We're both inside so I suppose now it is. Tell me though. Are you in trouble?"

"No. I just came from homework club."

Tension eases its grip on Rupert's stomach. "That's good then."

"I'm allowed to get something here, on the high street, I mean, every time I go to homework club."

"You want to look around? We have puzzles. Or Jenga? Have a look."

The kid unzips his jacket to reveal a shortened tie in a mess of a collar. "Could I have some of the coffee? With the syrup thing."

Dread seizes him. It is as though every item on display is listening, all the people who gave these things up are present, observing. He backs toward the stairs.

"Oh. Okay." The boy tucks his chin into his collar.

He looks so crushed, Rupert can't stand it.

"You can have coffee, I suppose, only a little because it is late. Nothing more. I'll ask Elaine to get hot chocolate tomorrow."

The boy follows him down the stairs. When Rupert gets to the bottom he looks back to see that the kid has stopped on the penultimate step and is unbuckling his shoes. They are caked in mud, with dull, creased leather.

"Sorry. I went through the park."

"Don't worry. Keep them on. I need to clean up soon anyway." He takes the kettle to the sink.

"How come you're always open? Every time I come by here it's open."

The kettle rumbles and steam plumes out. "Just a small cup for you."

"I'm not as little as you probably think I am."

"Oh yeah?"

"I'm sixteen."

"Right. And I'm twelve." He takes a mug and sets it

aside. "I'm very sorry. It was wrong for me to give you that drink so late at night. I wasn't thinking and I won't be doing it again."

"I'm okay. It's just coffee, right?"

"It's not a good idea to drink it late at night, even when you're old enough. Which you aren't."

The boy bows his head and fusses with his tie. It's striped with the blues of the comprehensive by the bus garage. "Going to look for stuff upstairs," he says.

The stairs hardly make a sound as he goes up. Rupert listens for the boy's steps between the bookcases and displays, the creak of the door opening or slamming shut. Nothing.

The coffee smells austere; already his mouth tastes bitter. The violet in the closest vial calls to him. A droplet or two will soften the coffee's edge. He'll be kinder after a proper drink.

"Are you coming?" calls the boy.

"Just a minute." He puts the vial down and takes the mugs upstairs.

The kid stands before the long mirror by the piano, trying on bowler hats, fedoras. One off, one on.

"Very smart. Like a young Al Capone. You can keep it."

A smile lights the boy's eyes. He comes over to the till and sits, gripping the counter. "These chairs are great. You could just do your work rolling around the shop. Only you couldn't go down the stairs, I guess."

"One of the good things about this job is that it keeps me on my feet. What shape I would have been in without all the lifting and carrying I have to do here. I'm not going to condemn myself to a sedentary life like an office worker. God help them, staring at screens all day."

"At school we have to spend ages sitting. So uncomfortable. And boring."

"Oh yeah?" Rupert lifts his mug. "Are you going to tell me about those boys? Are they from your class? Those boys that came running after you."

"Some of them." The lad glances over the till. And then he jumps and almost falls off his chair. He steadies himself. "No way." He stretches and takes the original framed drawing in his hands.

"It's something, isn't it?"

The boy holds the frame close to his face, and his bright eyes are reflected in the glass. "Do you think it's good?" he asks, speaking so quietly, he might have been speaking to himself.

"Sorry?"

"The picture. Do you think it's a good drawing?"

"Do I think it's good?" The question feels significant, as though this is a kind of litmus test. Rupert looks back, feeling watched, but there is only rain slashing silver streaks down the windows. He turns back and the boy is still watching, waiting. "It's special. Never seen anything quite like it."

Perhaps it was the wrong thing to say, for now the boy looks troubled, staring intensely at the picture.

"What is it?" Rupert asks.

"I did it," the boy says.

"You what?"

The boy places the drawing back on the counter. Tilts his head to look at it. "I did it. Years ago. Do you think it's good? You sell pictures."

Rupert takes the frame in his hands. It seems heavier. How tightly the scene hangs together. "I'm no expert." A queasy feeling spreads through his stomach. He raises his coffee and sips and lets bitterness stew in his mouth. No taste of syrup emerges. He definitely added nothing to his drink. It's fine. It is only coffee. Rupert, he tells himself, you are too sober to feel so paranoid. Not every Black person is somehow connected to Councillor Obi. "Who's your father?"

"My father?"

"That's what I said."

"He doesn't live here. Just my mum."

A little relief comes with these words. But Rupert can't shed the unease.

"Wow." The boy shakes his head, smiling. "Can't believe it's still here. Say I got my mum to come in here, would you tell her?"

"What? Tell her what?"

The boy's gaze travels from Rupert's face down to the picture in his hands and then back up again. He gets down from the chair, removes the hat, and leaves it on the counter.

"Bye."

And he is gone, out into the rain.

Rupert waits for relief to come, but the quiet remains taut, accusatory.

20

"Your teacher called," Ma tells him when he gets home. "Mrs. Nibley."

Kwasi freezes, one strap out of his backpack.

"She said we should encourage you to type your homework." Ma folds her arms. She is wearing one dangly earring and looks sleepy, unbalanced.

"Is that it?"

When Ma looks at him like this, just the two of them, it is as though she is watching from across an ocean, as though they stand on distant ships that are moving apart.

"What do you mean, is that it? She should not have to tell you this. She has told you this before."

"I know. I'll do it." Relieved, he hangs up his coat and goes toward the stairs.

"I've turned the internet off," Ma calls. "So don't try it. Just use a Word document to type up your homework. Focus. Do everything with purpose."

He has a good feeling, as he starts up the stairs, still warm from visiting the Chest. He is going to look at his old drawings from the summer he first went in there. It is mad that his drawing has been in that shop this whole time, that the shopkeeper liked it enough to put it in a frame, enough to keep it there. All this time, someone liked his work. Not just someone, a lot of people must have seen it, every time they went to pay for things. It was an okay drawing but he has done better since, and now this feeling is returning, he will do better.

But then, halfway up the stairs, his name is spoken, in the burble of conversation coming from the living room. He goes back down to listen.

They are debating his fate again, this time in English, so everyone can join in. A cruel sort of miracle. All their different countries and languages converge on this. He can't help thinking about the scene from the British Empire documentary, with cartoon faces of different shades of brown across the world, chattering over each other in English. Had Britain not held all their countries in one empire, the aunties' conversations might have meant nothing to him.

But then if none of them had grown up speaking English, maybe they would never argue in the first place. Auntie Becky and Auntie Madame and the other one from Gambia might have kept to themselves, and the two new Igbo women would talk only to each other. This house would be empty, maybe with just one woman and some cats, or a husband and wife. Someone else might be sitting on these steps now, spying on a totally different conversation.

Ma would not have met Da, and he himself would never have been born. A shiver tickles down his back.

"What more could he learn there?" Auntie May cries. "We have books, we have the computer."

Kwasi can feel his shadow self shrinking again inside. By the sound of it, if Auntie May gets her way, he won't be allowed to go to homework club tomorrow, maybe not until summer.

"The teachers are there," Auntie Aha says. "They said it's good for him to go."

"The same teachers are there all day. What more? For them it's a job. He is not their child."

"Send him to Obi. Obi said that he will help. Why don't you let Obi mentor him? Too many women are at that school."

"He needs his space, that's all," Auntie Aha says. "He wants space. Let him do his work at school. It is even wonderful that he himself brought the idea to go. He wants to take responsibility."

"Fifteen next year. Imagine. Almost fifteen and look at the way he walks."

"You keep treating him like this and he will never grow."

"It's true. Let him go."

"This is the age when he can handle trouble and learn. He has his bus pass."

"Even on the bus, people can be carrying knives."

"I'm tired," comes Ma's voice. "Imagine if he had attended school in Ghana. Just one year. Can you imagine it? I'm sure he would straighten up quickly. Sometimes, I really think about it."

"Oh no."

"Let him hold a proper phone. Probably he gave that old mobile back because his peers made fun of him. Give him a smartphone. Maybe that will help him become smart, aha."

"Will you pay for it? He'll be buying things there and distracting himself."

"It's true, he's not ready."

"Other boys smaller than him have phones."

"Let them stay on their phones. See if it will help them."

Heat floods his cheeks. Times like these make him want to escape, as he used to do when he first got his transit card, on Sundays, when the aunties were at church or visiting friends. Now and again he would go nowhere on a Tube train, watching the churn of travelers empty and fill the carriage. To feel unseen and to be ignored, to be left to himself.

It seems like a mercy that Da is not here to witness how far behind he is, and the stress it causes everyone. From what Kwasi has overheard, Ma mostly asks about the house when she speaks with Da on the phone, and about money transfers. She used to laugh a lot during these calls, and kiss her teeth with a fondness that made Kwasi smile. She used to end each call saying, "Come soon."

He pushes himself up into a crouch. Underneath the sense of doom is regret. The regret runs deeper than his mistakes; it flows thickly. Some of this regret belongs to Da, a separate current in his blood, cold with all the reasons why Da must want to stay away, that everything Kwasi was supposed to do, being born here, getting to move to a good school to have a new start, is coming to nothing. He presses his hand onto the step. The carpet here is thinning, and he runs his finger along the edge of a board underneath. Gray. It feels like this whole house is gray inside.

★

"Can I still go to homework club tomorrow or not?" he asks, when Auntie Aha comes up the stairs. He stands up, does his best to look brave. "The computers at school are much faster. I can type up my homework easier."

Auntie Aha glances back toward the living room. All is quiet there now. She turns back to him and rests an arm against the banister. "Go," she says. "Your mother worries too much. If she is upset, I will explain I told you to go. And buy food." Her sincere expression opens into a smile. "You are working hard, you should be eating more."

21

A crisp morning, acid blue sky; sunshine is balm on his cheeks and hands. The warmth in the light makes him stand taller, straightening as he waits at the till. Today's customers are in a cheery mood too. They trickle in and nod hello.

"It's so peaceful here," says a woman with thick-framed glasses and russet curls.

"It is," her partner says, and touches his hand to her back. He takes the thrillers she's considering, one in each hand, as though weighing them. "What a find. It's lovely here."

Inside, Rupert soars.

They have worked nearby for a month, they tell him. They are software engineers from the workspace by the station.

"I've not heard of it," he says. "You don't have offices?"

"Well we do, in Toronto, but we're taking a remote year, just to see."

"We're meant to be in Prague this week," the woman says. "But here we are."

"Traveling can be tricky," Rupert says.

"Because we're not ready for it, as a civilization," the

woman says. "The infrastructure. I think there's plenty of appetite for adventure though."

"Plenty of places to adventure locally. Have you gone up past the roundabout? When the weather's nice you can follow the trail by the brook."

"Oh, a nature trail?"

"We used to go out for picnics, my wife and I. Properly wild, not in a tidy manicured way, just thicket and bush. Gorgeous on a sunny day. All the dandelions."

The memory seizes him, a multitude of wishes clustered around stems, flowers with their yellow petals long gone. He remembers pinching stems between forefinger and thumb, blowing, giving flight to seeds.

"We haven't explored locally." The woman puts her chosen scarf on the counter. "We're following a guide to London from YouTube. There's so much to see. You have such a cute collection, honestly. We've been in charity shops all year. I'm challenging myself to live on reused goods and reduce my waste. I have a blog. Do you guys have a noticeboard? I'll leave a card."

The noticeboard is filling up. Turns out lots of people have things to share. Whether anyone stops to read it is another question.

When customers and daylight are gone, Rupert makes a cup of fruit tea and settles in the display nook upon a padded stool, watching people pass. Tulip's beloved berry infusion has its charm but is somewhat saccharine.

At least this way he keeps sober though. He is supposed to be heading to the library tonight, to register for the small business fund, but the past feels close and urgent. His memories are a muddle. He should not have started talking about it. Now it will come back to him at night.

A shadow sweeps over the shop. He pats his pockets for his keys, for his mobile phone. But when he looks back it's only the boy from Halloween, waving outside the back windows. The sight lifts him, brings something greater than relief.

"You've got to start wearing a hat and a scarf," Rupert says at the back door, welcoming him in.

"Yeah. I'm not a girl."

Rupert shuts the door and fans the tobacco smell away. "Gentlemen catch colds too."

"I have my tie. That's kind of like a scarf."

"And you don't even wear that properly."

The boy looks down at his shortened tie. "Anyway. Please can I get a coffee?"

"I have something better. But what's this? What have you got?"

The boy is unzipping his backpack, and now he pulls out a great hardback book. *Earth* is printed on the front cover, over a misty waterfall.

"You have the whole world in your hands."

"Oh wow," the boy says, and shakes his head.

"Well. Looks like it weighs as much."

"I need to finish this." He takes a folded printout from between the book's pages. "Can I do my homework downstairs?"

Rupert hesitates. "I'm not letting you have coffee again."

"I know. I don't mind about the coffee."

"Are you looking for something? A book, maybe? I mean, I'm glad you like the space. I don't mind you coming here at all."

The boy lifts his shoulders. "I just like how quiet it is."

"It is quiet," Rupert says. At the bottom of the stairs he stops. "There's a desk here somewhere. People keep bringing furniture, though I say I can't take any more."

"I don't need a desk." The boy squeezes past and settles on the floor.

"You can't study in darkness. You'll ruin your eyes." He lights more candles, until it's bright enough to look for the torch. The boy is already taking more books out from his bag.

"Is that geography homework?" Rupert asks. "I was good at geography, in my day. Maybe I can help. That sort of knowledge doesn't go out of date."

"French and math."

"You like math?"

"It's pointless, when we can just use a calculator in real life."

"Math is tricky." He sets the kettle to boil. "Useful though, if you want to go into business. Perhaps I should have tried harder at that."

"I used to be okay but now we have to mix letters in. And we have to do graphs. The other day, all I did was ask how you know how high up a y-axis should go, and our teacher said it goes up to infinity. So then I asked how high up that would be, then she explained infinity is forever, like in space. And that in space, you can see things way back in time and maybe in the future. That's when I gave up trying to follow it. All I wanted was to finish the graph."

Steam rises from the kettle. "That is a lot to think about."

"Makes me think about different planets you could get to, how they might look. Then I gave up on even trying to understand math."

"You came here straight from school? You must be hungry."

"I bought chips."

"Of course. There's no shortage of that about."

"Yeah, but the best chip shop closed. The fish and chips shop, I mean."

"Oh, not the Pattersons'?" Something dulls within him. He can't remember the last time he went into their shop. Perhaps a few months before Jada passed. He remembers the crackle and pop of hot oil, the mirror underneath the menu, and Jada's reflection there, her guilty smile when their eyes met, for her wavering commitment to vegetarianism, trying her utmost to resist the delicious aromas about that place.

"Yeah, the Pattersons'," the boy says. "They used to give me extra chips while we waited for our order. When I was in primary school."

"I had my first fish and chips there, when I moved here with my wife. They're a lovely family. I hope they're all right."

"I think they should have called it time."

"What's that?"

"Instead of space, the universe should be called time."

Rupert places a tea bag in each cup.

"Because you can travel through time, when you're high off the earth." The boy looks uncertain, as though the idea has just arrived, and then he nods, eyes glittering. "You can. It's true. In space, you can see things from hundreds of years ago, which is basically living in a different time."

"That's something." Carefully, he pours the hot water. "I suppose they call it space because there's no shortage of space up there." The deep red of Tulip's fruit tea blushes in the shallow teacups, with a gentle springtime scent. "Infinite space. Meanwhile, here everyone is scrambling to live on top of each other." He hands the boy a cup. "Careful, it's hot. Now. Let's see about a light."

The boy looks up and points with his chin. "Is that light not working?"

He follows the boy's gaze, looking up at the bulb overhead. "I forgot that light existed. It's been broken long enough." And again, there is this sinking feeling that he has kept away too long, that he has missed too much. "The wiring is bad—it'll be a big job."

The boy raises his tea and sniffs. "Smells like jam."

"What kind of jam?"

"Don't know."

"Guess."

"Strawberry."

"That's one of flavors, yes. See what else you notice there." He finds two more candles and a broken lantern. "I'll be upstairs for a bit, I have to add up the takings. You're welcome to come up. And shout if you need anything."

The shop is luminous upstairs. He thinks of what the boy said, standing by the glass, looking out to the edges of space, all the darkness drifting on high. In this moment, he can feel the emptiness beyond, how charged with possibility it seems.

Here is this burning inside again, the certainty they will make it. He looks back toward the stairwell, so much yet to unpack: furniture waiting to be repaired, polished, arranged; notebooks of ideas, parallel universes in which they are thriving, in which Jada is still here.

Rupert sits by the counter and opens his palms on the cool surface. Perhaps in another life he and Jada would have left this corner long ago. He could have followed her on her travels, resisted the feeling that the world was converging on London. They bought a house this far out, certain the liveliness of London would spread further north, would saturate the city to its edges. And here the opposite has come true; all the colors he loved have dulled. But even these colors might have appeared brighter, had Jada still been here.

"Strawberry and cherry," the boy shouts, startling Rupert. Tea, he remembers.

"Close."

"Grape?"

"Not so close." He stands and goes to the stairs.

The boy's face appears. He stands with one foot on the first step, hugging his *Earth* book. "I'm done with French and algebra. It's blackberry, isn't it?"

"Raspberry. It's late. You ought to get home."

"I can get home in no time."

"Are you going to teleport, then?"

"If I could do that, I would never get chased."

He waits, but the boy says nothing further. If anything, he looks like he regrets bringing up the chasing. He comes up the stairs slowly, keeping his head bowed.

"It's a shame that we can't teleport," Rupert says. "There is, however, a way to time-travel."

The boy stops, halfway up the stairs. "Not really."

"Oh yes."

"How, then?"

"If a building is tall enough, you can watch the sunset from the ground, and then hurry up to the top floor, from where the sun will set a second time."

The boy looks deep in thought. "So if you're high up you have extra time. Every day will last longer."

Rupert smiles. "Well, since we've spent so much time belowground, maybe we have even less time. Come on up now. Get home safe."

22

Saturday. The house is his. The aunties are bound for a function somewhere south. Giddiness tickles him, just from thinking of all he will draw today, with no one around to disturb him. He will start by finding the note he made on his homework sheet at the Chest, when new ideas rose in him. Ideas about space, infinity, seeing things that happened millions of years ago. He presses the sheet open on his duvet now; the writing he scribbled is tangled, so he can barely read it. He will draw in the living room, like he used to years ago, before everyone said he was too big, that he should be studying. He is going to try something in his old style.

It has taken the aunties forever to get ready but at last, by eleven, they are gathering in the corridor. Once they go, he will shower, listening to the water. No one will be around to rush him. After this, he will go through his old drawings, the ones pushed back under his bed, sketches he tried the summer he drew that scene inside the Chest. It might be fun to draw with crayons and coloring pencils again, as long as he can find them.

"Kwasi," Squid shouts from downstairs. "Kwasi, come down."

He goes lightly to the stairs and stops. Jericho's dad is by the front door, wearing a gray suit.

"Kwasi, are you still not dressed?" Ma says.

"I'm not going," he says. "You said I don't have to."

"You're not coming with us. We're giving you a lift to Jericho's house."

All the color goes from the walls. "What?"

"Are we not quite ready yet?" King Obi says. "Not a problem. Croydon will wait for us."

Kwasi looks at Ma. There are too many people in the house, too many fragrances mixing. "You said I didn't have to go."

"Jericho said you were happy to help out," King Obi says, "and it's been too long since you spent time at ours. Although I know you boys had fun at Halloween."

Kwasi bites his lip. Dips his head in a nod. "What's meant to be happening?" he asks. "Today, I mean."

"Kwasi, don't be rude," Ma says.

"It's all right." King Obi seems to find all of this funny. He has the same look Jericho gets, like he is orchestrating a prank. "I can explain. Today, I've got Jericho working on a nativity scene we accidentally volunteered to make. You like painting, don't you? You two can work on that while we're away. Better than sitting alone in different houses."

It is hard to pull air into his lungs. He grips the banister.

"We are wasting time," Squid says. "Kwasi."

"Come on then, shall we go?" King Obi asks. "We have everything you might need, and there's the Xbox if you finish early. You can order a pizza, and we have cake left over."

"Kwasi. Stop this nonsense and go and get changed," Ma says.

He looks to Auntie May. To Auntie Aha. Everyone looks annoyed.

His stomach churns on the short car journey, but not enough to actually be sick, to show everyone he needs to go home. It's been so hard to avoid Jericho this long since Halloween, and now the grown-ups have messed it up.

He can smell the twang of his own sweat by the time Jericho's house appears. He has an impulse to run as soon as his trainers touch the driveway. But Jericho is waiting in the doorway.

"Good luck," King Obi calls. "Don't get paint on the carpet."

"We won't." Jericho beckons Kwasi inside. "About time," he says. "My dad was up at nine. I told him your lot will take forever."

Inside, music warms the house. Jazzy melodies overlap from speakers he cannot see, a familiar refrain meandering beneath the hissing and rattling of cymbals. Kwasi hesitates, to hear if anyone else is around.

"Go in. We got Krispy Kremes," Jericho says. "And some dumb fruitcake. Hey. Take your shoes off."

It is strange being back in this house. The house King Obi used to say was always here as his second home. Last time he was here was for Christmas, in year seven. Two whole years ago. The wall between the living room and kitchen is gone. There used to be photos everywhere, but now there are only framed prints of what seems to be modern art. Only one photograph remains, of Jericho's mother; Jericho said years ago the whole family is in this picture. King Obi's shadow falls in the frame, leaning in the bottom of the photo, and his fingertip too is a blur in the bottom corner. Jericho is the swell in the dress that his mother's hand rests upon.

"It's here," Jericho says.

The nativity display covers the living room floor: so many wooden boards, different layers waiting to be secured together. "So basically, we have to paint it and glue everything onto the main background," Jericho says. "It's for a carol service."

The room has paused, even the music falls away. Jericho is watching him, one eyebrow raised.

"We have ages before Christmas," Kwasi says. His voice comes out smaller than it felt inside.

Thankfully, Jericho smiles. "Try telling that to my dad."

They sit on newspapers on the carpet and Jericho opens buckets of paint. Deep blue for the sky, browns and greens and yellows. "We have more in the garage. My dad is over the top. It's a mad story, the way I got volunteered."

The story is not that crazy, nothing compared to Halloween. Watching Jericho explain it is bizarre though. This is a different Jericho to the version that sneers at him at school. Even his voice is softer, quieter.

In the background, music quickens into rap.

"Start then, use the bigger brush," Jericho says. "What's happening with you? Is your dad still building that house?"

"Guess so," Kwasi says. He takes the larger brush. It fits snugly in his hand. The weirdest thing about this is that it seems like Jericho is just going to pretend like Halloween never happened. That night is still vivid, in faint aches all down his legs. He can still see Selim's brother's car pulling up, hear the screeching noise of it. His arm feels stiff and awkward as he touches the brush into the paint.

"It's cool that he is building his own house. He can do whatever with it."

"Yeah."

Now he is thinking about the pool Da mentioned on the phone, and about the children's voices he heard. It is silly to feel annoyed about a place he has never visited. It's hard to know which would be worse: if the house turns out okay, the aunties might stop making fun of Da, but then Ma might talk seriously again about moving to Ghana for good. Still, if the building work drags on and on, Da might stay in Ghana forever.

"Why do you look so stressed?" Jericho asks.

"Nothing." He makes an effort to set his face neutral.

"Tell me about this house then," Jericho says. "Is it near the beach?"

For some reason, Jericho is hungry for updates. Nothing is enough. And none of his questions even get near to Halloween.

"What music is this?" Kwasi asks at last. At least this could shift Jericho's attention off him.

Jericho inclines his head, listening. "You don't know who this is? Have you seriously not heard of Devilman?"

"He sounds weird."

"How can you have not heard Devilman? He's always sending for people. Who do you listen to, Bugzy Malone?"

"Don't really listen to music," Kwasi says. "I couldn't listen to this when I'm working. Too distracting."

"Listen when you're not working."

"So, when I'm sleeping."

"Nah, listen on your toilet breaks. For real. Is that why you never come out? What work are you even doing? Does your family not know child labor is illegal here?"

"Just schoolwork."

Jericho's gaze flicks over him. "Swear you're in the bottom set for everything."

"Yeah. That's why I have to do extra."

Jericho shakes his head. "I would be looking for bigger options. Your lot is too controlling, but in a way it's your fault. They won't let you do anything if you don't try. Like, if I hadn't suggested you come help me paint this, you would have been sitting in your bedroom right now, in silence."

"You should try living with my aunties."

"My dad does it too. Thinks he can have power over me. You know he told the Chicken Palace not to serve me?"

"Wow."

"I just get someone else to buy what I want. He has his people, I have mine."

They paint quietly, filling in the outlines marked upon the wood. Something about it, being here, the music in the background, makes Kwasi ache. It's not so bad and, in a way, he is still spending today on art. There might be time to paint something separate later. Still, alertness rings down his back.

"So you just stay at home, listening to your aunties."

"What do you mean?"

"You never go out. They have you on lock."

"I do go out." It just comes out, though he has not done this since spring. "It's not that hard. Like when everyone goes to church or sleeps in. I don't just stay at home."

"Yeah?" Jericho stops painting and considers him. "Where do you go?"

"Wherever."

"Okay then." Jericho dips his brush into the water.

"You think I'm making it up?"

Jericho glances toward the doorway. Something has changed when he looks back. "I could get you work," he says.

"What, painting?"

"Work that pays, idiot. With Selim."

The churning begins again, tugging his stomach. "I already have too much work."

"All I'm saying is, sure it's tragic how your aunties won't let you out. Just going to school and back is dry. There's money out here."

Kwasi lowers his paintbrush into the water. "You make money from stuff you do with Selim?"

"Course."

He stirs the water with his brush. The water is an infusion of deep blue. Lots of tiny particles, he remembers reading in science, moving randomly in chaos, making patterns by coincidence. Pigment moves through water like smoke.

"Going to make more next year," Jericho says. "I'm getting a keyboard, and a proper camera, and then we can start recording stuff. Big money."

"What are you going to do with the money?"

"Saving it. I'm not going to be one of those people who goes to uni and comes back to live at home. I'm going to travel. Actually, what I really want is to have these resorts, like holiday places but wild, where people come for music, photo shoots. Obviously, that's expensive, so. And when I've saved enough I can do something to balance everything out. I don't know, might set up a charity to help starving Ghanaians."

Kwasi flinches. "Hey."

"A joke," Jericho says, holding his hands up. "Or I could

let sad loners into one of my resorts for like, a tropical Duke of Edinburgh Award." Jericho's eyes go wide with this idea. "How sick would that be?"

"But what do you have to do? How do you get money? With Selim's brother, I mean?"

Jericho drops his paintbrush into the waterpot. "Enough talking. I'm hungry."

They order pizza and eat looking over the back garden, where they used to have barbecues to mark birthdays and to make the most of good weather. He used to imagine Da returning as a surprise during a barbecue here, so for a while he made himself keep coming, even though Jericho didn't speak to him at school. He used to imagine Da walking up between the flower beds, and all King Obi's guests turning to watch.

"You should come out with us," Jericho says. "Me, Wade, Selim. We go to the Turkish place, next to the park. You're not scared, are you? Because of Halloween?"

At last, here it comes. "Course not." It comes out faster than he can think. He wipes cheese off his wrist.

"Why are you avoiding us then? I called you and messaged. Do you not know how to use your phone?"

"Like I said, I just have lots to do. Anyway, that's not my actual phone. I had to give it back."

Jericho is shaking his head. "You are scared."

"Not really. I'm more scared about parents' evening."

"Parents' evening. Woo, some teachers are disappointed. What's the worst that can happen?"

"It's not funny. My ma might send me to Ghana."

"Shut up."

"Seriously. She used to say it, like as a joke. That if I

can't settle into schools here, if I didn't do well at the next school, she would send me to boarding school in Ghana." He shudders, thinking of it. He can hear it in her voice, saying a proper school will toughen him up, how teachers there will not be so easy on him, or so quick to label him.

"That's a lie. She won't."

"My dad's taking forever there. I guess he likes it better."

"Is this about the baby thing? How your mum wanted more kids?"

In his stomach, something twists. He closes the pizza box.

"What?" Jericho looks up with a faint smile. "Was it meant to be a secret? It was pretty obvious. Your mum was doing a lot, going to all these churches getting prayers and my dad paid for like, private treatment. She went off at my dad, you know."

"When was this?"

"Ages ago. Maybe in year six. I think that's when your dad fully took over the recruitment thing from my dad."

"Serious?" Kwasi lowers his voice. "Your dad used to work on it?"

"My dad worked on everything. I can't even say half of it. You remember that woman, one of the early ones they brought over, the weird one who never spoke, and she brought bad luck or something? Anyway, if your mum sends you to Ghana it won't be because of your grades. It will be because she has issues." Jericho gets up and takes their empty glasses to the sink.

From the photo on the wall, Jericho's mum stares at Kwasi.

"I used to hate going to yours," comes Jericho's voice from the kitchen. "Your aunties get so weird around my dad. And when your dad went to Ghana, seemed like your mum was going to try something. No offense to your mum. I did say maybe we could just adopt you, and leave the rest of it, haha." Jericho hesitates. "Playing games with you was the best thing about your house. What do you play these days? Do you play online? I'll add you. We all play on Sundays."

"Like I said, I seriously don't have time for stuff like that. And apparently screen time is bad for my concentration. I'm lucky if I get to go swimming on the weekend."

"Swimming is the whitest thing ever."

"Not really. The swimming instructor is Chinese."

"Nah. You are lost."

Shame rinses through him, mixed with annoyance. Everything pushes him away. Everything is too much but not enough.

23

It was bound to happen again. Flecks of white cling to the glass. From a distance they might be glitter. The smell hits when he opens the door: sulfur and rot. Eggshell on the pavement.

It must have happened just now, while he was downstairs. Egg muck is congealing, frosting to a white paste, drying like a great gob of spit.

The stench isn't just egg. He is standing in dog mess. He backs inside. Bits of eggshell are caught in the muck underneath his shoes. He can't bear to look at it and leaves both shoes by the door.

"What's all this?" Elaine asks, when she comes in. "What's happened? Good God. Someone's egged the front."

Rupert leans a hand against the wall for support. "I'll sort it out."

"Call the police. I'll say whoever let their dog do that knew exactly what they were doing. God. Put the kettle on, and I'll need detergent."

Down the stairs in his socks. He opens the cupboards under the sink and there it is: the box of not-so-fresh herbs.

A laugh escapes his throat. Feels like a lifetime since he hid it there, to keep it out of sight. All the flavors that could soothe him now. He straightens and grips the sink's edge.

"And grab a bin bag," Elaine calls.

"Actually." He rests a foot on the first step. "Let's take the day off. It's likely to be terrible weather anyway. I'll take care of cleaning up."

★

Rarely is he home at this hour. By day his house is changed. Here is the settee, hardly used, which he will soon sell. Here are the boxes returned from storage he can no longer pay for. They fill his living room once again: stacked into a brown wall and festooned with things he could not bring himself to get rid of.

Here is a familiar feeling: the urge to load everything into a van and drive to where it is sunnier, where no one will remember him. Laughter sours in his throat. He might do that, when he has a moment, and money to spare. Perhaps Jada knew she would not need to plan for retirement. But what is his excuse? Trust: that people would always give and buy and give.

On his table lies the landlord's letter, alongside a page he was supposed to fill with a draft response tonight. A prompt reply will lay the foundation for reassuring the landlord, if he is to have any hope of staying. More work must follow, to see if the landlord can cover fixing the wiring, to see what furniture they can salvage from the basement, what it might cost to clear and refurbish downstairs. He takes the pen. He will remember today not for what thoughtless kids did to the shopfront, but as the beginning of a bolder path, toward a solid place in whatever they are hurtling toward.

24

Even after how chill Jericho was at the weekend, at school he is unchanged, back with his usual spikiness. His gaze cuts all through class, and across the lunch hall, makes Kwasi certain he is in the middle of a complicated prank. And then at last it comes: outside the library after homework club, Jericho jumps him.

"Stop." Kwasi squirms free, grabs his bag.

"Ahahaha. Your face," Jericho says, and swipes for his head.

Kwasi ducks. The corridor beyond looks empty. No sign of Selim and the others. A cleaner advances ahead, pushing her mop trolley. He waits for the usual joke about his aunties, one of whom worked here briefly.

Instead, Jericho says, "Did you listen to Bugzy Malone?"

"Not yet."

"We'll listen tonight. Come, let's go."

Still there is no sign of Selim, but it's hard to relax, walking toward the exit; the school is vast and open, and anyone could be waiting round the next corner.

"Did you just have detention?" he asks Jericho, when the silence is too much.

"Nah. I'm doing this mentoring thing for year sevens."

"Did your dad volunteer you for that too?"

"Nope. My idea this time. Did you notice how there are so many more Black kids coming up? Imagine if we'd had mentors, when we started. But yeah, nothing to do with my dad. Year sevens are my people. They are so innocent but they all think they're bad."

"Are you going home now? Is your dad at the house?"

"Not going to mine. Going to Wade's. Hey"—Jericho pushes the double doors open—"when were you going to tell me about Gemma?"

Pinched by panic, Kwasi looks back. Still no one else is near. Somehow that feels worse.

"Hello? Gemma?" Jericho is giving him that look, like he seriously wants to know.

"I was just sitting at her table. There was nowhere else to go."

"You sat with her all week."

His cheeks flush. "Doesn't Wade live ages away? I'm not supposed to be out late."

"How dumb are you? Think. Would we be in the same school if he lived ages away? I'll show you where everyone lives."

"I have to go to the toilet."

In the cubicle he puts the toilet lid down and sits. It gets stranger, the more he thinks about it, how different Jericho can be. Sometimes it feels like everything he worried about was only in his head, but then he feels like it's just that they're working on a bigger prank. He folds his arms and rests his chin on them.

There was the time his aunties came to the school fair in

their church clothes, because Jericho told them the theme was heritage. They wore bright prints and gold jewelry and brought doughnuts and chin-chin for everyone to try. Thinking about it now still makes him shrink. The theme was supposed to be local heritage, but no one listened when he tried to explain. That was in year five, and everyone at school found it funny, more so after Jericho kept bringing it up. It got worse in secondary school, but at least it was easier to hide in a bigger school. Now it seems like hiding and keeping to himself has made it easier for everyone to make fun of him.

He gets up and grabs his backpack. It doesn't matter anyway, whatever Jericho is up to. He has a new drawing to show the shopkeeper. When he steps out he notices that the window by the dryer is wide open. It's not as small as it first seemed.

He climbs onto the windowsill, pushes his backpack out. It thuds close below. The one good thing about being small: he squeezes through easily, although it would have been easier if he had taken his jacket off first.

At last he falls through. Wipes gravel and tiny stones off his palms. Heart thumping, he grabs his bag and runs. Down the steps and up the walkway to the gates. Panting, he untangles his pass from his tie and scans it and hurries out into the street. There comes the drone of a bus—sometimes the driver doesn't stop, even when they see him, when it's only him. Luckily there's a woman at the stop, and she hails it. He gets on, out of breath, fumbles for his transit card.

★

The shopkeeper takes a sip from his mug and his face sours. He swallows with a grimace. "Far too sweet. Once you've had that, everything else tastes like cardboard." He puts his mug of hot chocolate down. "That's how they do it, how they keep people buying nonsense."

It's funny because even though he complains about sugar, the shopkeeper goes on and takes another sip. And another, like he enjoys having stuff to complain about.

"What's funny?" he asks.

"Nothing," Kwasi says. "I have a question."

"Go on then."

"After I go home, what actually happens here? I mean, do they pay you more to stay late?"

"Sadly no one pays me for working extra hard. It's my business."

"So you pay yourself."

"Only if work pays off. Raising money for charity and keeping this place running comes first. Unfortunately, it's not as busy as it was. When you go home, well, I get on with paperwork. Got new ideas for this place, to get it back to what it was. Not much time to turn it around."

It's especially quiet in the Chest tonight, undisturbed and still, like nothing has happened here in months. He can feel the edge of trouble looming, underneath the man's words. "Why? How busy did it used to be?"

"Oh. We'd have people coming and going until nine o'clock. Sometimes people would come in just to nose through our big books. We had two great books upstairs, you see, well I mean we still have them—the guestbook for general comments, and the book for charities to be considered for the vote. People would read the guestbook to see who had popped in, whether anyone had written anything alongside the entry they had left. And some people wrote down bands and singers they were listening to, and we would look through it each Friday—this was years ago—and add to our music for the shop. It's always been about variety here. Now we have too many clothes and books. And all this blasted furniture." He gestures back toward the stairs.

There is a quiet fervency about the shopkeeper tonight. It's sad in a way, like maybe most of the other people who remember everything that happened here in busier times are gone, and the shopkeeper is the last one, carrying all this in his head.

"Will you change things down here?" Kwasi asks.

"It would be wonderful to have more evening events. Need to sort the wiring, first. Anyway, that's for me to worry about. You worry about your homework. What are we doing today? English?"

"I did it at school already. I have something." Kwasi takes the sheet from his homework diary. "Here."

The man takes the page in both hands. Wide, pale hands, etched with rivulets of lines.

"It's this idea I had about a kind of underground river." It sounds weird, spoken aloud. But the shopkeeper looks intrigued. "Usually I just do comics. That's faster. I have a teacher who said to use my comics to remember things for history. Imagine if we could just draw for exams."

The man inclines his head, considering the drawing. "You'd do well." His eyes glint in the flickering light, their grayness sharpened to steel.

"Keep it."

"I would like to keep it. But only if you are willing to do something."

Kwasi folds his arms. Here it is at last. Everyone wants something. Everyone wants him to be more. At least he is going to hear it now, before he gets properly comfortable here. "Something like what?"

"I can't take this if you're not going to be working on more masterpieces to keep for yourself. You must keep on drawing."

Kwasi lets out the breath he was holding.

"You need to begin to choose what you want to make space for in your life. Whatever you focus on now will grow to fill your time. When you finish your homework, no matter how tired or bored you feel, draw. I might even have some paints. Do you paint as well?"

Thuds cascade above. Voices bellow.

Kwasi clutches his bag. Gets to his feet. "Is there a fire exit? To get out from down here?"

The man raises a palm.

They wait. There is no sound beyond his heart's pounding. As quiet thickens, his face rings numb. It could be the pause before the real noise starts.

"They've gone," the man says. "It's all right. Now. Are you going to tell me what's going on? With those boys from your school?"

Still, his body stays tense, as though it knows. "They could come back."

"Good. I'd like to have a word with them."

"No."

"I won't let them in." The man goes into the clutter of furniture. "Are they the same boys who chased you on Halloween?" he calls. "You said they weren't your friends. They know you from school?"

"They mostly ignore me. It was my fault for trying to do Halloween with them." He sips his hot chocolate, trying to seem calm. "Definitely won't do that again."

The man reemerges at last, holding a tall box. "How about a game of Jenga?" Without waiting for an answer, he continues. "That's another way it used to be busier here. We would have board games and puzzles. We would get so many children coming in with their mothers, see. Jada was wonderful with them. She had a school workshop, for girls. A workshop making fragrances."

"Only for girls?"

"Girls didn't have enough role models in the sciences, was the idea. Sometimes you need someone who looks a bit like you to show you what you can be. Or not even who looks like you. Someone who is like you in some way. Who you can relate to."

Kwasi hugs his shoulders. His chest feels suddenly tight.

The man places the box on the floor and lifts it up, so the tower of wooden blocks stands intact.

"Did you divorce your wife?" he asks.

"No, no. She passed away."

"Oops."

"That's all right. We had wonderful years. Right here." The man nods. "We did."

25

Work feels clearer walking home. Perhaps it was all the sugar from those hot chocolates. That game of Jenga took him back, and the stories about the Chest's best days that he shared won't settle again in his mind, now he has spoken them. He can see the Chest as it was meant to be, what it was at its busiest.

Sitting on his settee back at home, he is still energized, more awake than he has felt all day. He drafts a final response to the landlord, and reads it aloud.

Thank you for getting in touch. We have no problem paying rent this Christmas. We are doing much better and have registered for the council fund to support new projects we're working on. It would be a pleasure to meet in the new year and talk through our plans in more detail.

In truth, Christmas rent still looks shaky, even now that his settee has a buyer, though they've offered less than he hoped for. But he'll worry about that later. Rupert folds the letter and takes his box of seaside vistas to the settee. He looks through the glossy leaflets by the light of the corner lamp: sandy beaches fading into white-blue sea at

Cornwall, Devon, Norfolk. The country's edges, where it is warmer, quieter, where the land itself shrinks beneath the people fading there.

Thinking now of all the sleep he lost worrying for the nation's beaches when, as a boy in Mr. Eaton's geography class, he learned about Long Shore Drift. Mr. Eaton, a gray man with a gray voice. Rupert can still see him scrawling three letters on the board: LSD. Long and inevitable, the migration of sand, fragments of animal bones and stones and rocks and glass and dirt, little shards of everything, which he spent summers scooping into buckets and patting into fortresses. Every summer holiday, spent with cousins at the seaside, seemed somehow the same, the same striped paraphernalia and rainbow sticks of rock, endless fish and chips and dark arcade halls filled with chirping game-stations. That summer of longshore drift, devastated by the scale of the betrayal, when he had just learned that the land had its own journey of creeping departure. He blushed with furious guilt, sitting crouched in his trunks, watching waves come in and take, take, take. That they were going to run out of beach seemed the only certainty, a grim conviction reinforced when Father's interest turned to national parks, and they spent subsequent holidays exploring hilly inland retreats, wandering around lakes and biking trails with no sand or sea in sight.

It could be nice to retire and spend his last years by the sea. Although in a care home, if it comes to that, he might not notice where he is. The smell of salt and fish might be covered by the lavender sigh of diffusers. And the people: probably the same everywhere. Missing people too; her absence will meet him anywhere.

26

Draw. Something about how the shopkeeper said it laid bare the power of that word. Keep drawing. He has hardly even started with his drawings. Jericho is right. It's like he's not really trying.

So here it is: a plan. A plan that must be written, before it fades. There are fifteen days until parents' evening. As far as he knows, Mrs. Nibley hasn't called the house again, although he has another letter from her, which he will flush later tonight, when Auntie Aha has finished in the bathroom. Going to homework club is not going to be enough to finish typing up all the work or to make him better at math. There is too much happening in the library for him to concentrate, and Gemma is always staring. One thing they never covered at school is how to focus, how to make and then follow a plan. They just expect everyone to know.

The cupboards in Da's study are stuffed with expired plans. Long, detailed plans cover the backs of opened en-velopes and loose pages from notebooks lined and unlined. Kwasi spreads the pages out on the carpet. Chunks of notes have been scribbled and crossed out. Having a plan will not be enough; most of Da's plans are just wasted paper. But he has to try.

To try again, to go back to drawing as much as he used to—more—to try with everything in him, feels possible back at school, watching puddles reach across the playground from his spot by the window.

"Can I see?" Gemma asks later, in the hush of the library.

He pulls his pencil case nearer, as a barrier to his page.

"You're not drawing me, are you?"

"Why would I?"

"Don't know." She looks back to her book.

He is sketching a storyboard, of what needs to happen next. Not his best drawing, but it tells the story. A story in which his drawings get so good, Ma and his aunties run out of words. A story in which they finally see. He folds and folds the page, puts it in the secret pocket in his blazer.

Carrying it makes him giddy; his heart pounds behind the page's stiff shape. He contracts the muscles around his armpit, so they press against the paper.

The next day, it happens: for the first time since Halloween, he is assailed by Selim. Wade joins in, although Jericho is nowhere.

Their shouts fill the toilet. Elbows and fists pin him. They take his blazer, tie, and shoes.

"Your aunties have been slacking," Wade says, in Mr. Haye's Scottish lilt. "What kind of cleaners are they? This loo's in an absolute state—look, there's a great fat stinky turd on the floor."

"Aye. A big black poo." A foot nudges his back.

"Look how shiny it is."

His tie, they pocket. They will return it later as a blind-fold, after he has accumulated more demerits and chastisements for not wearing his uniform properly. They empty his blazer into a sink. Pens clatter and bounce off the rim and roll everywhere.

The blazer is thrown back and lands over his head.

He waits as footsteps fade. The only sounds are of drains and dripping, and the dryer *voom*ing from the girls' toilets next door.

At last he sits up. Pats the blazer until he finds the shape of his plan.

The shopkeeper has a plan too, he says, as they fold new old clothes still warm from the dryer.

"I was thinking about how lively it used to be here, after our chat the other night. I ought to put everything into this, just for a while, and now that I've told someone, I'll have to." The man's face wrinkles with a smile. "Three months to turn it around. We'll stop using so much water and heating, to save a bit. And then we have our new events."

"How much do you need to save?"

"Not an insignificant sum. But we're applying for funding, and we'll run new events." He goes to the tall cabinet by the stairs and returns with two sturdy notebooks. "These were my wife's plans. We didn't really think about making money out of events before, it was just fun. Everything was more spontaneous back then."

"Can I look?" Kwasi asks.

"Go ahead. If you have any ideas, I'm all ears."

"Ideas for making money?"

The pages are penciled with notes and brisk sketches,

lots of exclamation points and arrows. Crowds of stick men. Floating smiling faces.

"There is that. But it's about more than money. Ideas for making the most of this space. I'm learning to accept I'm a little out of touch. Good to hear what young people might like to see in a space like this. That was when the Chest was at its best, when it offered something to everyone."

Kwasi runs his finger down the page. "I like that it's quiet here. And that there's so much random stuff in here," he says. Something about the Chest settles him inside. It's open, yet closed away, and knowing there's so much movement, so many businesses close by, energizes him. The Underground's hum makes him think of all the people going across the city, all the ideas and plans they carry. It gives him more ideas for what to draw.

It is better with all the candles lit, new ones in colored cases that throw wavering hues across the ceiling. Teardrop flames jump and shrink and scents of cherries and oranges, ginger, honey and cocoa warm from softening wax. Flames pulse, and the basement, its wooden cupboards and chairs, becomes a forest of eyes.

Looking through drawings and notes, this much is clear: here is the perfect setting for an exhibition, to show his best drawings. The Chest has loads of unused frames, modest and ornate, packed amid the furniture.

He can see it: as his drawings go up over these walls, for a while, he will keep his identity secret. Like Banksy. If he draws well enough, all kinds of people will visit the Chest to see. They will tell their friends.

And one Sunday afternoon, on her way back from church, Ma will walk up, flanked by Auntie Aha and Squid, the three of them coming to see. He scribbles in his homework diary, ideas for new drawings to start when he gets home, of the Underground as a river of light stretching beneath the whole city, of a tea party scene down here, and of the Chest plunging back through centuries, like a time machine.

"What do you think about a kind of show? An exhibition?" he asks, as he gets ready to leave.

The man is writing in another notebook, with a calculator before him.

"Since there are all these frames. I have more drawings. And there are other drawings here we could use, that other one of the basement. We could sell some. You know, like an auction maybe?"

The man inclines his head, considering.

"I used to make collages." Kwasi hoists his backpack up. "I have loads of ideas. Every time I come here I get more."

The man sits back in his chair. "I have an assistant, Tulip. She has some artsy friends who might have thoughts."

"Okay. Good."

"Go on home then. It'll rain soon."

A test, in the living room at dinnertime the following day: "You know that shop in town, the Chest," he says, "it's not actually a charity shop. Even though it raises money for charities. It's not just a charity shop."

"So." Squid frowns beneath the storm of her hair. "I was right. You didn't just go to homework club."

"What were you thinking?" Auntie May asks.

He is thinking that perhaps this is not the best time to explain about the Chest. He should have anticipated this. The whole house feels gloomy while Squid unbraids her hair. Auntie Madame was helping earlier, to undo Squid's braids faster, but she got sent away for chopping too much off at the ends. Squid has been grumpy since.

"I went to get a book." He turns back to the dinner table and pokes a chunk of carrot with his fork. "They have tons of books and it costs nothing."

"Whose money have you been using?"

Kwasi's mouth turns dry. Auntie Aha is still away at work. That she did not tell the others she has been giving him money had not occurred to him.

"A book." Squid gives him a dark look. "You want us to believe you went to that place for a book?"

Ma drops the braid she was working on, and the room turns to him.

So now he must explain: it's a book for English, and yes, he tried at the library, but there are no more copies left, and at the Chest it only cost two pounds.

"You went to that man's shop? And he was there?"

"Kwasi."

"This is basic. What have we said about strangers?"

"He's a shopkeeper." He tries to speak from the base of his throat, from where his voice flows heavier. "He's just working, it's just like with teachers or any other shop."

"Did he say anything to you?"

"Where is the book you bought?"

"That man is trouble."

"We told you to come straight home."

"Is this the same man who poisoned his wife? Is he still working there?"

"Jesus."

"Kwasi, is this true?"

Rice turns to grit in his mouth. "Wait. Who poisoned who?"

"Did you go to that shop, the one where that old man is always waiting with his long face?"

He swallows his half-chewed mouthful. "I just went in with Kumar, right after school. Actually, it was his idea. He's been before and says the shopkeeper is really smart. We went straight back to homework club after."

"Is that so?"

"You are too big to be making up stories. It's not a game at this point. It is called lying."

27

The real work begins now.

Elaine shouts, as she leaves for the night, that the papers are on the counter. The full set of council papers, printed out to save him a trip to the library. He shouts back, thank you, but Elaine has gone. Sitting down, he leafs through the sheets. So many blank lines and boxes. His optimism is already waning.

"Have you read these?" he asks, when Tulip gets in. "Council wants us to . . ." He takes the page and squints. "'Evidence an ongoing interest in developing and improving efficiency, and enhancing customer experience.'"

"Yeah, I saw on the website," Tulip says. She seems even more cheerful than usual, sitting upright, fidgety.

"We need to put in here specific new things to try before Christmas. I don't want to ask the landlord for more time, but rent still looks tricky. I've been keeping the lights down too, got all the old candles burning. But." He lays the papers back on the counter.

"We can do it." Tulip bobs her head, eyes bright as two sparks. "We'll try new things over the next few weeks and it'll get people in before Christmas. And it will give us evidence to apply to the fund with."

"All right. What new things shall we try?"

Tulip falls quiet. She bows her head as she ponders. Having thought for a minute, she says she will think about it.

Rupert sinks further inside. That seems to be the trouble with graduates: imagining is as good as doing. He pushes the application papers aside and looks down over the dismal figures in his book. Despite the Reilly-Duffell boom, footfall alone is not enough. And the cost of running Christmas lights is not insignificant. He flexes his hands.

"Well, to start off with," he says, "we have your art night. That went well. Let's do that again. And I had an idea about a kind of storytelling night. We had fun back in the day, listening to people talking about their lives. It used to just happen, but maybe we need to put some work in to bring that back."

"That sounds cool."

"We still have deeper problems," he says. "It's as though nobody today sees value in anyone else's treasures. They come in, but they don't buy. Look at this."

He opens the black book, and Tulip gets up to see. "Last month's figures are worse than I expected, although it was busy."

"You still keep paper records?" Tulip leans closer.

"It works." He runs a finger over the figures.

"I'll put it on a spreadsheet." She unzips her bag and pulls out her laptop. "How does it work, actually? Do you give a fixed percentage of profits to charity?"

"Exactly that. Take a look. I've had to spend more on bills than I would have liked lately."

Soon, her fingers clatter over the keys. "Look." Slowly, the grid on the screen fills with numbers, with weeks and months of fundraising, records of items, and dates. She colors the table in red, green, and yellow. "I like the sound of those events. You did say it was community events that gave this place a buzz years ago. We have to create moments. Themed events, like you said, in the basement or up here, in the evenings and on weekends. The art night went so well. This is a perfect space for makers. Some of what we make could go on sale, or for auction—with most of the proceeds for charity, of course."

He tells her about the exhibition idea then, although he is certain he's getting it wrong, it sounds flat today. "I mean if your friends want to display their work here too, it will add color to the walls and showcase good things that young people are doing, that it's not all about loitering and crime."

"Maybe," Tulip says. "I don't know if anything we make is good enough for that. But if we can tie it in with a theme, it could work nicely as a one-off thing, you know, like those cool displays you guys used to put together. It's about wonder, isn't it? That's what makes this shop unique. Ooo. I like that. We could use that. We could make a statement with it."

"Well. I don't know about making a statement. We have the maps and photos from the consultation nights, maybe you and your friends can do something with those? You think people will come?"

"I do."

He presses his hand against the cool wooden counter. "Finished with the figures?"

"One minute." She transforms, in a flurry of taps, the

grid of numbers into a graph: not quite a ski slope, but just as he has known for months, the trajectory points down. These new events will have to be unlike anything before. Without a major change, they will be finished by springtime.

28

It was close today. Selim chased him as soon as he got off the bus. He had to run up the high street and cut through the park, and that was where Wade appeared, wearing the clown mask from Halloween. Kwasi ran so fast his chest locked tight, so he could only wheeze, nauseated, as he ducked into Sainsbury's. He was quick in there, it's almost funny now, now that he's outside the Chest. There is no way anyone could still be following him, not with how fast he was coming back down from Sainsbury's.

Before knocking, he glances back to the path. No sign of Jericho. Jericho won't come after him without Selim, and he lost Selim in Sainsbury's—he is probably still there. A sick feeling claws up Kwasi's throat.

He rubs his sweaty neck.

"You came through the park again," the shopkeeper says once he is inside, and looks pointedly at his shoes.

"Yep. I went through the mud to get you to clean up the basement. You said you wanted to clean up, anyway."

"I did say that." The man scratches his beard. "I did."

Kwasi removes his shoes to go downstairs, to feel the floorboards shudder when a train rumbles by. "Has anyone from my school come in here recently?" he asks, hoping to sound casual.

"Who's this? The same lads from Halloween? We don't get many young people in here at all. I don't think so, no."

"They were at the bus stop. It's like they knew exactly when I would get here from homework club."

The shopkeeper squints at Kwasi. "And they chased you? What is it that they want?"

He feels a new splinter of worry. "Nothing, forget it." If the guys follow him again, maybe the man will ask him to stay away. There is a slow crashing cascade in him, that the guys could win, could take this place from him, without even catching up with him. "It's fine," he hears himself say. "And I don't think they know I'm here."

"No?"

"Okay, I know they followed me on Halloween, but they don't know I've been back. I always go by the Chicken Palace first, so it looks like I just get off the bus here for chips. Sometimes I go to the park, and then come back." He gets his newest drawing out from his pocket.

"What's this?"

He smooths the page out for the man to see properly. "Three guesses."

"It looks like a planet. A planet with rings and many moons."

"Nope."

"A globe. Ah. A model of something. An atom, perhaps?"

"Yep. An atom with the different particles it has. I asked my physics teacher if we're really mostly made of nothing. And he went on for ages and then drew it out. We don't have to worry about it until GCSE, we just draw particles like circles, even though that's not what they are. And even the one he drew, the GCSE version, isn't real; particles aren't even like that. We'll learn more later, that's what he said, and probably then he'll just say it's something even more complicated and then you have to stay in school for years and years. Just memorizing lies forever."

"It's a model: a useful way of holding knowledge. You know"—the man goes toward the sink—"sometimes lies help us make sense of what matters. You have plenty of time to learn all the layers of understanding in any subject you like."

"I have something else." He gets the brownies out of his bag. He just about paid for them before Selim entered the shop and he had to run again. "See if you still hate sugar. These are so good."

"So many. You should have come earlier and met Tulip. She has a sweet tooth. I shouldn't be eating so much sugar. I haven't had my soup yet, I got caught up finishing with the numbers." The man considers the brownies. He looks like he is arguing with himself. "There's nothing but junk on this street. Used to be able to get a proper pastry from the bakery. There was a lovely Frenchwoman who ran it, I've forgotten her name. Those are full of preservatives."

"Try one."

"Well." He takes one, and goes to get napkins from the sink. So many napkins and paper plates, like he's planning a party.

"What did your assistant think of the exhibition idea?" Kwasi asks. "Did you find any frames we could use?" He goes to the top drawer of the old wardrobe and opens it. He adds to the small pile of drawings there his latest comic strips, portraits, a forest on black card stock, in chalk and green crayon. Gets a tingly feeling, thinking of them lying here while he's in school, drawings that now have their own life.

"I'll look when I tidy up. Tulip likes the sound of it. As long as we can tie everything together."

"What do you mean?"

"Well, when we have so much variety, it's good to find common themes, so everything fits together. Here. Your tea."

"Thanks." Kwasi raises a drawing into the light: women at the bus stop wearing the same face, different in height, coloring, clothes but there—the same weathered annoyance has made sisters of them. He puts it down and lifts another, a cartoon of the grizzly men who hang out drinking from bottles wrapped in dark plastic bags. "Good point. I usually just draw what I like."

"You have to think about how it will work with everything else on display, the bigger story you want to tell." The man is looking at the picture too now. "I like that one a lot," he says. "Men waiting for work. A van comes each morning and chooses workers. Odd jobs. Cash in hand." The man's gray eyebrows rise. He often wears this look: as though he can't believe what he is seeing, despite having seen it coming long ago, and now he is resigned to it. This too Kwasi must draw.

"Maybe you've seen this," the shopkeeper continues. He goes to a cupboard and takes out a box of papers. "Maybe you've seen this picture; who knows where else the council is using it." He selects a small card, a scene of greens and blues. The Chest's front window is filled with birds, a wooden model of a stork or something, paper cranes, books with birds on the covers, what appears to be a nest full of white eggs. Birds are suspended from a mobile, and people

195

on the street have stopped to look. "I wish we took more photos back then. I'll have to look for more at home, from our charity theme nights. That was my specialty, pulling together these displays, sometimes overnight. There was always a theme that held it all together, you see?"

Kwasi looks back at his drawing. "Men waiting for work. That could be the title. It goes with the one of the women. They're both about waiting. Maybe both are waiting to start their jobs."

"Maybe we're all waiting. We've certainly waited long enough for the Chest to be busy again. It's close though. I can feel it."

29

A walk, before the day begins: beyond the shifting fog, the sun is just rising, its amber light reaching over the park. The view—looking away from the city—yawns open, similar to the way the boy's drawings begin: a horizontal line across a luminous page. Rupert chuckles, remembering what the boy said, as he put his notebook away the night before: "I'm not going to finish it here. You can guess what it will become."

Rupert stops. Here is the Pattersons' chip shop. Gutted and empty indeed. Several properties above the shops down here are being advertised for rent, square signs jutting from the façade. Something is spreading along the street from here, up from the other side too, where the old Barclays stands, boards over its windows; a churn, a tipping that leaves emptiness.

Just a few years ago, the Pattersons would have been here, wiping counters, heating oil.

There is a new stirring in him, a viscous tide. He holds to the warmth inside, a little something, barely half a cup today, with the stingiest splash of syrup, to get him out early. They need to finish filling the application papers today, add in details for new events. Elaine said the council is already reviewing the forms it has. Tulip might have more thoughts for the exhibition, to make the most of the artwork the Chest already holds. Tulip will soon be in, to start early.

He takes a side road, to approach the Chest from the back. It does not seem so outrageous in this light to imagine a block of luxury flats rising here. The view from the top would be something. They might house hundreds of newcomers, and a new supermarket might follow, or perhaps more cafés.

The car park opens ahead, with the bins overspilling already.

He fishes his keys from his pocket.

And stops.

Crimson has splattered the Chest's back wall. Flecks of red explode way up from the step and over the back door. His hands find a bin lid, and he leans against it for support. Slows his breathing and waits as his heart falls into a more sensible rhythm.

"Come on now." He reaches out. Touches a red mark. It is crusty and rough and nothing comes away on his fingertips. He raises his hand to his nose. The smell is thin, like varnish.

He straightens. Unlocks the door. Inside, there is no sign of disturbance. He steps carefully around boxes he left by the till. Checks the bookcases, the hatstand, and jewelry display. Nothing has been taken. He fumbles for his mobile and presses Elaine's number.

His phone is still ringing when a hard thump falls outside. Rupert flinches. A flash of orange and lime fills the window—a construction worker in a high-vis jacket has tossed some rubbish into the bin. Their eyes meet briefly before the man walks away.

He shuts the back door with trembling hands, and hurries down into the basement. Which is silly. His phone cuts out.

Back upstairs, redialing Elaine, he sinks into the corner by the piano, out of sight. The mobile rings and rings. He looks through his contact list, for someone else to call. There are so many people who have moved away, still listed. Even some who have passed on. He doesn't have Tulip's number.

More thuds sound from the car park. Shouts. Laughter. He tells himself it is just his tea. He has kept sober for so long, a small helping has made him paranoid.

★

"Why didn't you call for help?" Elaine asks, when she arrives over an hour later, after seeing the mess at the back. "You should have called the police."

Rupert presses his palms to the floor and pushes himself up. "Nothing is broken." His legs are stiff from sitting so long. "It's just the bins. Idiots come out from all over to throw their stuff away. The depot probably threw paint out, splashed the wall by mistake."

Elaine shakes her head. "Vandalism. It could be from next door. God knows who's in there overnight."

"It's paint. I'll scrape it off."

"As far as I'm concerned that's evidence."

Tulip lets herself in. "Morning."

"Morning it is," Elaine says. "Thought you were having an early start today."

Tulip puts her satchel on the counter, unbuckles it, and takes her laptop out. "You are going to love this."

"I hope it's worth the wait," Elaine says.

"It's fine. We're still on time," Tulip says.

"It's fine," Elaine repeats. "Have you seen the mess at the back?"

"There's no sense in being dramatic now," Rupert says.

"What mess?" Tulip is already going toward the doors. Elaine follows her out and holds the door ajar.

"I've seen this before," Tulip calls. "On my run, near the park."

Rupert leans against the piano. "I'll cover it up. We were going to paint anyway."

"We were going to paint the *front*. And have you bought paint out of your own pocket? Why have you done that?"

"All this time you've been hassling me about decorating, and now—"

"Hassling. All right. Tulip. You're better off working at a café, or somewhere that wants to do business properly."

Elaine barges back inside and goes to the coat stand.

"Elaine," Rupert says.

She grabs her coat and bag, without slowing down to put either of them on.

"Elaine, just a minute."

"A minute. It's been years, Rupert." She grabs the door handle. Pushes her hair back from her eyes, blinking and blinking. "This isn't even a business now, is it? You're in here constantly, guarding the place. Hiding here like you don't have a home. It's not even safe. What if someone comes by late at night? Alice has seen boys hanging out around here at night, teenagers. Troublemakers. So many people have given their time to this place, Rupert. So many people wanted to see it . . ." And here her words run out, and she shakes her head. She pushes out the door.

★

A full session is overdue. May as well finish what he began. The box opens without a sound, and Tulip places the lid on the counter.

"That's cute. I love the sachets. Oh, it smells . . ." She frowns. "Strong . . . Wait. Oh God. Weren't you supposed to be detoxing?"

"This isn't the moment for detoxing. I may as well use my supply, since I already paid for it. It's not like I'm using it regularly."

"I don't know. I thought you seriously wanted to take a break?"

"A break, yes. And I have. Like I've said. It's perfectly legal. If you're going to judge me, I'll make it myself."

"I'm not. Hey, I want to try. I get it. What do I mix?"

And perhaps this too is paranoia: the feeling that Tulip also is here for hidden reasons, that no one who has worked here, calling themselves a volunteer, has straightforward intentions.

It is hard to think clearly, so close to a drink.

"Tea bags are in the fourth drawer under the sink. You can bag the leaves up, mix in a little of the loose black tea. Or you can mix them up together and brew it loose in the pot. There's a strainer under the sink. Mix whichever herbs and powders you like. As long as it fits in one tea bag."

"Okay. This may take a while. This is why I could never work in a café. With or without a wig."

"They're always in a rush at cafés. Take your time and do it well." The kettle starts to boil. He closes his eyes. "It

201

did look like blood, outside. I thought, maybe someone has killed a bird, or a squirrel, or a fox. What if they killed it and smeared it all over here?"

"Why would anyone do that?"

"I know what people think of me. Perhaps someone knows we're applying for funding and they want to scare us out."

There is a rustling as she opens the sachets. "People don't hate you." She must have filled the teapot already. The aroma warms him. "I reckon it's just those kids Elaine is always complaining about. Because the unit next door is abandoned, they're probably trying to lay claim to this space. Broken windows effect? We need to make it clear that the Chest is very much still in business."

"You think it was those kids? The same lot behind the eggings?"

"It's their own small resistance," Tulip says. "They don't see that we're on the same side. Oh. Will it get stronger if I leave it long? How long should I let it brew?"

"It's more an art than a science." He nods at the box. "You can't go wrong with this mix. It's like a tray of assorted psychological marshmallows."

She places a teacup on the table and goes to fetch the strainer. "That's good paint though." Her foot nudges the bucket of paint he left in the corner. "I have cheaper stuff in Dad's garage. Green. Dark forest green." She pours at the sink and brings him a filled teacup. "This is just a pit stop. We'll pick ourselves up and get back to it tomorrow."

Beneath the swirling doubt, there is still gratitude. "Thank you. It's a . . . a game changer, having you here. You're very bright. You don't have to be here, of course."

"Don't. I'm here because I love the Chest. There's no

other space quite like it. With everything happening next year, this is the one place where there's space to do something for the community." She rises. "Is there a spare socket down here for my laptop? I want your thoughts on the leaflets I'm making."

"There is, but the wiring is dodgy." He hesitates. "You might burn this whole place to nothing."

"God. Now that would be serious."

"I might even call the police then."

She laughs. "Yeah right. You're too stubborn. I bet you wouldn't even call the fire brigade. You'd try to deal with it yourself. You're so anti-authority at heart. I bet you would just let it burn."

"Well. If I let it burn, we could all go home, knowing we at least tried. That whatever happens to this place was out of our control."

"Rupert." She shakes her head. "Seriously though. It is much bigger than us. Everything about community is under attack. Real community, I mean. It's different, you know, connecting in person?"

"You know, it used to just happen, forming community. We'd find ourselves together, people opened up and got on. We didn't need all these papers and ideas."

"This place has given me so much, you know. I talked about it in my interview for university. It gave me a huge boost, knowing I had some experience. I remember reading on the student room website about how all the applicants to my course were volunteering, going to build orphanages in Africa and saving the rain forest in South America or teaching English somewhere, and just freaking out. But charity is charity. And no one's flying across the world to help our high street, to protect spaces like these, right?"

"We have everything we need right here, to make this place work," Rupert says. "As long as people want it to work, that is. Doesn't feel that way. Do you think we ought to involve the police, in case our vandals return?"

Tulip is shaking her head. "No way. And please don't take vandalism personally. Kids do it everywhere. Seriously. If anything, it's a sign the Chest is going to last."

"Maybe," he says. "I suppose we'll see."

30

A blank page is not neutral; surfaces he draws on affects how familiar shades appear. Loud colors look sleepy on squares of off-white card stock. The card stock is heavy, and soft as canvas. It's dizzying to think of how ink might turn out on real canvas. He would have to use proper paint then, and professional brushes.

"That looks good," Kumar, who is sitting beside him, says.

"Thanks." Everyone has moved since he last looked up, and no one is even pretending to be making Christmas cards anymore. They're forming two big groups, talking and messing about with glitter.

"Really." Kumar smiles.

Kumar is quiet too, but no one bothers him because he lets everyone copy his homework. He charges for essays and longer assignments too, according to Gemma. He must have done a thousand times more work than anyone else at this school. Now he looks over Kwasi's drawings. "The volcano would look epic in black and white. You should do a whole comic book like that."

Kwasi hesitates. It doesn't sound like a joke.

"What about people?" Kumar asks. "You draw people? In real life?"

Kumar is not like Selim and the others, but he is still different. Kumar has a tutor, even though he is already smart, has been getting the highest marks since year five. Sometimes Kumar looks at him and Kwasi feels Kumar sees all he is now but also everything he will and will not be.

"Are you going to take art?"

"Don't know. We don't choose our options until next year, isn't it."

"It's good to think about it though." Kumar looks concerned.

Beyond Kumar, the girls are tying tinsel in their hair. Jericho and Selim are by the laptop that controls the music, leaning into the screen's glow.

He has stared for too long. Now Jericho is up and coming his way.

"Uh-oh," Kumar says.

Jericho stops by their table. "Hey. Come outside for one minute."

"Why?"

"Just come."

Kwasi gets up. Kumar catches his eye and looks away.

"Miss," Jericho calls, "me and Kwasi are going to get more glitter from the art cupboard, is that okay?"

Outside in the hallway, Jericho has questions. "Why are you always hiding? Where do you go after homework club? When you get off the bus at the high street?"

Kwasi is all water again, ice this time, about to shatter.

"Hello?" Jericho says.

"Just to get snacks."

"So why don't you wait for us? We could go get food. We're just messing with you, the way you keep running is outrageous. Mad."

"I told you," he says, trying to sound calm, "I'm trying to sort out my grades. I don't have much time in the evenings. Mrs. Nibley called my house."

"Did she?" Jericho stops walking.

He hesitates. It is not really a lie, since it did happen, just not recently. "Yeah."

"What did she say?"

"I don't know. Ma only told me that I have to type up my homework."

"Listen. You know on Halloween, when you opened the bag. Did you do anything to it?"

"No, why?"

"Think carefully. Did you take anything out of the bag?"

"I just looked. Looked and zipped it up." He can feel the thing on his fingertips, even as he says it. He definitely did touch it, and there were no gloves.

Jericho opens the door to the store cupboard. Lots of paints and art materials are cluttered over wood shelves. It stings to think that Jericho has access to a whole other layer of the school, when he doesn't even like painting.

"What happened?"

"Leave it. Here." Jericho hands him a basket of glitter pens.

"Does your dad know?"

Jericho doesn't answer. He leans into the cupboard, turning his back. It is not clear he has even heard. Kwasi clears his throat but can't make himself ask again. At last, Jericho shuts the cupboard and turns.

"Let's go then."

The hallway feels narrower as they start the walk back, and heavy with noise from other classrooms, from other Christmas celebrations. The whole corridor is gluing, drawing, putting things together. Inside, it feels like parts of him are coming apart.

"Like I said," Jericho says at last, "my dad has his business. I have mine. Someone asked us to help and here we are. I remember you used to be on that Rambo stuff. Now you can't even hand a bag over."

He watches his shoes. He hates it when Jericho brings up Rambo. The humiliation of the sleepover in year four is rising again, the last sleepover he had, Jericho and another friend. Kwasi tried to explain about his drawing of Rambo, which was still up on the wall then. When they went back to school, Jericho kept bringing it up, and everyone found it funny, since he was rubbish at PE, and after that he took the drawings down from his bedroom walls, all of them.

"I actually rated you then. What is it now, are you trying to be like your aunties? You always act so babyish. You know what, forget it. Forget Halloween ever happened. Go back to your drawing. Go back to swimming."

"I can do better," Kwasi hears himself say.

Jericho hesitates. His gaze is softer now, it's like the version of him from the Saturday they spent painting.

Kwasi slows down. He tries to make his voice firmer. "We can get chips. I can pick up food for you, if your dad's still banned you from the Palace."

They are at the classroom door now. He can hear Selim's laughter in the noise from within. "Okay, listen." Jericho glances back down the corridor and lowers his voice. "You know that shop, Chest of Small Wonders? The one you ran into on Halloween?"

Kwasi nods.

"We're working on something around there."

"What?"

"I'll explain later. Go on."

"You should take art for GCSE," Kumar says, when Kwasi sits back down. "If you're serious."

Words are glue in his stomach. That Mariah Carey song begins and a cheer rolls through the classroom. Perched on her desk cradling a cup of tea, Mrs. Nibley smiles.

31

Evening has closed around them and the only light comes from the laptop. Rupert's eyes sting from its glare.

Tulip nudges him. "Thoughts?" She scrolls up the page. "Crafty Cosy Chest" is written across a midnight-blue banner. It matches the leaflet, copies of which she has left underneath the noticeboard. The web page is filled with crayon drawings of the basement that reminds him of one of the boy's drawings, all the furniture outlined in bright hues, like abstract art sculptures. Tulip has even drawn candles and shaded the silhouettes they cast over the walls. Since she found the boy's drawings downstairs, she's been full of new ideas.

"I don't know what to say." He's trembling slightly, anticipation or coffee. "It looks good. More than good."

"We used a ton of filters," she says.

"You and Natalie?"

"Lake," she says. "You'll like him. Digital artist. Mental."

"Ah." At the bottom of the web page is a map, and a dotted line leads from the Tube station. "Anyone who has a computer can see this?"

"Once it's live." She grimaces. "Is it okay?"

"It's more than okay."

She clicks and scrolls. "There's nothing about this place online. This will be the first time it's on the internet." The silence between them softens. "Jamie, do you remember her?"

"Jamie." He doesn't.

"She suggested crafts every weekend. Sculpting, collages. Knitting and mending. And they'll help with the exhibition. Let's do the exhibition in the new year. It will give us time to get more material together. We'll do the exhibition up here. If we push the shelves back."

He knows which of Jada's sketches they are both thinking of.

The sound of laughter comes from outside.

He looks up. Rain slashes the windows. Only rain. No sign of the boy. It would have been nice to tell him they will hold the exhibition in the new year, to ask if he has ideas about themes, before they finish with these forms. Still, the day has been long enough.

★

There is no sign of the boy the following night either, when Tulip's friends come by for an impromptu session playing with lights and cameras. Rupert waits upstairs, hoping the boy will not be scared off by the laughter and noise from below. It would be nice to let them meet, for the kid to have a say in how these new events will look. Tulip has been talking to poets who liked one of Rupert's old ideas, for a kind of interview night, personal storytelling.

He waits, but the boy does not appear.

It is the same the night after that. At this point, dust is gathering upstairs, as Elaine has also kept away. After locking the front, Rupert goes to look through the basement. He is running out of candles. No sign of the torch—only drawings the boy has left, and more from Tulip and her friends. Page after page, in drawers and cupboards, waiting to be framed. In the basement, cold gives way to bottomless quiet. Herbs beneath the sink call to him, as the warmth from his cup earlier is all but gone. But the boy might return tonight, so he stays sober. He fills a mug with hot water, to hold for comfort, and goes to sit in the window display.

Outside, shadows stretch along the pavement. Women pushing buggies, lads walking three abreast, shoppers overloaded with carrier bags. Christmas lights are up, the same ruby lights from last year, like cherries over everything in town. The reindeer that dangles over the post office will go up soon. He might walk up later to see.

He draws a breath and tests its mustiness, measuring the intensity of his own aroma, of sweat and laundry detergent and digestive biscuits. Something fundamental dims outside, and the shop becomes vivid. All its clutter, the delicate balance of disorganized order and chaos that has gone too long without a good cleaning, is illuminated, with no one but him to see.

No sign of Elaine.

No sign of the boy.

At home, the silence is crushing. It feels worse now his settee is sold and gone, with the empty space of carpet. He telephones Elaine. It feels like a miracle when she picks up; it's hard to remember what to say. The apology he prepared is nebulous in his mind.

"I know I can be difficult," he says, after a pause.

"You are," Elaine says. "And at some point I have to ask, is it worth my time? There are plenty of other places that need help. I'm already spending my weekends at church."

"Oh? I didn't know you still went." He thinks briefly of the other churchwomen who began volunteering alongside Elaine, of a Christmas spent drinking with them, how quietly they fell away.

"Found a new church, though it's not the same. People just want to have a nice time and give thanks. We already pay our tithes and cover the world with our prayers. He's lovely, our reverend, but he does go on about Britain's fall, people aren't going to church anymore, all the poisonous lies online. I suppose he has a lot to worry about, his own job included, but church should be about the Good News. Especially at Christmas."

"Ah." Rupert shifts the phone to his other hand. It has become awfully hot. "Anyway, I'm sorry, for how difficult I've been. I'm lucky to have you trying to help."

"I'll be back, don't worry. There is something special about that shop, about the spirit of giving there."

"Tulip's setting up a website. We can connect with more customers that way. And we sold my settee online, which will help with rent a bit. Not as much as I hoped, but it's something."

"Brilliant. My church has started sharing sermons online too. We had people listening from Sri Lanka the other day. They won't get the full experience though, you have to be there in person. It was so cheerful when Harry and I joined. They have a superb worship band and all the African women dress so beautifully, all the bright colors they wear. I could never—it'd wash me out. You'd like it. Harry can give you a lift if you want to try."

"Perhaps. I haven't made plans for Christmas yet."

"Harry wants to help the homeless. We've done food banks before. But honestly, most of the people coming in look perfectly sound. It's peculiar how they have ended up needing to come in. Teachers and nurses. They drag their children in, and they always have so many. And they have smartphones and the kids have their own gadgets. That's where all the money goes. So then they come to the food bank for their groceries. Time will tell what these children will turn out like. We're not built to be walking with our heads down. Ruins their memories—my grandson can't sit still and read a book. Can't finish anything. He watches everything in those short videos everyone's sharing. It's pitiful to live through a phone."

"Yes," he says. "It is." He shifts the handset again, presses its burning heat against his right ear. "You mentioned that there are kids who hang about the Chest at night. What exactly is happening? What's the latest you've heard? We are going to hold more evening events, and I don't want to put anyone into danger."

"Oh. It's just my son-in-law, Phil, mentioned seeing trouble outside the Chest, kids hanging around. That car park is an absolute state. It's waiting for troublemakers. If I were you I'd get the police involved. I wouldn't wait."

"All right. Anyway, I do appreciate all your hard work. Tulip's submitted our application, so we'll need all hands on deck to deliver. Got a new idea as well, for an exhibition. Sort of like the displays we used to have, but if the art is good enough, hopefully we can auction pieces."

"Well. That should give Tulip something to focus on."

"We'll hear back within a week. Do you think you'll be back then?"

"Oh, Rupert. I just don't want to waste my time," Elaine says.

"I have a good feeling," he says. "I really do."

32

This time Da calls after breakfast. There is no way out of speaking. Auntie May is getting a lift to work, so Kwasi has a ride to school. There is nowhere to rush to. He takes the phone to the study—Ma's smartphone this time. Messages from her friends keep interrupting the screen, so even though Ma is not outside listening today, she still feels near as he admits that no, he hasn't tried out for the football team yet, hasn't even swum in forever. Yeah, he is still in the bottom set for math. This might be their worst phone call yet. His answers come out flat and full of gaps. The gaps are the drawings he is working on, the exhibition that is not yet ready enough to mention. If he tries to explain it, Da will tell him to do something more practical or to spend time with his peers.

"Keep working hard," Da says, at last. "I will see you in the new year. Maybe summertime. I am thinking about bringing some of your cousins to London. They want to see how you are living. We can take them to Carnival. It's been a long time. Do you remember that time we went with Uncle Obi and it rained?"

"Yeah." He tried to draw it for ages after, the costumes

and the intermittent sunshine, lorries pouring music, a real street party, as King Obi said. He tried to draw it but nothing came out right. The day was too bright for any colors he had. He remembers the view from Da's shoulders, alongside Jericho, who was even higher up on King Obi's. None of the aunties came along. They said Carnival was dangerous.

"Anyway," Da says now. "Don't let me make you late to school. We will speak soon."

After the call, more messages flood in. Ma has an endless stream of friends. But maybe this is normal, for people who have smartphones. Adjacent conversations must be happening right now, maybe on these same apps, between everyone at school.

It is like a new invisible dimension. He thinks about it on the car ride, while Auntie May chats with her friend in the front. It was nice, for a while at Selim's on Halloween, imagining he could be part of their group. It feels clearer now, outlines of different versions of him inside, the version of himself that surfaced at Selim's house, that the communion loosened, a forgotten shadow-self. This part of him feels gloomy to think that Jericho has still not told him when to come over or explained what is special about the space behind the Chest. It is probably best to starve this part of him, to forget Halloween ever happened. He doesn't have time to feel this confused, waiting for Jericho to speak to him. Da probably won't even visit next year, let alone take him to Carnival. The exhibition has to come first.

He does not go into the Chest today. It is best to stay away, just for a few more days. Though he told the shopkeeper that no one knows he's been visiting, it is hard to know for sure. They were close, that time they chased him through Sainsbury's. It could be a good idea to make them think he was just out looking for snacks every time he left homework club early. And so today, after typing up as much as he can, he takes the bus to the high street and wanders through Sainsbury's. He buys a box of strawberry and raspberry tea. On the next shelf are packets of instant coffee. A laugh escapes from him. There are so many options.

It takes until Saturday to get the kitchen to himself. Everyone is in the living room, in the grip of a Nollywood film. The whole house is on edge, bound by the shrill note of tension from a synthesizer that comes from the TV. Kwasi closes the kitchen door, so the smell of coffee does not spread.

It's not as sweet as it was at the Chest; he should have added more sugar. Not that it matters. It's the feeling that he needs, the sharpening in his mind, thoughts zipping through constricted channels, until he can barely keep up with himself. He blazes through his French homework, and afterward he is too alert to sleep. He gets his pencils out and marks a faint outline. The shape of this feeling is tough to see, let alone draw. He suspects it should remain unbounded, with only hints of movement within, the tension and flows that give this feeling its heft. Simpler, perhaps, to attribute the feeling to an image of something he can hold. This is the same feeling of openness that awaits him in the swimming pool.

Drawing water is tricky. Anytime he tries to capture the way it scatters light, he finds himself drawing fragments of things nearby, so that the water is erased by everything that colors it. He thinks about what Jericho said, about swimming being white. Not really, was his response at the time. But thinking about it, in the water he relishes the feeling, of becoming, in fluid strokes and roaring quiet, not white at all but transparent, colorless.

"Kwasi," Squid shouts. "Kwasi, your da is on the phone. Come and say hello."

"Again? I just spoke to him a few days ago."

"Come down."

"I'm working," he shouts back, and then in case that is not enough he adds: "It's for a test. I'll talk to him tomorrow."

He works on the water idea until nine. Even then, he could go on. His pencil hovers over the page. One last idea to test for now, a bigger idea, the world as someone smart, someone like Kumar, sees it. He sketches, on an A3 page, the street old-fashioned, but also the present and the future. In the future scene, he draws jetpacks and hoverboards. Shops crowned with domes that control weather. All kinds of potions for sale. Everyone will be allowed to paint and powder their faces, to mix whatever fragrances they like. All will decorate their ears and color their hair. He can imagine in the future there will be no limits to how or what a person can be.

He draws new iterations through the night, lying on his stomach. One version places the three vistas side by side, like portals, so you have to choose one at a time. He draws another—this one takes hours, and even then it's not quite right—where past-present-future cover different zones of the high street, so the bus stop is old-fashioned, the middle just before the split in the tarmac is as it appears today, and the final stretch that tapers into park carries the future.

A third version he draws while the aunties are at church the following day: everything is jumbled here, in layers laid over each other showing all three time periods at once, so you can't tell what belongs to when.

He tries with chalk, with crayons, smudging with his fingertips. He tries with marker pens.

"K," he pencils in the corner.

Here he is at last. The version of him that comes out in these drawings feels closest to the truth, settled and bold. At last, he feels ready.

On Wednesday, he returns to the Chest. It's time to put all his art together, to settle which theme to use for the exhibition.

"What do you think?" he asks, presenting his newest drawings to the shopkeeper.

The man squints at the future scene, in the drawing with three portals. "This is different from your usual style. Astounding."

"Took me ages." He feels like he could dance.

"Shall we have some tea to celebrate?"

Downstairs, the man has made coffee again. It's on the counter. The bitter smell is everywhere.

"You were meant to be giving up coffee."

"A little coffee now and again doesn't hurt. I've only added honey."

Little silver flasks are out by the sink again. It's clear that something more has slipped.

"Trouble is, I started young. Once you learn how easy it is to change how you feel using a drink, it's a slippery slope."

"How old were you when you started ..." He doesn't even know how to finish this question.

"I was about your age when I first got drunk. I had brothers. Never stood a chance."

"Did you and your brothers ever fight?"

"Did we fight." The man smiles. "Let's sort out some frames for your pictures. Good to know what we might need to order and what we already have."

Looking at all the drawings together, it's clear not all are his. Some are small as postcards; others are rolled up A2 sheets. Twenty-eight finished pieces in total. Even those that aren't his match the colors and styles he has used. Even his trickier drawings, composed from smudges of things aunties left in his wardrobe: ochre, coffee and bronze powders, deep purple lipsticks, even his drawing of tiny pencil *o*'s, have been copied in smaller pieces.

"Imitation," the shopkeeper says, "is flattery. Lemon and ginger tea?"

"How about hot chocolate?"

"I suppose we've got that too."

Kwasi thinks of all the strangers walking by outside right now, wrapped up warm. In a few weeks, they might be looking at his drawings. The largest frame rests on the floor, the only place it cannot fall from. He crouches and runs a finger along its edge.

"Did anyone from my school come here, while I was away?"

"Why?" The shopkeeper looks back at him. "What's happened?"

"Nothing," he says.

"Don't think anyone came by. But maybe I missed them. I've been busy myself. I was reading about the council's plans. That Councillor Obi is really meddling with things."

"Does Councillor Obi ever come inside this shop?" Kwasi asks, watching the shopkeeper carefully.

"Now and again."

"Do you think he would come in, if we held an exhibition?"

"I think so. He'll want to know what we're up to. That could be good for us, as long as he doesn't make it about politics. Some of the art you've made with these postcards—I think he'd enjoy these. You know, he brought those photos here in the first place. Brought some old maps as well. I'll look for them. Perhaps he'll come to our next event. We're interviewing local people, starting with a poet. Maybe one day we'll have to interview him."

"Councillor Obi?"

"He would enjoy that. Everything else aside, it's good that he's so visible, Councillor Obi, good for young people to see. People make a lot of noise, say you can't do this or that if you look a certain way. I don't see color. It's about what you can do."

Kwasi looks down at his hands, at the pink flesh of his palms. He wishes the shopkeeper had not said that.

He goes into the toilet. Feels like he could be anywhere, as long as he is inside this little room. He runs the tap for a while, watching water circle the drain. He imagines himself transparent, clear and easy as water. When at last he goes back out, three ornate frames lie on the floor.

"Three futures framed in gold," the man says. "A triptych."

"Triptych," Kwasi repeats, wiping his hands in his trousers. A riddle of a word. The gold frames are too big for his drawings, but it's lucky that there are three. He feels a bit warmer again. Feels like this could be good.

"Our street in parallel universes."

"I was thinking about how someone who is really smart might look at this place when I drew them," Kwasi says. "How much more they would notice."

"To think of how someone smart sees things, you must be rather smart yourself."

"Or good at pretending." Kwasi looks over the pictures, and then around the dusty basement. "People might think they're for sale, if you put them upstairs."

"We'll keep them down here for now."

"How much would they cost, if they were for sale?"

"Not too sure. But if we hold an auction, they could raise more than any price we recommend. We'll make it a special day. Really memorable."

He tries to see these drawings in someone else's home. More than showcasing them here, the exhibition could give each drawing a new life, somewhere he may never see. They should talk about it soon. If they sell his art, some money could help keep the Chest open. Some will be for Shelter. He should get to keep some too, although how that bit works isn't clear. But what is clear is that first, everyone will see what he has been working on. He tries to see through Ma's eyes. Sad eyes. He starts to think of how Da might see it, if he actually does visit in summer.

"Are you all right?" the shopkeeper asks.

"Yeah."

"We're getting there. If we get funding, we'll decorate

upstairs and down here, so we can hold more events. All very exciting. You should head home. I don't suppose you carry an umbrella. All your aunties must be worried."

"I told them I'm volunteering." This much is true. He doesn't say that he told them he was volunteering at a mentoring workshop at school.

"Toddlers will be volunteering soon. And how did you end up with so many aunties? I've seen them coming and going. One of the houses on Broad Avenue?"

"Yeah."

"That side really has changed. More of the houses are sublet. But there's a nice mix of cultures. Much more interesting. Maybe some of them will come to our events."

The man says he can remember when the boy's school opened. He shows Kwasi the old map that King Obi donated. "So many families moved here to the edge of the city to avoid the London toll."

"The London toll?"

"Stunted lungs from toxic air. Always being about three meters from a rat. Living in a decrepit flat with strangers. Noise. Too much light. Coughing and sneezing all winter thanks to all the germs riding the Tube. Damp. I could go on."

"You should tell your life story," Kwasi says. "You know you said we might interview Councillor Obi? We could interview you." He is thinking too about his aunties' warnings, how they kept him away from this shop when he was small, all the rumors around it. Being interviewed at a storytelling night could be a chance for the shopkeeper to set everything straight.

"I don't know about that."

The man lends him an umbrella, a long one with a curved handle. "Don't let the wind get hold of it."

The shopfront looks like it's melting, washed with the deluge. Kwasi glances back toward the stairs. Leaving always feels abrupt. If he had more time here, he could draw so much more. And it would help the Chest. "Could I work here? For the Chest, I mean," he asks. It would be impossible in practice, but in theory, it is dizzying. "Just over Christmas break. I could help tidy up and wash new clothes."

The shopkeeper has a way of smiling that slants his features, though his mouth rarely curves. "You enjoy the holiday break. Get ready for a new term in January."

"I can help tidy the basement. No one will see me."

"You've already helped plenty. Go on home."

Disappointment follows, but it is not crushing. At least the shopkeeper didn't laugh, didn't dismiss the idea completely. "Okay." Kwasi grips the umbrella and pushes the door open. "You should go home too," he says.

33

There are days when he feels intensely alive and grounded, even while sober; when it feels as though time has not only stalled, but deepened too, plunging him toward something vital, something that charges the cold air. Such is the day the news is out. Councillor Obi arrives moments after Elaine pops out for lunch, so Rupert hears the news alone.

Obi arrives with more stickers and a wedge of leaflets under his arm. "I wanted to congratulate you in person."

Relief rinses through Rupert. He sinks onto his wheelie chair.

"Bravo. Bravo."

Rupert rubs his neck. Weeks of exhaustion weigh across his back. "Well. We haven't got anywhere yet."

"We're holding a drop-in session tomorrow, gearing up for the next stage. The final deadline is the eighteenth of January, but we will be reviewing submissions on a rolling basis." Councillor Obi's hands come from his pockets and clap together. "Future is bright."

"Yes."

"Tulip was at our drop-in last week—great to see local young people engaging." He rubs his hands and looks around. "And rumor has it you still have the toilet downstairs?"

"That space isn't open to the public yet, but yes, I'm working on it. That's why it's in the application."

"Wonderful. We need more public toilets."

He almost says something sharp, to remind the councillor that the Chest is not a waste center, but stops himself. This is a moment to stay positive. "Thank you, Councillor," he says instead. He keeps his gaze on the framed drawing of the Chest, its tentative colors.

"I've not actually read any applications, to be clear," Councillor Obi says. "Officers review the forms. But we have an engagement map showing which units might be up for refurbishment and I was excited to see the Chest."

"Early days," Rupert says. "But thank you."

"Elaine mentioned you've had some antisocial behaviour here."

And just like that, the shop withers around him. There it is again. No matter how charming this councillor appears, there is something more beneath his mask. Always some point he has to make. "No trouble. We're just busy. That's all."

"Of course. Appreciate what you do, Rupert. We're all feeling squeezed."

"Yet council tax is up again."

"I know we've had our disagreements. But we both want things to improve. Between you and I . . ." Councillor Obi glances back to the door and lowers his voice. "We'll have to get used to austerity. We're having to do more with less. People do need homes, new homes, and new flats will mean more taxpayers, which helps make up for all the cuts we've had. It means more people to spend their money at new cafés and bars. The Tube station means we're forty minutes from the city. Do you know the value of this place?" He goes to the door. "Best of luck with it, Rupert."

After the councillor leaves shame descends, and then thins into annoyance.

"I am grateful," he tells Elaine later. "But every time he visits, I get stuck on what happened in the past. I am grateful. Just for some reason it won't come out."

"You've been here too long, Rupert; you forget that years have passed," she says. "Most people are muddling through the present or worrying for the future. He's probably forgotten about your license disagreement. You should focus on the future too. There's a group online calling for more flats on the high street, saying they like the leaked council plans. We're not in the clear yet."

"We won't be until February or so."

"Did you mention you're sober?"

"Why would I tell him that?"

"He'd be happy for you."

"Well. Like you said. We're not in the clear yet."

★

To celebrate, before heading home, he picks up ingredients. Sugar, flour, eggs and butter and cocoa powder, chocolate, in dark and white. Almonds. By nine, the aroma of brownies fills his house.

Even with all this sweetness, lying awake between dreams

he will forget, he feels for the memory of their first tea party, in the basement of the Chest. It would be so easy to return; when he drinks his inky tea he melts into warmer times. When sipping coffee, emptiness expands and takes over, wears him as a hand wears a glove.

34

Even after Selim and Wade jumped him in the toilets, after they chased him through Sainsbury's, still Jericho acts like nothing is up. A frosty Sunday afternoon, and he is back at Jericho's, finishing the painting they started over a month ago. They only have to add a small detail into the nativity scene, so it should not take long. Unfortunately, it turns out drawing an angel, even just sketching the outline right, is tough. Jericho has a stencil, a cardboard silhouette, but it looks dumb, too chunky and rounded. The patch they have painted blazing white, in the corner of the display, remains undefined.

"Apparently," Jericho says, reading from his phone, "angels are covered in eyes. Look."

The search page is tiled with alarmingly geometric entities overdecorated with eyes. Kwasi has the feeling he's going to see them in his dreams. "That's a lot," he says.

"Explains why everyone's scared when angels appear, huh."

"We could just leave it as it is. Like, as a flash of light."

"Yeah. Maybe it's the moment right before the angel fully appears."

They both consider the absent-present angel, the brilliance of it.

"Or it could be like the angel is there, but it's so bright you can't see its shape."

"Let's leave it to the audience to guess."

"What about the rest of the paint?"

"Do you want it?" Jericho gets up. "I can sell it to you." He goes to the kitchen, and moments later, the microwave starts its drone. "I'm kidding," comes Jericho's voice. "Take the paint, it's yours."

They eat leftover wings from Nando's, so hot that tears sting Kwasi's eyes.

"How are your grades? Parents' evening this week, right?"

He hesitates, but Jericho doesn't seem to be mocking, seems like he wants to know.

"Not great, to be honest, but I have a plan."

"What, buy answers off Kumar?"

It's annoying that it is so obvious. But also reassuring, like it's not a bad idea.

"Maybe, maybe not," he says. He has also spoken to Gemma, who is going to help with his history project. Best not to tell Jericho this bit though. Although it would be nice to have advice. Gemma said she's open to different kinds of payment, so he needs to decide what to do. Maybe she wants him to draw something, with the way she kept asking what he was working on. "But I have a question for you," he says, shifting the conversation back around. "What's going on? You said something was going to happen, near that shop. What's it called. The Chest of Small Wonders."

Jericho gets up, and Kwasi braces himself. But Jericho

just gathers their plates. "One sec. I'm getting popcorn," he says, and goes to the kitchen.

He has left his phone on the carpet, where it buzzes. Selim's face is there. Kwasi turns the phone over and wills Selim to give up calling.

"Turn the Xbox on," Jericho shouts from the kitchen. "I'll explain everything while we play."

Kwasi gets up. He has a bad feeling about the Xbox, about joining a gaming session with everyone. The console lights up rapidly, like it's waited for him all day. He sinks onto the couch. He needs to know if there's going to be trouble at the Chest.

He closes his eyes. Something of a prayer is trying to unroll. Although parents' evening will be tough, everything could balance out. He will help save the Chest. If he gets money from selling drawings, he could pay Kumar for more homework. Not just worksheets and math, full essays as well. Kumar would be one of his people then, and in a way, the shopkeeper would be too. His own people, separate from Jericho's, and from whatever Selim is planning.

"Can you please explain it?" he says, as soon as Jericho reappears.

"Put *GTA* on first."

"I haven't played it before. I'm probably rubbish."

"You haven't played *GTA*?" He puts the disc into the Xbox. "This is why you need to get involved. I guarantee your aunties aren't going to be sponsoring your snacks after you get destroyed at parents' evening."

"What do you want me to do? Because if it's something serious . . ."

"It's good. It's good. You won't get caught, not with your

face. Look. We're just supplying a demand. It's perfectly legit."

Kwasi looks down at the controller, so Jericho can't see his face. "It's drugs?" he asks. He can't help but think of the shopkeeper, the drinks he is trying to quit. "It's against the law. So that means it's actually not legit."

"Do you hear yourself?" Jericho asks. "If you think the law is a way of deciding what's legit, you're lost. Were you asleep in class? Did you not see all the stuff that was legal during the Empire?"

The doorbell rings.

It is Selim, with bags of Haribo and crisps. Wade follows, hugging bottles of Lucozade. "Can't believe you're having a party without us. Why didn't you say you had a free house?"

"I'm actually surprised my dad's not home yet. He'll come any second though." Jericho puts the drinks on the table.

"Text him. Ask when he's coming." Selim grabs a handful of popcorn. "You lot playing *GTA*?"

"Special K came to help—I was supposed to add an angel into this." Jericho nudges the nativity scene aside with his foot. "How would I know how to draw an angel? Who else is coming?"

"My brother," Selim says. "He's getting drinks."

"We won't have time," Jericho says. "Plus, we have nine a.m. math."

"Chill. Chill. Mr. Never Missed a Day."

"Ay, K-man." Wade lands on the cushions next to him. "Are you sure you know what you're doing?"

"Just exploring," Kwasi says, doing his best to sound easy. "Driving around." He offers Wade the controller.

"Keep it. You need the practice more than I do."

"True," Selim says. "Maybe you should stay in the game, at least if you mess up here you can just start again."

"Guys, my dad will lose his mind if he finds out I even have *GTA*." Jericho glances to the window. "I guarantee he's walking."

Selim shoves more popcorn into his mouth. "Do you have *GTA* at home, Kwasi? Do you mess up weapons in the game too?"

"What do you mean?" Jericho asks.

"They're still saying we messed up on Halloween," Selim says. "They won't say what exactly happened. So I'm just thinking, hmm. Who was the last person to look in the bag before we handed it over?"

The doorbell rings once more.

"I'm going to pee," Kwasi says.

"No, you can hold it. You've learned that now, haven't you?" Selim's voice swells louder. "Oi. Remember that summer K-man peed himself?"

The room answers with laughter.

Kwasi looks to Jericho, but Jericho is heading for the door.

"Yoo-hoo, I'm talking to you," Selim says to Kwasi. "You opened the bag. Why would you do that? Did we ask you to open the bag?"

From the hallway comes the rumble of older voices. More voices, so deep Kwasi feels them in the soles of his feet.

"So you opened the bag, messed something up, and you

can't even admit it. And you think we're going to just let you in, suddenly you want a part?"

"I need to go." Kwasi gets to his feet.

Selim gets up as well. "To do what? You don't do anything. When are you going to do something?"

He grits his teeth and walks on, out into the hallway. More guys have arrived, blocking the entrance.

Someone prods his back.

He can taste the heat from his Nando's. Da's words scream in his head: fight back; always fight back.

35

"Just almonds?" the customer asks, considering the last three brownies in the tin. "They look great. Only I have allergies."

Rupert lowers the lid. "More for someone else then."

"I didn't know you guys served food."

"Can't promise it'll be regular. But if you come back it might be. Plenty more surprises coming in January. And if you're around on Christmas Eve, we have an interview with a local poet."

"Yeah?" The customer pushes the woolly hat he bought into his backpack. "Sounds exciting."

"We'll put updates on the noticeboard. If you live nearby, come along."

"I just moved from Luton. Haven't done much here locally. Appreciated your window display. Thought I'd kill some time."

They both look to the window, where empty boxes wrapped in silk, ribbons, and tinsel are arranged around a tree, the tree Rupert picked up from the market, a precious little fir, hung with fairy lights and crowned with paper-cone angels. A productive morning, trying to make the most of this buzz, the elation of getting closer to securing funding. He can't wait to tell the boy and see how he likes the display.

"You're always welcome here. We welcome most of whatever you may be trying to get rid of too. Any Christmas gifts you get that you could do without, books you've already read and sweaters that don't fit, bring them down. More for someone else."

"Someone's in a good mood," Elaine says, after the customer leaves.

"Business is up. The display is helping. Should have thought of it earlier."

"You found a use for that fabric. I heard you were giving out brownies too. No extra ingredients, I hope."

"Of course not. We have a real chance here." He locks up the till. "People have been generous here lately."

"Generous? In a charity shop? Never." Elaine shakes her head.

"Well. They're going over and above. Tulip's friends came by at lunchtime, took some photos for the website. They're going to record our events too, for the landlord, and anyone else who doubts we're serious."

"That's good. Good news."

"Now. Do you want the last brownies?"

"You have them, Rupe. Don't stay late. The real work is just beginning."

He won't stay late, just long enough in case the boy comes by. This too is why the Chest must remain: this space is needed, open and undefined as it is, responsive to whatever customers ask of it.

He is rummaging through the box of old notes and

sketches from when they first opened the Chest when knocks sound from upstairs.

The boy is standing out by the bins, without a coat. One of his eyes is swollen shut.

Rupert shuts the door behind him. "Are you going to tell me what's happened?"

"Nothing."

"You're limping."

The boy drops his bag on the floor.

"What's happened to your eye? Was it the boys from Halloween?"

"It was yesterday. It's fine." There is a tremor in his voice. "I didn't come here to worry about that stuff. I just need to concentrate on the exhibition."

Rupert hesitates, uncertain. Seems that the boy does not want to talk about whatever trouble he has escaped. "Well. I have some good news," he says. "We're through to the next stage for the council fund."

The boy freezes. "Serious?"

"Yes. The ideas we put in the form, we need to demonstrate what they'll be like."

The boy has both hands on his head now.

"Are you all right?"

"Yeah. This is good." The boy lowers his hands and looks around.

"We're not out of danger yet, although we're definitely on the way."

"Do we get some money already, to fix things up for the exhibition? We can make it really nice."

"We don't, unfortunately. We'll have to be creative with what we have. But that's always been what the Chest does best."

"Like the Christmas stuff at the front."

"Exactly."

"It's good. And if we get the funding we can have more exhibitions."

"Exactly. Other events too. I'm curious to see how the storytelling night goes—ArteFacts, we're calling it. That will be special. Plus we'll be able to repair the wiring, fix up the steps, and stop worrying about bills. And Tulip's friend is recording a video, to let the landlord know what we're planning, like a film trailer, I think. We'll mention your exhibition. We'll do that in January, just before we hear back from the council fund."

"January. Okay. What do I need to do? Like should I help look for more frames? Or should I just work on more drawings?"

"You keep on drawing. Don't worry about the exhibition too much. Enjoy your art."

The boy gets his notepad out. "I'm going to look upstairs for a bit, to see if I get any new ideas."

After he goes, Rupert remembers the brownies. He knows better than to press about whatever's going on with the other kids. Jada would have handled it better, by creating space, leaving room for the truth to surface. But at least he can offer something sweet.

He gets the tin from beside the sink and calls up the stairs. "I set some brownies aside for you. And for your family."

The boy races back down. "So you do like brownies," he says.

"Only when they're natural. No preservatives, and a bit of cinnamon. It's been a while."

The boy opens the tin, breathes deeply. "I feel like I'd be into baking if I had grandparents here."

"Are your grandparents overseas?"

He takes a brownie and accepts a napkin, perches on a box of books. "They died, years ago."

"Sorry to hear that."

"I didn't really know them." The boy eats his brownie carefully, breaking off small chunks. "That's why my da went in the first place, because of their funeral."

"Your dad's overseas too, isn't he?"

"Yeah. He went for the funeral and then he got business ideas while he was there, so he's still there."

"I see. So you live with your mother? And your aunties. Are they all family?" He remembers asking before and not getting an answer. It's worrying enough that the boy's schoolmates keep hassling him. But now it seems that things might be complicated at home.

The boy looks up from the crumbs on his napkin. "Maybe if they were family they might not get annoyed with me all the time. Actually, they probably still would. They work all the time. It puts them in a bad mood."

"That's the advantage of grandfolks. They have more time to give away."

"That was really nice," the boy said. He sweeps up crumbs from the floor on his napkin and folds it carefully. "Thank you."

Rupert gets up, goes to the drawer of expired technologies. "I know things aren't easy for you at school. I have something." The Walkman looks good as new, although the headphones are long gone. He selects two cassettes. "This tape my brother made for me, after my first big heartbreak. Charlotte. Moved to the country. I got into a fight not long after she left, broke my arm in two places. I had a lot of frustration in me, missing her. This music helped me muddle through my sadness and anger. There's a theme to these songs, but it might not be what you think it is, when you first listen."

The boy takes the Walkman carefully in both hands.

"I wonder if you'll think of a word for it, the themes across these songs. And the second tape, it'll take you through all the classics, Bowie, a bit of Prince, Led Zeppelin too. The Beatles, of course, you have to start with them. You can hear the progression, you can feel the world changing."

"Thank you," the boy says, getting up. "An actual mixtape. Wow. I have a thing at school tomorrow. I'll probably need something to listen to after. Apparently my grandma liked the Beatles."

"Are you going to be okay walking back?"

"Yeah. My leg's fine. I forget it hurts when I'm walking." He gathers the brownie tin, Walkman, and tapes. "So, definitely January? For the exhibition?"

"Second week of January," Rupert says.

36

It goes like this: Squid sits beside him in the place where Da should have been. He feels even smaller at her side. The night outside is all rain, the roar of it on the hall roof is a kind of mocking applause. The hall is filled with teachers all talking at once over desks to parents, and the room is unsettled with gesturing and nodding. Too many words are being passed back and forth.

"I would have liked to have spoken earlier," Mrs. Nibley says, "to have a little more time. I still think it would be helpful, if you're able to come in for a meeting. I don't know where to start with Kwasi. He has potential. I think sometimes he has difficulty concentrating and following instructions. There have been a number of times he's come in late, or without his tie or blazer."

They are all looking at him, considering. He thinks of being colorless, even as heat flushes his face. He thinks of having a pool all to himself, a lake, an ocean. He thinks of how thinly he could spread, if he could loosen and expand in the water, if he could dissipate.

"Thank you," Ma says when it's over. She's holding a sheath of leaflets Mrs. Nibley gave her. Mrs. Nibley looks apologetic, sorry in that courteous distant way. Kwasi knows better than to meet her gaze. His worry is turning to anger and has an edge and over the edge is a flood.

"Let's use the toilets before we go," Ma says. In this moment they are the same: she is filled with water too.

In the toilet the window is larger than ever. He thinks of all the buses going across the city, that will keep moving through the night. All the places he could go to, if only he had the courage.

On the bus Ma and Squid converse in glares and silences. Each ding that brings them closer to home pinches him inside.

When at last they are home, the house seems withdrawn. Its walls lean apart and all the photos cringe away from him. A nature documentary is on, showing a snowy mountain range. Everyone looks fed up.

"So," Ma says. She puts her handbag on the table. "How many letters have you kept hidden?"

"What did we tell you about lying?" Auntie May says. "Kwasi. What were you thinking?"

"Am I laughing? How can you stand there and smile? Is this funny?"

Kwasi tries to stop smiling but can't. He is smiling because it stops his lips from quivering.

"Do you know what we would have given for the opportunities you have here?"

"These next five years will be the foundation for your future. Just five years, Kwasi."

"You can be anything, but you say what? You don't even know. You carry on and you will become like your father, just following ideas and talking."

"When I was half your age, I worked to send my brothers to school. Every day I woke up at four and went to the market and sold slippers, so that they could learn in years what you learn in one term."

"We know that you have been hanging out after school. We know you have been messing around with Jericho and those other boys, going into shops when we told you to come home. Are you surprised? You think we can't find out where you have been? Jericho is honest, at least. Yes, he told us—you have been hanging about with those boys after your homework club. Those boys are not failing their classes, are they?"

"We worked the farm, six of us in lines, and when we finished, we went into town to wash cars. This was to pay for power. And power was always cutting out anyway."

"Jericho is taking his GCSEs early. Is your head made of something different? Do you not have eyes like Jericho? Are your ears closed?"

"Eat your dinner, we have to plead with you. Come straight home after homework club, we must beg. Study so that you can have a good life; do you expect us to pay you or what, before you consider that one too?"

Ma says, "Call his father. Call him." Ma is like him, her sadness is anger too.

Squid passes him her phone.

"Good evening," Da says. "How are you? Every time I call you're busy. How are you doing?"

He can't think where to begin.

"Hello? Kwasi, what's going on?" Da sounds echoey, like he's in a bathroom.

Ma takes the phone. "Come and see your son. He hid

teacher's letters from the school." She loses her patience and switches to Twi.

★

Auntie Aha comes into his room at bedtime, with a tall glass balanced on a plate.

He takes his earphones out, pauses the Walkman.

"I haven't seen you drink water today. You know, your daddy will return soon. He is working hard; he would expect you to do the same."

"Soon." He pulls his covers up.

"It's not easy. When you are older, you will see. You know it's been tough for your mama."

There is no point in arguing. They will always have tougher things to talk about, from their lives before. They will never get how hard it is for him. Better to just concentrate on what he can do. The exhibition will happen in January. It will say everything he can't. That he does care, and he does see. He sees how lucky they are to be here, how much it still costs.

★

Late on Saturday morning he tiptoes to the bathroom and runs the shower hot. Steam blurs his reflection away, until the mirror over the sink is a square wooden frame depicting nothing. He works the pebble of soap to lather in his sponge and scrubs carefully around the newest bruises on his leg. They look like stains now, ones that might be washed away. Their darkness sits layers deeper though, and nothing but time erases them.

A man is made once and endures. The aunties make

themselves daily, sometimes many times a day, powdering and braiding each other's hair. How flat and small his body is.

He goes down the stairs, quietly. Everyone is already up, waiting in the sitting room.

"Do you understand," Squid says, "why we are not happy?"

"I know. I messed up."

"What you did, hiding those letters, was very bad," Squid says. "We all work very hard. If you cannot do your work, if we hear one more problem from you, annoying your classmates, or causing trouble in school, or going where you should not be, or missing deadlines for homework, you will come home that day and there will no longer be a place for you in this house."

"You will be returned to Danfa," Auntie May says. Kwasi feels it under his heels, like the floor is falling away.

"You will go and live with your father's people. Then you will learn what work is."

"We will not move you to any other school here."

"We have moved enough."

"You know at the last school, what they said? They said, we are concerned that Kwasi has behavioral and learning disorders. They said, this boy needs to be on medication. They said they would only keep you as a special-needs child."

A rumble of outrage fills the room. The ceiling presses lower. He imagines the air turned to stone, all of them sealed in a stone tomb.

"If you want to misbehave, that is your choice. We will say this just one more time: We are not moving you to a new school again. If they exclude you, or if you fail any exam, we will send you to Danfa."

"You are already behind," Auntie Aha says. "Jericho has offered to help. You will study with him at Uncle Obi's house, starting from next term."

He looks to Ma. Ma has not spoken. She is watching the window.

37

Tulip has a new job. Or rather many little jobs. Freelancing, she says, and insists it's no big deal. She works on her laptop all afternoon at the till. Designing posters for people she has never met.

"Are you sure you don't want pay while you're here?" Rupert says. "There's a fine line between exploitation and volunteering."

Tulip looks up, with a faint smile. "What now?" she asks. "You think I'm being exploited?"

"Did you know that there are over a hundred thousand slaves in the UK?"

"Didn't know that, actually. Where is this from?"

He opens his charity suggestions book, looking for the pamphlet on his mind. "Yes." He finds it, folded twice over. "Eight million in India," he reads. "In Russia, close to a million."

"What is with you today, Rupert?"

He closes the suggestions book. Brushes dust off the leather cover. "It's getting toward the time for our next vote," he says. "January. I was thinking we could invite suggestions at our ArteFacts night. So we make sure charity stays at the heart of this place. And as it'll be our last few weeks fundraising for Shelter around the time of the exhibition, we can have a real push for people to donate there."

"Definitely. And we can make a statement about housing. You know the council is still talking to developers, about putting up flats?"

"We shouldn't get political. If anything, we are making a space where people can take a break from all that, focus on good things that are happening."

Tulip runs her hand back over her head. She does this when agitated, as though with this gesture, she is sweeping grievances to the back of her mind. "Who's in the running to be our next charity? Let's see."

They look through the book, leafing through pages of scribbled charities and campaigns people would like the Chest to support. Notes and leaflets, folded between pages. Some are very niche, campaigns to fund research for conditions he has never heard of.

"We've had a few of these," he says, and smooths the creases from a leaflet about refugees.

Tulip studies the leaflet. It is printed with block letters and photographs of children.

"Again. Best not to get political," Rupert says.

"Oh come on. The right to a safe home is hardly political. Refugees need help to rebuild their lives."

"As do homeless drug addicts," he says. He looks out toward the street. "How many of these refugees could be working to support themselves?"

Tulip gives a tight-lipped smile. "We can put recommendations online."

"Not everything has to be online."

"We can link to charity websites so people can learn

more. We could even let people vote online. We'll get people involved who don't live locally, maybe. And then if they're ever in town, they'll visit. We could live-stream the vote." She gasps. "We could set up a fundraising page."

"What's that?"

She shows him: a website where strangers pledge money to each other. People are raising funds for medicines, for funerals, for holidays and businesses, for novels. "What do you think?"

She scrolls down the page. People have left comments, encouragement, and questions.

"Is this why you won't take pay?" he asks. "Do you have people on here sponsoring you? Looks a lot like organized begging."

"Rupert. Not at all. Jamie and Lake pay rent to me. Less than they would have paid otherwise."

The door groans open. Cold air washes through the shop. Three boys troop in, puffer jackets zipped over their chins, and disappear down the aisles. A fourth boy lopes in and pushes his hood back.

"Hey," Rupert calls. "We're not open."

"Sir. Is this a charity shop? How do I donate?" the boy asks.

Rupert scoffs. "Out you go. We're closed."

"Oh, come on. How can a charity shop close? People need help all the time."

Laughter cackles from the bookcases by the stairs.

Tulip closes her laptop and slides it off the counter, out of sight.

"So," the hooded boy says. "Do I just bring stuff in, to give to charity? Do I just bring it in a box?"

"Out," Rupert says again. "We're closed."

"Doesn't say closed."

"Ay, there's a piano."

"Hey." Rupert raises his voice. "All of you. Now."

Another boy appears from the shadows of a display. "We're just browsing."

"I don't want you here browsing. On you go. Come on."

"What? We didn't do anything. Ay. Come we go downstairs."

All four of them head for the stairs.

"I'm calling the police," Tulip says quietly.

He grabs his cane from behind the piano. "Out."

"Whoa."

"Relax, man."

"We're going. You can see we're going." They sidle past, hands raised.

"So much for charity, man."

After they leave, silence rings in his ears. His hands are curled white around the stick, and tremors are shaking from his elbows.

Tulip touches his shoulder. "Sit."

She goes and shuts the door and locks it. Leans her back against it. She is shaking, too. The silence is a quivering emptiness. It presses in his throat and makes his eyes tear up.

★

He tells Elaine, the following day, that tickets for their first event, a second crafts night, are selling fast online.

"They'll clean up after themselves so no need to worry—"

"I don't worry. I haven't the time." She gathers her detergents into her trolley. "I hope you're charging them enough. Ten pounds at least. And use Tulip. She has half an art degree. We can put that in the application."

"Half? In art?"

Elaine looks smug. "She quit her accounting degree. En-rolled as an art student but didn't tell her family. Imagine. The neighbors heard them yelling. And then the parents packed up and left. Left the house to her—she has to pay rent and get tenants. That's something, I suppose. You can't be a child forever."

He looks over the polished counter.

"It won't be a waste if she brings in more people and calls the craft sessions *classes*. And get her to take that exhibition seriously. It's not a chance for her and her friends to show off and feel good about themselves. We could hold practi-cal classes here if people are interested. I know a thing or two about knitting. You could get Mrs. Maple in to teach sewing. Might find a use for the rest of those fabrics."

After she goes, a sinking mood falls over him. A drink would lift him up; he deserves one for all he has put up with today. But he'll need to see how the storytelling night and the arts event unfold, to know whether it's worth making them regular and find frames for the exhibition. He and Tulip spent an hour scouring the web for larger frames. Tulip's digital artist friend is snapping photos along the high street to display. They are close. Jada would be with him, staying level and sober too. Perhaps she is watching over him with pride.

38

He stretches his legs and plays the third cassette on the new-old Walkman, listening through decades, as advised, in order, apart from the Beatles. He is saving their songs for later; he fast-forwarded through the first part. He has met David Bowie, Prince, Led Zeppelin, Michael Jackson, and he already knows their songs, without knowing how. He meets ABBA, remembers aunties who sang these ballads. Wonders if they are still singing now, in the new homes they moved on to.

When he looks up, Auntie Aha is standing over him. He waits for instructions, or chastisement for some forgotten offense. Perhaps he left something where it should not be. Mud from his trainers on the doormat.

But instead Auntie Aha prompts him to use the computer. She has turned the internet on for him, she says. "You have been so quiet. Why don't you play a game? Thirty minutes and then you'll get ready for bed."

Alone with the computer. He opens six tabs and loads games. Old games. He has to download plug-ins just to make them appear. But the games he played with Da and Jericho years ago look cartoonish and flat now. Still he plays, waiting for the thrill. But it seems that part of what made these games so fun was sharing them, in taking turns and competing.

A glance at the office door confirms no auntie is in sight. He looks back to the screen, where the cursor ticks in an empty search bar. Selim showed him, on his phone, websites where you can watch grown-ups doing it. Bodies quivering and mashing together again and again. He looks back, and still no one is outside. But time is limited.

He types into a search page, "The Chest of Small Wonders."

It has a website. A photo of the Chest in black-and-white, taken recently, since the mannequin is wearing the blue hat with the huge flower on it. A picture of a teacup that looks like a fancy wineglass. It makes him think of the shopkeeper's syrups.

He clicks to the Events page, which is mostly empty as well. The ArteFacts link takes him to a new website, where he could buy tickets. The "Cosy Crafty Chest" link leads to a similar page, but it says tickets have sold out.

There is no page linked to the final listed event, the "Exhibition." Still, he has this swirling feeling inside, that it's actually going to happen. He takes his hand off the mouse. He can feel people watching, especially when he shuts his eyes. He cannot tell yet if this is a good feeling or not.

He opens a new search page, and types:

Is coffee a drug
Could you poison someone with herbs mixed with tea
or coffee

Are herbs mixed in coffee or tea legal
Penalty for using drugs
Penalty for supplying drugs

"Kwasi," Squid shouts from downstairs.

There are too many words. He follows the links with words like "natural," and "healing," and "inspiration" first. He will read the negative stuff later.

"Hey." Squid is watching from the doorway. "What are you looking at there?"

Panic seizes him. "Homework," he says. "Biology." He closes all the tabs at once.

"You shouldn't look at screens too late. Shut it down and go to bed. Get up. Oh. You need to tidy your room. For Christmas, you will sleep here with the children. Auntie Rosanna and her husband will sleep in your bedroom, and we'll put the mattress up there, for Auntie Jackie to join them. Tidy everything. I don't want any last-minute halfway job. All of the clutter under your bed, all the junk on your windowsill. I just went in and I don't know what you are doing with the foil scattered everywhere—you have to clear all of that rubbish away. It should be like a hotel."

Shadows are falling over him, over the whole house it seems. He was playing at molding the foil into figures, but now it seems like a dumb idea.

"Do you hear?" Squid asks.

"Okay. I'll tidy up."

"Oh. Before I forget, Jericho phoned."

"What?"

"He said you can join him for the carol service on New Year's Eve. You painted the nativity scene for this? I told him you're not doing anything that day. You will have to work very hard next term. Go and have fun before that time. Better than sitting here on your own, isn't it?"

39

Their first public event is a success before it starts. Sold out, with a waiting list. Selling out is not what makes it special though, is not the reason for his smile. It is Tulip's event. The same Tulip who came to the Chest years ago, bookish and nervous, yet also assured, determined. The basement twinkles, candlelit. Just six candles and one lantern, but with the mirrors out, ovals and square panes, strategically placed, the whole room is alive with light.

Here come twentysomethings in dungarees, baggy shirts, Christmas sweaters and beanie hats, thick-framed glasses and trainers.

"Welcome to your living room," Tulip says. She asks them to leave their trainers and boots at the door and offers them cheap slippers they may later decorate and purchase.

Delighted, guests don their slippers. An aroma of cinnamon and wine wafts up from the basement—the mulled wine is nonalcoholic but smells just as good.

Tonight the Chest is restored, all its liveliness is below, as it used to be. Rupert's shoulders feel tight, and he hugs his arms and rubs them. Best not to think of Jada; she would have wanted him to enjoy, to be present.

He pushes the door and looks outside. Tightness spreads up his throat. People are coming up the street, bent over phones, glancing up at the shop signs. They pass by and return and pass again before they accept that this must be it. Their faces are bright and unlined. Colored hair peeks from hats, jewelry flashes in ears and noses.

"Just leave your shoes here, I promise we won't sell them," he says. "Although we might have to sell yours, goodness, what a remarkable pair of boots. Rupert. A pleasure. Welcome to the Chest. She's downstairs, they're all downstairs. Here, let me hang your coat. Of course you can. Plenty downstairs. We're your home away from home, so get your slippers on."

They shed their layers and shoes and go like moths to the glow rising up the stairs. Rupert follows and watches as they settle on the rugs on the floor. Their skirts pool around them. Pages are distributed, yellow in the candlelight. They lean over sheets and canvases.

Two lads set up speakers. Hissing pours from black mesh fronts. They laugh, unplug and reconnect cables. Music breaks through static, a flurry of notes, with a rhythm that makes the building tick, pulse impatient and disturbed. He rests against the banister.

They sway as they work on their sketches.

After a while, he waves to Tulip. She rises and comes over. Turns her sequin eyes on him. "Ginger tea?"

He shakes his head. "I'm heading off." His voice does not sound like his. "I'll leave you to it." Leaves the keys on the shelf of a bookcase. "Lock up, won't you?"

"We will."

They look over the glowing basement, all the business unfolding.

★

So many kids are on the corner tonight, at least a dozen standing in the freezing cold, looking at their phones. He wonders for a moment if they are looking for Tulip's craft night. But no. These are local kids, in puffer coats with hoods up. Troublemaking sorts.

He unlocks his front door and steps inside. All he can think of now is the Chest, ticking on without him. Liberated. He could laugh.

When she was diagnosed, he said, "It's a good thing we have no children, since you're not sticking around."

And she said, with laughter in her eyes, "Well if you'd given me a child, I would have had a reason to stick around."

She once told him to think of life as a bridge. "A bridge, and say it looks like it's flat when you're walking toward it, or on it, but it's not." It begins low and rises, and then declines, gracefully as a bird swooping to land.

And everyone is trying to lengthen it. To make it last.

40

Wind harasses his eyes as he paces to the station. In his old Nikes today, gray tracksuit and the huge jacket Uncle David left last winter, which he found when tidying his room, heavy as a duvet. His shadow, obese, edges over the pavement.

The Victoria line is the best, just takes a while to connect to it. Its velocity shrinks the city, pinches Walthamstow and Brixton close, plus it's hot. In the carriage, his palms burn with the sudden heat. He rubs them together: how cold his fingertips are.

On the map, the Victoria line is a bright blue current. You wouldn't believe how busy it becomes, how quickly people pile in, then minutes later, the carriage is his again: an elongated sitting room. People linger by doors, though there's plenty of room. Only the elderly or pregnant settle close to him. Most people are busy with their phones. A girl two seats away is secretly taking photos of the woman struggling to keep her twins in order. He sees it all—reflections of screens in the perennial black of the windows.

He was supposed to be meeting Jericho to help set up for the carol service; they were meant to start from the

Chicken Palace. He wonders if they are still waiting for him, expecting him to show up. He can't help but smile. There are other ways to fight back, and sometimes distance hits harder. He is in uncertain territory here: since the fight, they have ignored him. But they are watching still, deciding what to do with him. There is no way Jericho seriously intended to practice singing Christmas songs today.

He imagines all the lights in different parts of the city, what it might look like from the center, from a bridge over the river, looking north and then south, the constellations of Christmas colors, all the people wandering in their unfathomable lives. There is a big park in the city where people go and do festive things. He imagines people dressed as snowmen, as elves. There will be sleighs and reindeer, girls and boys and maybe Tim, and his not-so-new sibling. All of them drinking hot chocolate from paper cups. Maybe there are rides as well, ice-skating and music. He imagines Auntie Baby there, holding hands with her boyfriend, her long braids swinging. Her laughter, the way her speech will mist the air. He crosses his arms over his aching chest.

The Tube has reached Brixton. One day he'll surface here. It looked nice online, lots of music places. He sits and waits for the cleaners to come and go. A new driver boards, and the train runs back up. Kwasi jots ideas in his notebook. He sketches scenes for a new comic.

For variety, he changes to the Jubilee line, which feels dirtier and slower. Up to Stratford and out into the warmth of the shopping center. He went up to the wrong platform once where the trains were going to places like Norwich, Colchester. Wild to think he could have boarded the wrong one and been shunted out of the city.

The shopping center at Stratford feels closer than it

is, because he can get here without walking under open sky. Here, he feels colorless, easy. It's like moving through water. Even the adverts here show people who look more like him. He buys a cinnamon pretzel, warm and soft, and eats it as he walks by shopfronts, considering the different ways a person can present. Tattoos, webs of them, and dreadlocks. It is cozy—the warmth and light and smell of different foods—but sad, like he could keep walking and keep finding options and all of it would blur and there would be no reason to choose one over the other. And he has no money for anything anyway. He has just enough for a present for Ma (a scarf and a pair of earrings) and a present for the house (a Christmas angel decoration and chocolates, as standard).

He rides the Tube back west, watching the churn of passengers. Back on the Victoria line, it's crammed, hard to watch people without feeling watched in return.

After ten, late enough for the aunties to begin to be concerned by his absence, he makes his final journey north. Surfaces into the gnawing cold. Walks, paces, jogs up the street. Frozen hands fumble for the biggest key on his fob. He hesitates in the living-room doorway. They lean out from their sofas and he does his best to smile.

41

This event is Rupert's, but everyone has contributed. Even the name—ArteFacts—was Tulip's idea. The first speaker they are interviewing is a poet friend of hers. This one did not sell out, but it's Christmas Eve, and they were ambitious about how many they could seat in the audience. What a thing to see the space reassembled, new, yet more familiar than before, matching Jada's floor plan from years ago, as though he has stepped into those pages.

Tulip and a friend lift benches and chairs up the stairs and arrange them in six rows. They lay out cushions, blankets, and beanbags. They drape donated fabrics over shelves and mannequins.

He asks Tulip to take a picture of this view, for future leaflets, but more than that: for Elaine to see how those rich cloths have become useful again tonight. Perhaps the woman who donated them will see, if they share the photo online. Tulip shows him how to use her phone camera and he takes some pictures of his own. The camera is so sharp, the shop through its lens is pristine, greater than he could have hoped. His head feels fuzzy, looking. He backs to the staircase, standing tall to capture the full scene.

"Careful," Tulip calls. "We need you to judge how tonight goes. Don't fall!"

"Doing my best," he says.

Lake—a mixed-race lad with dreadlocks past his chin—arrives carrying speakers, and with some of Tulip's friends. They begin setting up a camera to record, to get yet more footage and photographs. Tulip said it will help promote the Chest online.

Rupert recognizes Miri, who came to last week's craft night in unforgettable boots. She nods hello and goes and sits upon the counter. Lake gives her a bulky microphone, and from time to time, she taps it. Raises it to her lips and says, "Nothing is. Sound. Sound is. Hello." and "Good evening, lovely humans. I'm your host for tonight." Outrageous violet lipstick against pale skin, no eyebrows he can see. Tulip watches her with a tender gaze.

Miri stays swinging her legs from the counter as newcomers trickle in. She's still there when the event begins, when the audience is seated, at least forty guests. Familiar faces from the last event, but plenty of newcomers. No sign of the boy. Most of the guests look twentysomething, but a healthy number look middle-aged. Several of the men have the same haircut, the same carefully trimmed beards. The last event felt more diverse, perhaps because the numbers were smaller. He should have eaten something firmer than soup, now his stomach feels unsettled.

From the counter, Miri interviews ArteFacts' first guest—a tall, slender woman.

"Yes, now it is my legal name. Lemon Bridge." She waves and the bangles on her arm chime. She has lived just by the park for almost twenty years. She sits barefoot and cross-legged in the rocking chair. Her hair is bleached sunny by the standing lamp. Lake has done a great job with the lights: bulbs glow ruby, sapphire, and emerald.

". . . always a Christmas Eve tradition. I'd just published my first collection. I'd always had this fantasy of living as a hermit, hidden in the country. I'd like to read a verse from my first collection, actually."

In the reverent hush that follows, Lemon opens her book. "And of course, if you do like it, you're welcome to buy a copy—you'll have to order online as I haven't brought printed copies. I will donate fifty percent to Shelter, whose work, sadly, is only going to become more vital." She clears her throat. "Limestone bridge of waterlogged bones/Runs under and above/And the forest's mines of dormant night/Kept in chambers ever between."

Rupert closes his eyes. The rhythm of her words. He had forgotten this.

". . . and I ended up in the Chest, soaked. I'd never seen anything like it. There was a cocktail bar below at the time—it was only there a few weeks, sadly, but it was *fantastic*. Jada mixed her own infusions. And they served teas in delightful little cups. Jada was an angel. She just *collected* good news, whenever someone came in with rumors of trouble, she listened and gave them positive stories in return. We were all devastated when she was diagnosed, but she kept working. She loved it here."

He grits his teeth. Rises. Steps toward the door.

Outside, he finds himself tangled in conversation with a crowd of latecomers. People he half remembers and has not seen since Jada's death.

"You look well," they tell him. "This is a wonderful idea."

Meera and her husband arrive. They draw him back

inside. Everyone wants to sign up to speak. Tulip looks up from where she sits in the corner, drawing a courtroom-style sketch of the speaker. She gives a tiny smile.

★

Afterward, stacking chairs:

"We have totally got this," Tulip says.

"It was all right, wasn't it?" Rupert says.

"Definitely one to do again. A few people said they'd like to hear from you. As in an interview with you."

"We'll see. Best to focus on the exhibition now."

"The exhibition will be easy. Let's not plan it too much. It should feel spontaneous, like those displays you and Jada put together? We'll do it on the fourteenth of January, a Thursday, yeah? We have so much art. Eek. I've been thinking. People keep asking about Jada's cocktails. What if we put it in our application for the next round? We'll be a space for people to unwind, connect, and create. Your syrups are so soothing; it's like therapy."

Exhaustion is a new layer, ossifying under his skin. "We can have a think. The council weren't keen on it at all, last time Jada and I tried."

"That was years ago though. And they're more open to new ideas now."

"It's still the same Councillor Obi. Some people never change."

"As long as we don't go crazy with it, it shouldn't be a problem. You guys had natural herbs too, right?"

"It's a tricky one. I'm really trying to stay present, to stay sober, you understand?"

By the door, Lake zips his speakers into their padded cases.

"I'm not saying we should go all out. Councillor Obi has a grid of what they're judging businesses on. Here." Tulip loads it on her mobile and hops over to show him. "Brings people of different backgrounds together. Brings people of different generations together. Addresses social isolation. Provides opportunities for people to learn new skills. Promotes mental and physical well-being. We could start a listening service. It would suit our charity focus—we could call it . . . heart-to-heart in the Chest."

"No, no."

"We could try—"

"We're not qualified for that."

Lake and Miri shout goodnight and blow kisses as they leave.

"Seriously," Tulip says. "You're a good listener." She pauses. "Speaking of—did you hear that? I thought I heard someone knock."

He approaches the door, pushes it, and steps out into the cold. "Are you there?" he calls into the night. "Hello?"

The boy steps in from the alleyway. Smartly dressed with tapered black shoes and pressed trousers. "They're still following me," he says. He looks beyond, across the car park. "They went round the back."

Rupert locks the back door. "How many were following you?"

Tulip says, "What's happened? Who's this?"

The two of them stare at each other, and then glance back to him.

"Here we are," says Rupert. "You meet at last. Go on down and put the kettle on. I'll lock the shutters."

★

When he gets downstairs, Tulip is lighting candles.

"Have you introduced yourselves?" he asks.

"Yep. It's Kwasi, right?" Tulip says. "I feel like I'm still saying it wrong."

"Kwasi."

"Kwasi," Rupert says. He cannot remember saying it before, all this time.

The boy looks startled too. Something is changed; the moment feels sharper.

"Is that it, Kwasi?" Rupert asks.

"Call me K if you like. It's not that important. What happened upstairs? Did you see them?"

"I did, with their hoods and hats. It's Christmas Eve, for goodness' sake."

"Who?" Tulip asks, sitting down.

"Troublemakers. Kids messing about."

"How many? What do they want?"

"A good talking-to, is what they want. Teenagers, old enough to know better. They'll get the trouble they're looking for soon enough, if they carry on like that. Only three or four of them, tall lads." He sinks into his armchair.

"Are these the kids who egged the front?" Tulip asks.

"Let's not worry about that tonight. We'll not give them that power. They've cleared off now." Rupert does his best to smile reassuringly. "We used to sit for hours here, smoking, before they banned it," he says. "Jada and I. Then she started mixing drinks." He shakes his head. "I don't think we should bring beverages back, Tulip. We had no clue what we were doing."

"You did fine," Tulip says. She returns and perches with a cushion on her lap. "In the end."

"I'll have you know, my end is yet to come."

"To a very distant end," Tulips says, and raises her mug. "We could have fun with the concept of teas, of secret ingredients and mixing. We could call it 'Specialteas,' as in 'teas'?" She lifts her mug again.

"Oh dear," Rupert says.

"We could make it exclusive too, like a limited number of guests, and maybe only once a month. And it could be super ceremonial."

"Maybe later," he says. "Let's keep things simple now. We need the council on our side."

"The same council that undemocratically decided to build flats no one can afford? They'll never really be on our side. We could spend forever diluting our vision trying to win their approval. Let's have some fun. Come on."

"Well. Let's not let worrying about that spoil our fun at the moment," Rupert says.

"Okay. I guess we have a fair bit on, over the next few weeks. So, Saturday the ninth, we have our second Arte-Facts night, and we'll need a speaker to interview for that. And then on the Thursday after, the fourteenth, we have the exhibition."

"That's good. That will keep us busy. I'm also meeting our landlord at the end of January, so hopefully by then we'll have a solid plan, and funding."

"It's on a Thursday?" the boy asks. He looks troubled.

"What is?" Rupert asks.

"The exhibition. Does it have to be on a Thursday?"

"We can move it. Are you busy on Thursday?"

"No. But. My family will be busy."

"Thursday evenings are best," Tulip says. "We can join

in the Throwback Thursday hashtag with some of our posts, since there will be lots of nostalgia. We should stick with that."

"Well, we wouldn't want your family to miss it," Rupert says. "Let's see about putting it on the weekend, Tulip."

"On a Sunday, maybe?" the boy suggests.

"Sunday won't work," Tulip says.

"Let's leave it for now," Rupert says. "We can talk about work another day. It's Christmas. Haven't you kids some-where better to be on Christmas Eve?" He turns to the boy. "Your family don't celebrate Christmas?"

"They do. I told them I'm singing carols with my friend. I was going to. But my friend wanted to do other things."

"Lying to parents. No wonder everyone thinks I'm trouble." Rupert shakes his head.

"Doesn't have to be a lie," Tulip says, putting her cup down. "We can sing."

42

On Christmas Day, it is hard to relax. Once again, this is a different Jericho, who can't even remember that Kwasi ducked out of the carol service. This Jericho smiles so much he looks dumb. He's wearing a red sweater with a reindeer face and lets the toddlers take turns to stroke or pat its brown fur. Kwasi keeps his distance, busies himself bringing trays of snacks up from the kitchen and replenishing the kids' cups.

Cousins: in sibling sets of threes and fours, with the same curling eyelashes and matching beads in their braids, the same button noses and shy grins. They stare and talk behind their hands. As if they know: here is a boy who is on his final warning, a boy who may be sent to Ghana in the new year. Everyone knows it. Uncle Stewart, who Kwasi remembers only vaguely from a funeral in Edmonton, cornered him by the bathroom earlier, asking if he's ready for hot weather, if he will attend boarding school or stay with his father. Uncle Stewart went on and on, about how boarding school builds character, how important it is for young people to spend time far from their families.

"You can return here for university," he suggested. "Return when you are older, when you know where you come from. You can even study in the States. It's just the foundation that is tough. The system is not in our favor. When I was your age, we carried ourselves like men. Here, you don't have any place where you can carry yourself properly. It's a very serious problem."

He and Jericho are the eldest, but when the grown-ups want something, it's Jericho they call. After Christmas lunch, Squid shouts for help to get the new speakers working.

Only then do Jericho's eyes meet his, briefly. "Okay, everyone stop—listen to Uncle Rambo." The children look to him, long enough for Jericho to slip out and vanish down the stairs.

So now Jericho is playing music from the laptop downstairs, highlife and soca and gospel songs, and Kwasi is stuck watching the kids play on the computer. All their sticky fingers jam the keys and fight to hold the mouse. Did their mothers sleep here years ago, or perhaps in the sitting room? Do they know they would not even exist, if Da had not helped their parents? All the houses they'll return to, are those houses bigger than this?

Most have traveled from south, others from further away. They sleep in the office, snoring. Lying on the edge of the mat, Kwasi stares at the ceiling while his stomach cramps. All the greens they forced him to eat are coiling, sprouting roots deep in his bowels.

For New Year's this time they mark the day at Jericho's. It sounds like it's Ma's fault, from what Squid said to Auntie

May. She left it too late to get a ticket for the watchnight service at church this year.

As much as he hates to do it, Kwasi stays close by Squid and waits to see if Jericho will confront him at last here. The house feels larger with more people, like he's seeing it for the first time: strikingly detached, with brilliant white walls, oak banisters, too many rooms. Tonight the living room is illuminated by a real fireplace, where King Obi roasts literal chestnuts. A Christmas tree towers in the atrium, dressed in lanterns and baubles and shimmering with tinsel, lighting the corridors and stairs in pulsating yellow, emerald, and red. So many gifts surround the base, they must be fake. But they are not.

The good thing about Jericho's dad is that he doesn't send kids to entertain themselves far from grown-ups. Everyone sits in a circle and talks about their favorite thing that happened this past year. Afterward, they have to go back the other way and talk about their hopes and resolutions. When his turn comes, Kwasi imagines himself in drama, playing a different kid for a short time. "This year I learned how to do simultaneous equations," he says. "Also algebra."

Most mention small things: they've been getting up at six every morning, they no longer eat chocolate. They are learning Spanish, learning to dance salsa, learning to cook—it's never too late! They are starting businesses, helping at a food bank; they are dating again. Squid announces that this year, she wants to stop eating meat.

Conversation rolls around, dizzying, as all the aunties who share his house introduce themselves and what they are striving to do.

"It's going to be a brilliant year," King Obi says. "Twenty-sixteen. I feel it."

"Amen."

"When I came to this country. God. The police. And my parents, despite having been invited to rebuild the country, they found no place to rent. They were told"—he inclines his head, a bitter smile lights his eyes—"No Blacks, No Irish, No Dogs."

Around the room, a murmur spreads. Kwasi tenses and draws his shoulders in.

"I remember drinking in a bar near Kings Cross with my friends—celebrating our twenty-first birthdays the British way, to our parents' dismay. And as it got busier, livelier, we were asked to move downstairs, and then later, told to leave. Simple as that. We were hardly tipsy, weren't giving anyone trouble. Look at us now. This is our time."

"Preach!"

"It's not going to be easy. Black, white, yellow, green—the recession hit us *all*. And people want someone to blame. We see more and more of the same stories: Black youths are violent, Black youths are killing each other. Black fathers are negligent. We have a government that cuts and slashes. And they have a hostile environment. This is what they openly call it. They will use the Syrian refugee situation to come after all of us."

Squid's arm curves around Kwasi's shoulders, and she hugs him to her side.

"Be generous, but be smart. You all know I like to talk. If I didn't have to wrap up by midnight, I could go until sunrise. But really, I love people. We all have something to give. I try to connect with everyone, but I've learned that lots of people are not open to connection, because they fear. Try to reach them if you can, but first care for those who can respect you.

"We are brothers and sisters. Let's hold each other to account. We are here, after all. We have to make it worth our while, for our children, and for those who went before. When we meet again next year, we celebrate growth."

Kwasi has heard King Obi speak enough times to know what will follow: a ritual, an exercise in sharing, a turn-to-your-neighbor situation. He wriggles free from Squid's embrace and gets up. Ignoring the eyes on him, he goes across the hall to the bathroom.

The bathroom is bigger than his bedroom at home. His reflection, framed in an oval mirror, looks alarmed. It takes a moment to understand why. He looks like Da. If Da could see him now, see his collar and his smart navy sweater, see his gleaming cocoa-buttered face and the sheen of terror that makes him appear alert, he would be startled too. He squares his shoulders. Bright and tense like this, he looks kind of smart.

A huge bathtub and all the tiles throw back his reflection. It smells like vanilla, like freshly washed clothes. He puts down the toilet lid and sits. Closes his eyes.

★

Back in the main room, the little ones are tearing paper and distributing gifts. Music beats beneath laughter and chatter.

"There you are," Ma says. "Kwasi, come and say thank you."

King Obi must have asked Ma's permission beforehand,

yet Ma and the aunties watch appalled as the sleek black phone is unboxed. It's the phone from the advert, the one that always plays before the news.

Inside, Kwasi is spinning. "Thank you."

"Give it. Come," Jericho says, and helps set it up while the grown-ups dance. The phone's screen fills with icons. Younger kids crowd to see. Their hands reach to touch the black case.

"Can I see?"

"I want to play."

"Can I try next?"

"Hey. Can I try it now?" Kwasi asks.

"Come, come," Jericho says, and gets up. "I can't hear anything you're saying."

In the hallway by the Christmas tree they perch on the radiator.

"Why do you talk so quietly?" Jericho asks. "No one can hear anything you say. Look, look. What's your email?"

Kwasi recognizes the colors of the site Jericho is about to log in to. "I'm not allowed."

Jericho smirks. "Choose a password and put your email in."

The phone is so light in his hands. Kwasi hesitates.

"Relax. You'll like it." Jericho takes the phone and turns its camera on him. "Smile."

The camera crunches again and again.

"Nice," Jericho says. "Festive."

"Let me see."

Jericho dodges. "Wait for it. I'm setting your profile pic."

Kwasi glances back but none of the others have followed. "Did my aunties ask you where I go after homework club?"

"Ages ago. They're like the mafia. My dad called me down and there were like three of them just standing there."

"What did you say?"

"You're with us. What? If you're not with us, you're against us. Hey. Is it true that you have a Walkman?"

"It works. And I got it for free."

"Nah, that's not right. I can't have family carrying museum technology. Look, look. I'll send you music, you can just listen here, or here." He points to two icons on the phone screen. "As long as you're online. I made a playlist—I made the one that's on now. It's sick, right? Afrobeats is going to be everything this year. Trust."

The music sounds familiar, like the Ghanaian songs that beat through the house on endless summer evenings, but sharper and sunnier. Kwasi finds himself nodding.

"Why did you run away, when we went to the carol service? You always chicken out. I swear I wasn't going to invite anyone. Selim is always out—I was just saying hi."

"You saw what Selim did at yours. And his brother."

"It was a good fight," Jericho says. "Are you still not over it?"

"Why did you let them come?"

"When we were playing *GTA*? How was I supposed to know they were coming? I don't control them. What did you want me to do, not let them in the house? You could have fought better. You always chicken out. Stick around, you might learn something."

"Maybe I would if—"

"There's no if. This is family business. You don't choose when you stay or go. You have to invest in your people. So here's your New Year's resolution: Stay with Your People."

Kwasi starts back toward the main room, but Jericho grabs his wrist. They go in together. It is four minutes to midnight; everyone is leaping and twirling. The house is one puffed-up chest.

43

Taking everything down is the hard part, but someone has to start. Pain tugs on his joints as Rupert lifts his arms. That's what he gets for drinking and eating to excess.

The hall is two stories high, and all its beams and poles are festooned with winking lights, tinsel, and festive bunting. That's a sign of a good display, when everything hangs together as one, when there is no way of knowing how it fits together or what was put up first. Or how to unravel it.

He rubs the soreness in the small of his back. Stretches—carefully—and unwinds the snake of silver tinsel from the beam that supports the projector.

Boxes of baubles surround him. Best to keep them separate so they are easier to unpack next year.

Across the hall, late risers are rolling up their sleeping bags. Some are wandering off with them. The church will need to buy more sleeping bags at this rate. That's the only part of clearing up anyone is helping with.

Elaine comes and stands at his side, one hand on her hip.

"Shall I go and have a word?" he asks.

"It's fine." She shakes her head. "They can keep the

sleeping bags." She's wearing another Christmas sweater, with a sequined elf on the front. She peers over her glasses at the boxes of decorations. "Honestly though. Lots of them have friends they're staying with. They just came for the food, didn't you, Al, you sausage."

Al stands, a sleeping bag under each arm. "I'm off," he says. "Going." And ambles away.

"See that? Not even a *have a nice day*. When you're finished, take the decorations out to Harry's van."

"Does he have a ladder in the van? Unless a team of angels put these decorations up."

"Don't be silly. I'm not letting you climb a ladder. The caretaker will be here around noon. You can have another coffee. Thanks again, Rupe. I know it was last minute, and honestly, I don't know what we would have done without you."

She would have been fine without him. She just wanted an older man around; most of the volunteers are women. He did suggest they ask Tulip, for her friends would certainly have been keen to help host a Christmas sleepover for homeless people. But Elaine would not have it. "They're not believers."

"I haven't been to church in years."

"But you do believe. You said you do."

He dared not argue. It wasn't as though he had anywhere else to go.

"Don't worry about it," he says now. "Hurry on home to poor Harry."

"It was his idea to help out this year. He would have been wonderful. Has a way of sharing the good news in everything he does. But that cough." She pats his arm.

"I've got to see if we have any more devotionals, be right back."

The hall is still emptying. People leave in groups, hoods up and caps pulled low over their faces. But wait—is that . . . ? Rupert peers more closely. It's definitely him, the man from Camden, so many summers ago. Phineas? Phil? Felix? It has to be. He's pressing his sleeping bag smaller, pushing it into his backpack.

Rupert goes over, picking a careful path between the boxes. Phil. "How are you doing? Let me help."

Phil's pale eyes look over him. "All good, cheers. Thank you."

"Phil. It's Rupert."

"Sorry, did I mix you up again? Thanks, Rupert. And thank Elaine too. You lot are saints."

"Rupert. Remember me? Rupert and Jada. We met in Camden? You were busking and Jada was selling herbal tea. We did it. We opened our teashop. Our bookshop. Gift shop. You should come and visit."

Phil's eyes look past Rupert. His face has grayed and fallen.

"Did you get the tattoo?" Rupert persists. "What was it, something in Latin? Or a map of something. A map of London. Yes, you said Big Ben."

Phil's eyes light up. He shrugs off his jacket and unwinds the blanket he's wrapped underneath. "How do you know about that? What's your name again? Jay? Albert?"

"Rupert. And Jada. We married. She's . . . You remember Jada? Her herbs? We had a lovely time by the canal. You had that awful bedsit over the nail salon."

"Jada." Phil's face clouds. He rubs his arm again. "Impressed that you remember. But then"—he grins—"it is a damn memorable tatt." He pushes his sleeve up, revealing bruised skin, networks of blackened veins, so many little scars. "Silly me." He smooths the sleeve back down, his other sleeve up. A mess of ink, tattoos over tattoos. Somewhere under all that noise is London, the eye, the face of a great clock.

"Remember Jada?" Rupert asks again. "American?"

Phil's eyes light up. "The tea lady. You still dealing those tea bags? Whirlwind in a cup." He laughs and coughs. "Maybe I'll come by. If not, see you here next year. And bring Jada!" He smiles, falling into a memory. "What a God-awful voice she had. You have to get us guitars as well. Next time we do Christmas here, get us a proper band. I can't do much with an organ."

★

He goes out to the garden for fresh air, with a cup of bitter coffee. Just reminiscing with Phil has stirred his appetite, awakened a part of his mind that waits for escape. Tulip made a salient point, that it's legal, and it was a sort of spiritual release. Dr. Hyde has sent his seasonal discount text message. Rupert makes a mental note to call, a compromise, if Jada is watching from the other side, if angels can have a say in the course of what transpires, he'll leave this one to her: if Dr. Hyde can deliver within the next four days, he'll go ahead and try one last time, to see about serving Specialteas in the Chest.

For now, he sips coffee. Just the aroma is making him jumpy. Every blade of grass cries out to be seen.

Something stirs by the gravestones. A rodent, perhaps. But no: a dog. A scrawny mutt comes and sniffs at his trousers, and doesn't make a sound. Someone must have left him behind.

"We'll keep him for a few days," Elaine says, when Rupert leads the poor thing inside. "And if no one comes asking we'll take him to the shelter."

44

Kumar is one of his people, among the first. A short conversation, forcing the words out, and the arrangement is secured. Kumar shares his working-out sheets for math and detailed notes for science. In return, Kwasi draws comics to illustrate Kumar's holiday stories and the convoluted dreams he recounts. Kumar lends him a book about impressionism and pointillism.

At parents' evening, they said he should speak more in class. This should be an easy win. But again and again Kwasi sits wrapped in sentences that have no beginning, no end, and no way for him to hold and give them sound. He thinks, I'll wait before I say this, I'll wait until I know how to say it just right. And then the lesson finishes.

Words flow more easily after school; he takes his homework to the Chest, and Tulip and her friends help him. They are his people too. They don't laugh at his handwriting or complain about how quickly he gets bored. While they fill his worksheets more neatly, he draws new ideas. He considers their long necks, their narrow wrists and pointed noses. Girls like these would tease him at school, tear bits of paper to throw at him, tall girls, white girls with tidy smiles and long legs.

But they don't just want to help with the homework. One evening, during the first week back at school, as he stares at his geography book, Tulip asks, "What are you doing?"

"Learning," he says.

"You're reading the same passage again and again."

"You're not trying to memorize it?" Miri says.

He nods.

"But you don't understand it." Tulip leafs through his book. "You've just copied it out. Could you try to turn it into a story? Interpret it. Try to tell the meaning to yourself."

"Draw it," Miri says. "Here."

They start out drawing water cycles, rain becoming rivers. After this, drawings spiral into silliness, beasts with wings and claws and feathery hides, creatures with tentacles and too many heads. Sometimes they draw serious portraits, with skulls in the background. Skulls are important, Tulip explains, to remember that everyone, no matter how majestic, dies.

"We should go to the National Portrait Gallery. Or the Tate. Have you been to the Tate?" Miri asks.

He shakes his head. "Don't think so."

"Not even on a school trip?"

A memory stirs of school trips years before, the horrible moment when the teacher told everyone to partner up, the crowd sorting itself into pairs, the sick feeling boarding the coach, terrified of who would sit behind him, how they might make the journey hellish, going away in his head, imagining himself elsewhere. Times he pretended to be ill, so Ma would let him miss a school trip. There is a dull anger in his gut now, remembering all that he has missed.

"You okay?" Miri asks.

"Yeah. No. I mean I don't think I've been to the Tate."

"We'll go," Miri says. "It'll be fun."

*

In music, he finds more of his people, more voices who get it, who have felt what he feels, at his freest and heaviest. Their words come to him over decades, carrying a little of his truth. Listening to Jericho's playlists, he wishes he had looked these songs up earlier. Each track gives way to a stronger song, and he can't stay still. But if he gets up to move, the floor creaks and Ma comes up and stands outside, glaring at him. Then she goes away into her silence, like she's decided it's best to act as if he's already in Ghana.

Music this good deserves more space. It's understandable now, why Jericho always has music in the background, why cars go by thumping with sound. There might be a way to play music at the Chest, like Rupert did on Halloween—maybe Tulip will let him stream on her laptop. Music might help Rupert. When Tulip and Miri are around, Rupert falls back like a shadow. Maybe he doesn't want them to notice he is drinking heaps of coffee again, and adding syrups to them, despite announcing he will stop. There is even a new item on the website last time Kwasi checked on his phone, that makes it look like Rupert plans on using yet more teas. He loads it again, and sure enough there it is: "Specialteas," underneath the row for the exhibition. "A night of radical empathy and hyper-presence. Unlike anything else you will ever experience. More information coming soon. 21+ only."

"Kwasi."

Startled, he looks up. Pulls his headphones off. Squid fills the doorway, still in her work uniform. "Why did you stop?"

"I didn't. I'm still working." He opens his math book.

Her eyes narrow. "That song you were playing."

"Sorry." He only played it out loud for two minutes before putting his headphones on. It wasn't even loud. He just wanted to see how different it sounded when played outside his head.

"Well? Play it." Squid takes a pen from the shelf and scratches between her braids.

"Again?"

"That song. It's Nigerian, isn't it?"

He scrambles to connect his phone to the computer speaker.

"Turn the volume up," she says through her smile.

"Is it Nigerian?"

"Of course," she says. "Can't you hear the pidgin?"

He lifts his shoulders.

She claps. "This one. Send it to me. Send it to my phone." She goes away, dancing.

The artists on Jericho's playlists are not named. When Kwasi looks them up, typing out lyrics, he finds names and faces in music videos and recordings from live shows. Interviews, karaokes, freestyles. He wishes he had been born earlier, so he could go to those shows now. Seems like the best tracks are from years ago. Grime is funniest, and whenever Squid catches him grinning with his headphones on, she asks what he is plotting. The aunties can't stand grime, even stuff that's slower, like poetry.

"It's so rough."

"Why are they so angry?"

"Where is the tune? Me, I like something I can sing to."

Kwasi does not push it. It is nice to keep some things to enjoy alone.

There is a mood of generosity about this time, an easing in these final days. One night, Auntie Aha lets him go out, after he comes home early. "Buy something nice," she says, and gives him a ten-pound note. "Maybe a nice notebook, aha? If you can stay on top of work at school this term, you will have more time, and also peace of mind to enjoy your hobbies."

"Thanks," he says. "I might do art next year, for GCSE. Just thinking about it."

Auntie Aha frowns. "GCSE? We will have to talk about that. It's important, the subjects you focus on. Here you have more options than you would have had Back Home. Maybe that is part of the problem, aha. Too many options. For now, do the very best that you can."

He tells her he will, through the thickness in his throat. Turning away, the corridor blurs. If anyone was going to see how being good at art might help him, it was Auntie Aha. He can only hope that seeing it all on display in the Chest might help reassure them. Especially if someone buys something he made.

He doesn't need a new notebook. He has a better idea for the ten pounds. Rupert mentioned that he would like to get a dog someday. If he had a pet to take care of, he won't have time to drink so much. He might even cancel that Specialteas event. And so Kwasi takes the bus west this time. Dogs are expensive, but maybe talking to someone at the shelter will help him work out how much he would need to save up to get one. He gets down at a petrol station and checks the map on his phone. He is two minutes from the dog shelter. He should hear barking soon. He hurries over the crossing and turns left.

And stops.

Selim and Jericho are sitting on the wall by the bus stop, with some year elevens. Now they're shouting, waving.

"I have to get bread," he calls.

"Come. Just a minute. Come."

He grits his teeth. They might want to fight again.

"Oi."

He starts slowly toward them. This is part of survival. A ritual of maintenance. At worst, this fight will be better than the last one.

"Why didn't you get bread in town?" Selim's quick eyes look over him. "Swear you live ten minutes from Sainsbury's."

He looks to Jericho, but Jericho is reading his phone.

"You were hiding at the Chest before." Selim's voice is still breaking and it keeps going wobbly. Kwasi bites his tongue to keep from smiling. "Yeah, we know about that. So what are you doing here? Did they kick you out?"

They know, of course they know. His mouth tastes of blood. He pushes his shoulders back, tries to appear easy. "Just getting stuff for the house. I'll come out later if I'm allowed."

"Wait. What are you doing in that shop? Seen you going there like every day."

He looks back down the street. A woman is standing by the curb, waiting to cross. Kwasi rubs his shoulder. "Community service."

"You know he killed his wife?"

"What?"

"The old guy in that shop."

"He killed his wife. He's into the weirdest drugs."

"Mad drugs. I rate it though," Wade says. "I mean it's weird because he's old. But if you think about it, he's mixing his own stuff and still running that shop. I rate it."

"K-man," Jericho says. "Who are the girls who go there?"

"Girls?"

"The white uni girls. How do you know them? They working there?"

He shakes his head. "Nothing really. Just boring charity stuff."

45

The rakish Dr. Hyde is here, against all odds, at short notice, in person. It is a sure sign that it is time to go ahead with Tulip's Specialteas idea. Dr. Hyde has aged splendidly. In he sweeps in his tailored jacket, felt hat, and black patent brogues.

"Long time, Rupert," he says.

"Too long. But only because I've been satisfied." They go into the sitting room. Rupert offers tea.

"I'm all right. Can't stick around." He looks over the boxes. The empty space where the settee was. "Time is currency. Are you moving? Finally had enough? Is that what this is about? You want to stock up and vanish?"

"Not at all. Although I do want to stock up." Business at the Chest, he explains, is ramping up. They'll need herbs, syrups for new cocktails, and baked goods. They're going to run a tea and mindfulness club.

"My. Jada would be proud. I was beginning to think I had lost you."

"We haven't started yet, but it was one of our original ideas. I've been assured people are keen to try, apparently everyone is microdosing."

"They are. Business is booming. Not least . . ." Dr. Hyde takes a handkerchief from his breast pocket and dabs non-existent sweat from his brow. "Not least because our highs are to be banned."

Rupert goes cold inside. "Excuse me?"

"You don't follow the news? Our honorable friends at the Home Office are cracking down. They've played it well. It looks like the end. I'm afraid it's a blanket ban, this time. Laughing gas, synthetics, salvia. All of it. All my headshops and dealers are ordering in bulk. Customers are stocking up for life. If business is on the up, Rupe, you had better make the most of it. Dark days ahead."

Rupert cannot speak. He backs up, but the settee is not there for him to sink onto. He leans against a box, while the room turns to vapor around him.

"Chin up. Final straight. Listen. If things are really picking up at the Chest, you will want to keep your energy up." He leans closer. "I have just the thing."

46

There are really good times with Jericho, the best times they have shared, in these last days before. Something has changed since Christmas. It doesn't matter now, so Kwasi tells himself, that people wear different masks, that sometimes they need to. Sometimes, when they surprise him, the twist is interesting.

Like today, when they are supposed to be at King Obi's, studying. Instead, they are out, with two bags of Doritos and Mars bars and Lucozade from the corner shop.

"Where are we going?" Kwasi asks.

Jericho's strides are so long it is a struggle to keep up.

"Seriously," Kwasi calls. "I told my aunties we would be at yours."

"We are," Jericho says, swinging his blue carrier bag. "This is a field trip."

Kwasi hurries after him. The air is charged and close, with the promise of rain. Maybe snow or hail. And his backpack is stuffed today. Squid made him take a bunch of biology textbooks for Jericho. "He is taking time to tutor you," she told him. "Give something in return."

"Slow down," he says now.

Jericho waits. "Hurry up."

The park opens ahead. Bushes border the far end, and sometimes year elevens hang out on the swings, by the netless goalposts covered in bird poo.

Kwasi is out of breath, sweating. His armpits itch. "Wait." He reaches under his coat, unknots his tie, and yanks it out. Pushes it into his pocket.

Jericho is walking backward now, watching him. "So unfit."

"Leave it. I can't run in these shoes. They're too tight."

"Remember when we used to play 'it'?"

He smiles, remembering how much he hated that game. Mostly it meant being slapped a lot, endlessly chased.

"Run. To the swings," Jericho says.

"Wait," he says again. He doubles over, hands on knees.

"Come, come." Jericho helps him up, tugs off his coat, and bundles it with his own. "Go."

They run together for about six steps before Jericho flies ahead. Feet pounding, Kwasi shuts his eyes and runs blind. Trips and falls onto slimy grass. Mud on his hands as he pushes himself up. To cheers.

Sure enough, there's Selim, Wade, and Sean D. More guys are on the swings, sitting on the rusting roundabout, wearing hoods up over their balaclavas. Selim's brother jumps up and swings from the goalpost. His arms bulge. There is a new thickness across his neck and back.

"About time," Selim says, and waves. "Is anyone else coming?"

"Let's go," Wade says. "I want food soon."

Music tears from two baseball-shaped speakers that Wade holds to his chest like boobs. Everyone shouts over the noise, so Kwasi can't even hear the beat. Six, nine, twelve.

Older guys from the Halloween party lean out from among the trees, filming on their phones.

"Rambo, get in. You're not in the shot," Selim says. "No, no. Wear the bandana. Ay. Do you want my glasses? You don't need a mask, trust. Looks better without."

Kwasi clutches Jericho's arm. "What are we filming?"

"We might not even use it." Jericho shakes him off. "Just visuals for our new track. Can't just put it out with no video, can we? Honestly, just for once. Chill."

"We're shooting on Saturday too. We need more people. Bring your cousins." Selim's brother seems shorter, now that he is standing so close. "All your aunties have kids, right? Bring them through. We've got bare Ghanaians in hiding here. You lot are shy but you have to come out, support your local and that."

Jericho elbows him.

"We should shoot later, on the way back. We should shoot on the street," Selim says.

Kwasi winces. He wishes they would stop saying "shoot."

"The street. What's on the street? Wasteman."

"We could get outside the Palace."

"Outside the station," Jericho suggests.

"That's bait. The track is three minutes anyway. If you want more shots you lot need to deliver more bars."

"Yeah but we need to post it by, like, Monday. They just put another video up, did you see? It's dead, but it's there."

"Upload it tonight then."

"Who?" Kwasi asks. "Are we battling someone?"

"Battle, you know. No. We're obliterating them."

"Let's go. From the top."

Useful. There is joy in this. There is freedom in adding his voice to theirs, masked, anonymous. With the bandana and glasses, he could be anyone. Jumping, shouting to the camera. Jericho's arm on his shoulder. All the people who pass at a distance, people dragged out by their dogs or pacing to the bus stop, glance their way.

At some point, the rain stops. On the walk home, spinning from too many energy drinks, he feels lucky.

As preparations for the exhibition become real, with new frames stacked in the corner, with sketches of how to lay out the space, signs of luck are everywhere. Just like his three scenes framed in gold, there are three piles in the basement by the washing machine: a pile for clothes that can be saved, another for clothes that will need a lot of work but could maybe still be saved, and a heap for clothes to be repurposed. Kwasi can choose from any; he gets first pick. Tulip and Miri are upstairs, choosing poetry for the exhibition, pages of it printed out over images of the street from years ago. He is thinking about what to wear, and if he will be in photos, or if he should still try to stay anonymous.

"Like it?" Rupert asks.

"I won't keep it," he says, as he buttons up the shirt. Tie-dyed, with blotches of pink and lime green over the white.

"It's good quality, made to last. Sadly, it's out of fashion."

"It will come back into fashion," Miri shouts before she vanishes again, up the stairs.

"It might." Rupert unfolds a patterned skirt. Its colors have run from many washes; it is impossible to know what it was, what it was meant to be. "Maybe in some other part of the world it's already trendy again."

"Somewhere sunny," Kwasi says.

"Indonesia. Hawaii."

"It looks like it might glow in the dark."

Rupert sits back down on his leather chair. "That's true. You know, you can get fluorescent dye. You can make all kinds of magnificent T-shirts. Have you ever been to Camden Market?"

Kwasi frowns. "Northern line, right?"

"Indeed. You'd fit in dressed like that. Leather trousers and boots. Best to wait a few years for that."

"Purple. Hmm." He twists, looks at his reflection in the dressing mirror. "Like Prince. Why was Prince called Prince, do you know?"

"It's a good enough name." Rupert lifts his mug and slurps. "He's had many other names. He was the Artist, at one point. And the Artist Formerly Known as Prince." He chuckles. "Tora Tora. Something Starr. I've forgotten most of them."

Kwasi selects a velvet cloak next and pulls it over his shoulders. Feels like he could cast a spell in this. A spell to get the funding, maybe.

"Keep it. No one is going to buy it, unless you can make it look smart on the mannequin upstairs."

He unbuttons the cloak and takes it off. "Stuff looks better down here."

Still he fears that his drawings won't look good when the exhibition comes on Saturday. Tulip keeps adding so many other photos and prints. He folds the cloak and places it on his stool.

The aunties are going easy for now, although they are still watching. Ma, in contrast, hardly looks at him lately. She only speaks in Twi now; even her words have turned from him. He told Squid to make sure everyone is home next Saturday.

"Are you worried about something?" Rupert asks.

"Just thinking about stuff. I had an auntie years ago who used to play dress-up with me."

"Oh yeah?"

"She let me choose clothes for her and draw her. I wish I had kept some. The drawings, I mean. I threw them away."

"Why did you do that?"

"I don't know," he says. But he can feel it even now, the biting clarity of it: he could not bear the thought of her dressing up somewhere without him, or perhaps not dressing up at all. Because he could not decide which was worse. There was no goodbye, no promise to meet again, and she never returned with gifts or stories from her new home. Everyone pretended she never existed, until they began gossiping.

All those spices.

The girl was forever cross about something, never grateful.

She was speaking fluent English on the phone, can you imagine?

And she threatened to send for the police.

Well. Her passport is waiting for her here. I suppose she will become a new woman now.

"What's on your mind?" Rupert asks.

"Doesn't matter." Kwasi goes behind the mirror to take off the shirt. "Do you ever find clothes that you like here?" He steadies the heap of to-be-mended clothes, to stop it toppling. "And do you only wear them when you're not here, in case whoever brought them here comes back?"

Rupert laughs until he coughs. "Perhaps that's why I always wear the same clothes. Maybe the rest of my wardrobe is made up of things I've pinched."

The floor shudders as a train rushes below.

"You think your auntie would like this place?"

Kwasi nods.

"Invite her for the exhibition. Invite your family to ArteFacts as well. I bet they have more interesting stories than the rest of us put together. Plus we have a surprise guest ready to talk about his life. Tickets are going fast."

"It's not Councillor Obi, is it?"

"I can't say. Otherwise it won't be a surprise."

Kwasi looks down at the floor, at the dark lines that run between the wooden boards.

"What's the matter? Are those boys giving you trouble again? Seems like they're out later every night. It's terrible, the way they intimidate people. That's what kills business, when people don't feel safe. They should be in their houses. And their parents aren't helping. If you can't keep your kids in the house, can't take care of them right, you shouldn't have had them. Better that than leaving them to walk the streets at night."

Kwasi lifts his face. Something viscous is seeping down through him. "Do you actually think that?"

Rupert raises his mug. It has been so long since he last took a sip, his drink must have gone cold. Still, he slurps, and lowers the mug again. "A little responsibility goes a long way."

"I mean, I'm not at home."

"Well, no. But you're not a troublemaker."

"They're just hanging out." The basement feels tighter, brittle and old. Rupert is avoiding his gaze. "I mean, it's nice, being out. Plus they don't have their own houses— only their parents' houses."

"Well." Rupert gets up, turning his back. He goes to the sink, limping again. He runs the tap, letting water rush away, not even washing his hands. He says: "Anyway. Do you want to get Miri and Tulip and we can settle which pictures you want to put in those new frames? Saturday will come up soon."

Back up the stairs, Kwasi's phone buzzes with new messages. Auntie Aha has sent a picture, of rice and corned beef stew. Jericho has sent a message that everyone is at the Chicken Palace. "Are you coming?"

Inside he is tipping. The message was sent half an hour ago; they might still be out.

"Hello? Sorry. What do you think?" Tulip asks him, waving. He puts his phone away.

"Of what?"

"Oh actually that reminds me," Tulip says. She rummages in her pockets. "Maybe you should give us your number? So we can chat about stuff like this when we're elsewhere? Oh damn. I left my phone downstairs."

"And we still need to go to the Tate. I keep forgetting," Miri says.

"Okay, let's focus on getting this done now." Tulip claps her hands. "I was saying we should keep the shrine for Ms. Reilly-Duffell, at the exhibition."

Behind her, Miri is shaking her head, her eyes scrunched shut.

"It will look good. It'll blend with Lake's black-and-white photographs on this side. Gives a spooky dimension, like we're haunted by the past, the past is still with us, you know? Plus, Rupert was saying it was since this woman passed away, and since all her stuff came here, the Chest has been doing better."

"Tulip," Miri says. "Can we just put everything up? The pictures downstairs? See how it looks?"

Tulip looks at him. "Should we?"

They are both looking at him, and in their gazes there is a new recognition: they are his people. And there is room, here, to move and recolor everything. It's different with Jericho, more like there is already a script for him there, like as long as he follows it things are not so bad. Here there is no script.

Outside the shop is darkness. No one is out, across the street, at least not yet.

"We should put the shutters down outside," he says. "So no one can see us in here. It should be a surprise, right?"

47

"The city was taking off," Rupert begins, and then he lifts his face—too soon—and the lines he rehearsed are lost.

Rows and rows of faces—expectant, listening—are illuminated under a sweep of yellow light. The Chest has never been busier; people are standing at the back, all of them here to listen. Rupert shifts forward, careful not to disturb his clip-on microphone.

"The city was taking off, and there were no rules. Let's see. I wanted to start with the city, the business of finance, that is. I've just lost my train of thought. Yes. The city was taking off, when I came of age. It brought out the best and worst in men. Clive—my oldest brother—made a fortune, then lost it. And we were ordinary, my father was a chauffeur. My mother a nurse. Hard workers with their ears to the ground. Both witnessed the nation changing. They saw our empire crumble, saw the nation devastated by war. Saw children return from evacuation, Britain rebuild herself. And of course, the Commonwealth people who came to help rebuild our country and brought much more besides."

He sits back. There was more to make of this point, it

was supposed to flow into something else. Opposite him, Miri raises an eyebrow. Shall I jump in? her hesitation asks.

"It was an extraordinary time. My father lived in anticipation, watching to see what we might become. He educated himself, always kept the radio on, and listened to conversations of the businessmen he drove. He knew the city—the center—like instinct. He saw all the transfusions of foreign money, and new ugly buildings that rose, built to be functional, all square-edged concrete and glass. There was a great rush, you see, to raise homes, and *better* homes. Simple things you take for granted now: indoor toilets, central heating, double glazing. Councils did all that.

"We were reared on dinnertime lectures. Our father taught us that while we must make ourselves useful, every one of us has a gift, what we're drawn to and good at. There is a duty to cultivate it, to refine it and give from it."

Miri raises her microphone. Alas, his words won't stop.

"Folk aspired to work in offices, to play games of risk and luck. Betting on fluctuations, on how flows of wealth might react. Granted, there was some math—some pattern—to it, but only Clive went to grammar school and on to do A-levels. The key thing, it turned out, was knowing someone. It takes no gift to go and gamble on ups and downs. I wanted to work with people."

He uncrosses his legs.

"I considered teaching, but I wasn't smart enough. Hopeless at exams. And my father wouldn't have me teaching—said it was women's work. And it was, more and more. Women liked it because it gave them time to watch their children after school, and there was a view that working with children came naturally to them."

Light falls over the audience again. All these faces and

yet the boy is nowhere to be seen. Rupert lifts his glass and takes a long sip of water. Sobriety threatens: the awareness he is here, surrounded by strangers, dozens of them in rows.

"I took a job in a bookshop. It paid, and we were sure books would soon be more popular than music. Everyone was going to school and more and more from ordinary homes could get on to do A-levels. He predicted appetite for books and ideas would grow exponentially. He was right; it did. And the people I met. Anarchists. We were always out drinking. And dancing. That's how I met Jada."

He closes his eyes. Six pounds for a seat to hear the story of his life. The first ArteFacts session of the new year. Sold out. Because they like the cartoon version of him Tulip drew for the poster, or whatever stories Tulip's been telling on her social media websites. Elaine said he had to charge or homeless folk would come, but they came anyway. Lake welcomed them in and they are sitting in the back row by the heaters. Phil is with them, wearing a gray beret.

"But that wasn't your question. Ah. Thatcher. It was a difficult time, people forget. I heard that when the Jubilee line extended east, there was a decline in life expectancy for each stop. Horrid living conditions.

"Thatcher shook everything. Some of us fell into lucky places—went from council tenants to homeowners. Others never recovered—the mines, unions. It was every man for himself and it was terrifying. But what a thrill. Trying to get ahead, to *make* something. It was easier to try things, to start businesses. Used to be all markets up this street, and bookshops and florists. A chocolatier's. Whenever Jada and I argued, I'd dash out to get chocolate and flowers from neighboring shops.

"So Jada and I, we applied for this Enterprise Allowance

Scheme. We got a little help with business costs. We set up shop and sent out leaflets saying we were selling miscellaneous gifts. We sold a lot of the junk my father got from the gentlemen he drove. Statuettes and vases and decorative tea sets, little gadgets and novelties.

"Many people were new in town. Everyone wanted to donate. And when recession hit, many people moved out, to Essex, to Kent. New people moved in. Different people. Indians and Greeks and Jamaicans and Africans.

"Everyone loved Jada. Her family had come from America to lecture. She was obsessed with finding ways to improve moods with fragrances and colors, with the senses. She made scented candles and sold them here. She had so many friends, mostly from traveling. International volunteers, students on endless gap years. We fundraised for everything: anti-apartheid protests, women's rights, better homes and jobs for all. Jada brought people together. She had followed musicians around, traveled through Asia. Some of the herbs she used in her soaps—and later drinks—were from her trips. Britain was special, in her eyes, since it was plugged into the world, and at a unique moment, where it could become something new."

The high is wearing off. He rolls his shoulders and his back clicks.

"And the river. There was a river—something like a brook, up where that phones-for-you place was. It was a sad sham of a river: lads were always pissing and tossing trolleys in it. The council forced it underground to make space for retail. I suppose that's what made our little town truly urban. Now our only river is the Thames. That has always been the story, all of our stories, becoming part of a greater whole."

Again, Miri leans forward to interject. A new question perhaps, or a comment of her own. It was supposed to be more of a conversation, but he cannot stop, and the audience is motionless, rapt.

"Sometimes, I think Jada is lucky not to be around to see where we are now. It was the transformation she'd prophesied but it's beyond anything we'd imagined. We have people visiting from all over the world, but everyone's on their computers. And the high street has been dying ever since."

"Rupert. Thanks so much for—"

"Jada was happy here before she passed. I'm sure you've heard stories about her last days. Well, she was happy. She loved this place. She never imagined it could struggle. Town always reflects what people want most, and people always want something. You lot know what it will become next, much better than I ever could—it'll be whatever you want most."

"Homes," says a freckled lady on the second row. "We want homes."

A smattering of applause.

"To live in. Not to sell as investments."

"We know what's coming." A woman gets up. "I'll tell you what 'change' we'll see: this very shop will be the reception for a block of flats, with a gym and a sky garden, so the residents don't have to meet us in the park. Soaring views over the city—yes, there's a council paper on how our sky space is an untapped resource—stack enough boxes on each other and the ones at the top will have a view. The funding they're offering businesses now? You have to meet criteria, don't you? Eventually they'll 'recommend' that you turn your lot into a block of flats, or maybe a workspace."

"People need workspaces."

"For empty jobs," Lake calls.

"Hardly," another woman says. "If someone pays you to work, someone values what you do."

"Someone *thinks* they value it."

"If you think you value something, you value it."

Rupert closes his eyes. When he looks up, audience members are on their feet.

"... of a self-checkout machine. Anything that can be repeated will be automated."

"People want work. What world do you live in?"

"People want *security*."

"... that when everything is automated ..."

"... council just wants to take—"

"We are the heart. We make it."

Rupert raises his clip-on mic. Tilts his collar until it emits a keening cry. The room stills.

"Please," he says. "This is a space for peaceful exchanges. And sure, it's good to be honest, and many of us have concerns. But all this noise helps no one. We have a tradition here. If you have a dispute, settle it over tea. I have a wonderful tea set at the back, and paper cups if you'd like a takeaway. You can donate as much or little as you'd like. But let's all just slow down, that's the magic of a cup of tea, and we can finish our conversations with a bit more kindness."

Elaine tells him he handled it well. But as he sits, cradling his cinnamon tea, rumbling rises below, like water beginning to boil. It is a good thing, he thinks to himself, that the boy did not show up after all, to see adults throwing tantrums. A flash of light startles him. A couple of Tulip's friends are outside, taking pictures of themselves, arms stretched out ahead. He sits a little lower, to make sure he is not caught in the background. But more people inside are also taking photos of themselves. He gets up and goes down to his basement. The new order of sachets he brought in has been left open. He was sure he put them away, after he showed Tulip all he had bought. He turns to go back up the stairs, but exhaustion pulls him. He goes to the sink and lifts the kettle under the tap. One cup for Jada, he tells himself.

48

He is repacking his bag—water bottles and crisps and a notepad rolled up to fit—when the doorbell rings. He hesitates, and then tugs the zippers on his bag together.

A plan: to disappear underground and emerge at Southwark Station. From there he will walk a little way and go into the Tate. There's no point waiting for Miri or Tulip to finally have time to go with him. They didn't even remember to take his number, and today this feels like a good thing, gives him some distance from the Chest, so he can step away from the noise online. The website says entry is free; the only cost will be travel. No one will find him there; he will turn his phone off so no one can get to him. That should be enough time for things to go back to normal.

The doorbell rings again.

Holding still, it is possible to feel every movement in the house. It feels empty today; nothing whirrs in the kitchen and the television is off. Sunday mornings are simple: aunties either wake up early and go to church, or they stay in bed until eleven.

The doorbell rings again.

From the sitting room comes a groan, and then the creaking of furniture. The door whines open.

"Morning, auntie," comes Jericho's voice.

Cold wafts under the door and tickles Kwasi's feet. He creeps out of his room and goes into the bathroom, back into the warmth and steam left over from his shower. The tiles are fogged and the window is misted white. He locks the door.

He runs the shower, hums a tune to let them know he cannot hear anything they shout to him. He undresses, climbs into the bath. In the tumbling water, he imagines dissolving like sugar, being carried down the drain, down through pipes. Mixed with dirt and dead skin and hair from houses all over town, flowing further south, mixing with the city's waste, joining the river, as many tiny parts.

Jericho must have seen. On the internet, everyone is writing about the Chest—and there is his drawing from years ago, shared again and again, as a background with words in capitals over it.

He ducks out of the shower and loads it again on his phone. Sure enough, the drawing is still replicating online.

Empower communities.

People first.

Support small businesses.

Love local.

They have changed the colors in some cases. Some have added in hearts and flowers. But it is definitely his drawing.

The phone slips from his hold and his heart plunges but

he scrabbles to catch it and just about does. Shaking now. He only saw the image by chance, looking to see what people were saying about ArteFacts last night. He wanted to make sure no one was saying anything rude about the man, or about the Chest.

It's quiet when he emerges from the bathroom. He sways into his room and stops.

Jericho is sitting on his bed.

Back to the bathroom. Grabs his towel from the floor and shuts the door. Cheeks burning, he winds his towel about him. It could have been worse. He might have gone back to his room without his pants. He makes sure the door is locked. Waits there for his body to cool.

"Ay." Jericho's voice is clear, like he is right outside the bathroom door. "Why so dramatic? I've seen everything already. Bubble baths at your old house with the green ducks. Remember?"

Kwasi tucks the towel tight under his armpits. Glances at his reflection. Last time they hung out was fun, but he has the feeling whatever Jericho is planning for the next few days is going to ruin this fragile peace. He was supposed to meet them at the Turkish restaurant yesterday, but he couldn't do it, told them Ma took his phone. He had planned to go to ArteFacts, especially since the shopkeeper said it would be special. He couldn't even do that; the thought of seeing some of the people who might soon look at his art, who might consider buying some art to help the Chest, actually seeing them in real life, was too much.

"Your mum used to powder us," comes Jericho's voice now. "Do you remember? Talcum powder. I remember she'd pat us down with it until we were white. And we pretended to be ghosts. You should have come out yesterday. We found a scooter, by the swings. Took it back to Selim's."

Kwasi steps out and pads into his room. Tugs his shirt over his towel and struggles into his shorts.

Jericho is going on and on about Selim, about his brothers' friends, how one has a pit bull, and how the dog kept hanging its head out the car window as they rode to central in someone's Lambo, and they filmed another video, and Jericho keeps talking and smiling that same dumb smile from Christmas Day, and Kwasi can't listen anymore.

"Why do you have to be like that when Selim is around?"

"What?"

"Like different."

"I'm not."

"Yeah you are."

Jericho shakes his head. He looks pretty annoyed. "You do it too. When you go to that shop I bet you act different."

"Not true."

"They probably just want you there because you make them feel good about themselves." Jericho lifts his face. "You know, I'm getting paid. Your dad's paying me."

"Why would he do that?"

Jericho groans. "You *are* stupid. I'm being paid to tutor you."

His stomach hurts. He was going to get a cookie from the coffee place by the Underground station, a soft one with chocolate chips that would have melted on his tongue. He was going to try to make it last until Green Park.

"You don't cream yourself?" Jericho asks. "You're just getting dressed?"

He shrugs. "Sometimes I put lotion on. Don't have time now."

Jericho's gaze roams over his bed, over his stuffed backpack. "Where were you running?"

"Nowhere."

"Going to meet someone? Gemma?"

"No."

"Going out on your own?"

The smell of burning toast rises from the kitchen. From the sitting room comes faint singing.

"You should cream yourself. No wonder your elbows are always dry."

Kwasi rummages through his drawer for clean socks.

"And dark," Jericho says. "You remember? How dark I used to be?"

Kwasi looks at him. Jericho looks lost without his smirk. He stares until Jericho's face blurs into a rounded square. If he stares harder, if he never blinks, he could make Jericho fizzle into nothing.

"Thing is, you don't try. You want everyone to feel bad for you when you don't even try."

He pulls his socks on.

"Just because you survived parents' evening doesn't mean you can chill. If you don't get into the middle set this year, you'll have to sit foundation."

"What?"

"Foundation. GCSEs for dummies: best you can hope for is a C." Jericho turns his attention to the foil sculptures on the desk. "These yours?"

"Don't touch," Kwasi says. "Look, I'll come downstairs in a minute."

"I'll go downstairs too. Right after you."

Kwasi gets up to look for his comb.

"You know those girls don't rate you, right?"

"What girls?"

"At the shop." Jericho picks up a foil man. "They don't like you. Think. Why would they?"

Someone is creaking up the stairs, slowly, probably that new auntie who never removes her headwrap. She is probably texting on her phone, taking forever.

"It's not like you have anything to give them." Jericho tosses the foil man high, catches him, and tosses him again. "Is it?"

Kwasi combs his hair. He should cut it soon, maybe just on the sides to grow it thicker on top.

"Oi." The foil man flies at him and catches his cheek.

"What?" he says to Jericho.

"What are you giving those girls?"

"I'm volunteering," he says. "We help out together."

"So you're not even getting paid?"

He picks the foil man off the carpet.

"What's the deal? My dad says that guy, that old guy at the Chest, is a crackhead."

"He's not."

"Okay, maybe not crack, but he's obviously on something." Jericho takes another foil figure—the alien warrior— off the desk. "What are you doing in the shop? For real."

"I'm not going to talk about it. Like I said."

Footfalls approach his door. They both freeze. The bathroom door opens and the fan clicks on.

"Unless you're ready to say what's special about the space at the back."

"Honestly I feel like you might mess things up if I tell you too early. That's the only reason. As soon as it's time to play your part, I'll tell you."

"Why would I mess it up? Actually. Forget it. I'll work on my project and you work on yours."

"Cool. As long as you know those girls don't like you. No matter how much you want them to."

"I don't," he says. "I don't care. It's just useful for my drawings. You'll see." The ease with which this lie comes out is mortifying. It sounds true to his own ears, the best and worst lie he has told, a lie that smiles to him, that says he has not just a plan, but a master plan, that he is outside everything. All the threads that tangle around his bones are gone. For a moment, he belongs only to himself. He is bigger in that moment, and he has many people, like pieces on a board game, whose claims on him are turning to dust.

Maybe Jericho feels it too. He squints, as though watching from far off. "Hey." Jericho places the foil alien back onto the desk. "Do you draw portraits?"

"Maybe."

"So you can draw me."

"Depends."

"On?"

"How much your dad will pay me."

"Well at the moment you're wasting your dad's money. Come then, let's study."

After Jericho goes downstairs, Kwasi checks on his phone again. On the Chest's home website too, gone is the photograph, in its place is the drawing. His drawing. He sinks back onto his bed. The feeling is of being turned inside out. Everything is leaking away too soon.

"Are you coming?" shouts Jericho.

He presses both hands over his ears. There is the sound of water, of being drowned.

49

Nothing he hasn't seen before. In a way it's a relief: he was not wrong after all, to suspect that applying for help from the council would be a waste of time. He should have told Tulip. Her determination blinded him for a while, over these last few weeks. It always ends this way. Each generation rises up hysterical, claiming life has never been so dire, certain revolution is imminent.

"What are you thinking?" Tulip asks.

He clears his throat.

Tulip looks up from her laptop. She has shaved her hair low again and startles him each time she meets his gaze. "Rupert?" she asks.

"Another coffee." He gets up.

She declines the cup he offers so he drinks a double helping. Too much too early in the day. But the best way to get through a comedown is to avoid it.

★

"What exactly did he say?" Tulip asks. "When he said we're not getting funding, how did he say it? I'm going to write it up for reference."

"For reference. What would that mean, to put it on the internet?"

"Do you remember what he said?"

He shuts his eyes. Councillor Obi's words are soup inside his head.

"He should have put it in writing. It's so unprofessional, just calling you up to say it's over. And before the actual deadline. It's like they brought it forward just to spite us."

He wishes he did not have to see this part, and to watch futile determination toy with Tulip's face. The shadows under her eyes. All the friends she has rallied to make this work.

"Do you remember what he said when—"

"He said applications were competitive. Said we need to be more commercial. Our revenue goals are too low. Something about omni-channel so and so."

"More commercial, more online." Tulip nods. "He didn't mention Specialteas, did he?"

"No. But I'm sure it was on his mind."

"Okay, what else did he say?"

"He also said footage from ArteFacts was found on a hard left website, an extremist site. I expect that was your friend Lake."

"What? I don't think so. I mean he has his own projects, but that's nothing to do with our application."

"Wish we had this in writing," Miri says. "We could print copies and, like, stick them over the photographs, over the charcoal drawings too, so it's about bureaucracy, and—"

"Genius," Tulip says. "Could we ask for it in writing?"

"Rupert, can we see Jada's notes again? Can we take pictures?"

"Hysterical," Rupert says. "Arrogant beyond words."

"Sorry, what?" Miri looks uncertain as to whether to laugh or take offense.

The anger startles him. It comes in flashes, glimpses of it through the mist in his head.

"Could we see Jada's notes again?" Miri asks once more.

"I heard. I'm getting them." He gets up.

Brimming with his fifth coffee, he stumbles up the stairs with Jada's plans.

"Go on," he says. "Take all the photos you want."

"It's going to be fine. We'll finish the exhibition. You should have seen the support K's sketch of the Chest got online. We'll sell heaps of stuff."

Tulip and Miri leaf through Jada's files. Tulip gnaws her fingernail as she reads.

"We promised we'd do the exhibition," Rupert says. "Doesn't change the council's plans though. It was always going to come to this."

"The flats? People hate that idea."

"Your friends hate that idea."

"Everyone does. It's all over Twitter, and—"

"And *Twitter* won't be voting, or paying taxes here." He puts his cup down.

"We already have a plan," Tulip says. "And people love our events. We just need to convince the landlord it pays, right?"

"Yessir," Miri says.

"We'll raise money to sort the basement out *ourselves*. Otherwise we'll have done all this for nothing."

"We'll have music nights and poetry. This is just the transition."

He doesn't notice when the boy arrives, but suddenly he is there. Tulip orders pizza. They have moved into the basement, tidying up. Putting the last of the black-and-white photographs into frames. Copying lines of poetry onto canvas in black and red paint. Lines from Jada's journals. Miri takes photographs of the pages. Each crunch of the camera startles Rupert.

Now they are helping him into his coat.

Tulip and Kwasi walk him home. Everyone they walk past stares. Everyone knows what he has done, what he did to Jada.

"In the basement, under the sink. I should mix something stronger," he says, "to get rid of those highs. Can't just leave them here. They won't be legal forever."

"We're taking care of everything. Lake and Nat are coming. You rest."

Here is his front door. He has flown too high, skipping time once more. He is going to lose his grip.

"Do you have your keys?" Tulip asks.

He finds them at last. Unlocks the door and stumbles in.

"Whoa. This is all yours? No one else lives here?" the boy asks.

"Rest, Rupert," Tulip says. "Don't worry about the shop. And please, please, please drink some water."

50

The smell of sizzling meat fills the house as he dresses. Black T-shirt and black jeans, and a shirt he might put on later. He checks his phone one last time, and sure enough the exhibition is still up on the website. It says this is not a ticketed event, come by and say hi. The date is for this afternoon.

Down the stairs. In the kitchen, Squid leans over a steaming pot of stew. She lifts the lid of a small pan and meat crackles.

"You've given up?" Kwasi asks. "That was fast."

Squid glares at him, although there is a smile about her eyes. She has braided her plaits into one chunky rope that tapers to a stop halfway down the back of her yellow T-shirt.

He grins. "Can I get the Nando's sauce then?"

"Why not? Bring it. Maybe it will taste more like meat that way."

"Is it not meat?"

"It's vegetarian. It's not even February and you think I have given up?"

The fake meat looks pale. "I bet Uncle Obi won't even

remember any of the promises you guys made. He seemed drunk at the end."

Squid laughs.

"And we won't go to his place next year, right? It's only because we had no tickets for the church thing."

Squid wipes her hands in her apron. "Do you think this is for Uncle Obi?"

"No, but—"

"I wanted to try it for years. Every time I suggested it you people only laughed. Shame on you."

"I wa—"

"And when the food is ready, you will all come up from your hiding places and be here making noise." The meat sizzles and crackles. Squid turns back to the stove. She nudges the meat through grease and vegetables with the wooden spoon.

"Is everyone still going to be free this afternoon?" Kwasi asks.

Squid doesn't seem to hear. "Let me tell you something," she says. "Obi likes to talk about community, about supporting each other, and that is important, but . . ." She knocks the spoon against the pan and puts it on the tray. "It is never only that." She reaches to the back hob and lifts the lid from the rice. Its expansion startles him every time: a miracle of water, fire, and time. "Uncle Obi is very helpful; your father would have been homeless without him, and he would not have met your ma." She smiles cryptically. Goes to the sink. "Uncle Obi is good to us, but he is not family. After all, he is a Nigerian." She sucks her teeth. "As a matter of fact, he is not even Nigerian. Not even African."

He climbs up and sits on the worktop, swings his legs.

"Jamaica. That is where he was born. When his family came, people gave them trouble. They were told to go to Africa." She shakes her head. "Funnily enough, Uncle Obi, when he traced his ancestry, found his people were Nigerians. That is why he took Nigerian names. Even married a Nigerian. Jericho's mother. Maybe she never told him though, that Africa is not just about community. It is—always is—every man for himself. Even your own God-given mother and brother can turn against you if they choose. I am not turning vegetarian for Uncle Obi, not even for your ma. This is for me. You must do the same. Don't wait for someone to watch before you walk correctly. Do you hear?"

He nods.

"Now. Get down from there." She threatens with the wooden spoon.

★

These days, no one asks where he's going. They only tell him to take his phone and to respond as soon as he sees their message. At the end of the path, he turns the internet off. Jericho has just added him to a new group chat. He also sent pictures in which he wears the Shanga costume—gold bands and cuffs and chains, a gold plate over his stomach, and bands around his ankles. Hanging from his waist is a bloodred garment.

"Can you draw me like this?" Jericho messaged.

And again, worryingly, "Hey. Come park tonight. Bring your transit card. Big things coming for you."

He puts his phone away and zips his pocket. If everything goes well tonight, he'll be busy at the exhibition, and his aunties will be there, and they will not want to leave once they arrive. King Obi might even make Jericho cancel his plans to come see.

It is bright for six. Summer will begin before he knows it and the Chest will be mad busy. He jogs to the crossing.

The Chest is in darkness, although the shutters are not yet down. That means Tulip's still setting up. He presses his face against the glass door. Light blushes up from the stairwell. He knocks.

Seconds pass as minutes. Finally, Tulip opens the door. She hugs him. She smells like strawberries.

Some of his sketches and comic strips and portraits and collages are already on the walls. Thick frames that may or may not be gold. Frames with curling spirals and studded with brass discs. Frames of gleaming black wood. He feels a thrill of excitement. But something is off. Drawings framed last night lie on the floor, leaning against the walls. Cloths hang over bookcases, and the mannequins are gone. Several drawings are missing. The past, present, and future ones, all three of them in their golden frames.

"So," Tulip says. "I know I said to open at half six, but a buyer came in like half an hour ago. I told him nothing was for sale yet."

He backs up. Grips the counter's edge.

"I don't get it. Where are my drawings?"

Tulip takes a sharp breath. "This is why I said we need your number, in case anything happens. I didn't have any way to let you know."

"Let me know what?"

"So this guy came in, as I was setting up. He's alumni from Miri's flatmate's university and he said he's a producer. He's been watching this whole thing blow up online. And this is insane, but he wants to work with us. We could do something huge, with all this momentum."

"Something like what?"

Tulip runs her hand over her head. Her eyebrows are heavier today, and not quite symmetrical. It makes her look angry.

"Like what?" he asks again.

"Okay, not sure yet. But he wanted to buy a few up front as a guarantee. I tried to give him my copies, all the versions I drew."

Kwasi's head feels fuzzy. It's like he's watching himself from above. How small and silly he looks. Words are swarming up his throat, with a sting that is blurring his vision.

The steps creak and Rupert's gray head comes into view.

Kwasi tries to ease up, but it feels even worse, that Rupert has been here the whole time.

"House rules," Rupert says. "No arguing. The pair of you. Come down and have a cup of tea."

★

The basement feels abandoned, with all the paintings moved upstairs. Kwasi sits on the edge of the armchair, studying the cracks in the leather.

Tulip's gaze is still on him. "I'm sorry."

Rupert turns to look at him too. The man looks so tired, standing by the sink.

"But I don't get how this is disappointing. You *gave* your work to the Chest," Tulip says. "We both did."

"No raised voices," Rupert says. "Sit closer if you can't hear each other."

Kwasi's heartbeat rocks him. His tongue is swollen. All those drawings, gone.

"This producer, he *really* liked your drawings." Tulip reaches across and touches his arm.

He leans away from her. "The point was never just to sell them. We didn't even hold the exhibition."

"Can I at least tell you how much he paid?"

"How much then?"

"Three grand."

Everything goes numb. He no longer has a face or a body—or a sound to make.

"Exactly, right?" comes Tulip's voice, from somewhere beyond. "He's coming back. And he has experience working on campaigns. Have you heard of Occupy?"

At last, a sound comes out. Something like a squeak. And then laughter. He shakes his head.

"It's the right thing. If you had been here, if they had been my drawings, I hope you would have done the same."

"Here you are." Rupert is offering him a teacup on a saucer. He wipes his cheeks and takes it. Something to focus on. Something to hold.

"Thanks," he says. The drink is a peculiar shade of green.

"It's green tea. Very calming. Let's take a moment to settle down, remember who we are."

After a few sips, he can meet Tulip's gaze. She keeps blinking, like she too is trying not to cry.

"I get that you're angry," she says, "because it feels like we stole from you." She lowers her teacup carefully onto the floor. "Rupert's told his story. Okay. Here's mine."

Rupert pulls a chair near and joins them, with a mug painted with flowers. "Go on," he says. "We're listening."

Tulip's gaze stays on Kwasi. "When I saw your drawing

on the counter I decided to keep trying. I mean. I am what, eighty thousand pounds in debt. I can't drive. I can't get a proper job, I messed up my degree because I had to draw, to study what I love, figured I might as well since I was paying so much. The only guy I liked left me to be polyamorous. Like, and super confused about everything. And what else could he be? We were *lied* to. We were told we could become anything but everything is being programmed away. When I look for illustration work they want to know what I can do with *Photoshop*. But then I walked into the Chest and saw your drawing by the till." She gives a tiny smile. "I had forgotten: not everything has to be crazy. And all the time we spent here—why do you think I copied your drawings? I wanted to learn. I wanted to see."

He looks down at the water in his cup. How cool it looks, despite its searing heat.

"We can make sure you get proper credit for everything," Tulip says. "I get that it feels like I've just taken your ideas."

He shakes his head. "I wanted us to have a proper exhibition. If you just wanted to make money, you should have said. I was going to get my family to come, so they could see everything together." He can't say any more, or his voice will break.

"But this is huge," Tulip says. "Bigger than an exhibition would have been. And your family will see. It'll be different from what you had in mind, but they'll see. I know it's a shock, and it's not happening the way any of us planned, but it's happening. Right, Rupert?"

It's hard to even know what to feel now, what Ma will think if she sees his work all caught up in some kind of protest. It could make things worse.

"Rupert?" Tulip says again.

Kwasi looks to Rupert. It's sad to look at the man's eyes. He seems blurry, a vanishing presence holding himself away.

"We've had a lot of excitement," Rupert says at last. "Why don't you get on home now, K? Tulip and I will have a word. We'll sort it out. We all need to reflect, think about what we want, why we are really here. We all need to be a little more honest about what we are trying to do."

51

Walking—stumbling—back, with this weight pressing, a weight that is a compression, such that his body no longer fits. With each step he folds, in neat lines doubling on himself. He fumbles in his coat pocket for his phone. It's almost seven. It's hard to know who to be annoyed at. It's Tulip's fault, for cancelling the exhibition, no matter how she phrases it, the exhibition is cancelled. It was meant to happen today, inside the Chest. And Rupert should have done something; it's supposed to be his shop.

Kwasi hesitates at the crossing. The road is ocean-wide tonight. He feels small enough to drown in it, in business and headlights. At last the green man lights up, beckoning a way across. Heavy and muffled, he walks, like it is the only way to go. Like there is not a braver version of himself who is turning round, walking back to the Chest.

On the other side of the street, everything is wrong. Tulip is using all his work for something completely different. Something she can't even explain, only assure him it's important and pressing. Feels like he's caught in a big web, like he is small again, watching Da read newspapers, with a vague sense of dread, of huge and complex shapes cooling into new ceilings high over his head. She was the one who convinced Rupert to mix those drinks again, those drinks he tried so hard to quit.

Still. Three thousand.

The number is all sparks in his head.

Just like that, his heart is racing, trying to catch up with his head.

Across the street, a figure steps out from the shadows by the café. Jericho.

Kwasi freezes.

Jericho stops at his side, grips his arm, leans in. "Hey. Did you hear me?"

He rubs his eyes. Tries to shrug Jericho off. "I'm going home."

"Yes, go home," Jericho says. "I've left two bags in your room. Either you collect them from your room, get down to Liverpool Street, and take the ten-thirty to Ipswich, or they'll be found by your ma, when I text her where to find them and tell her this is what you've been doing for that old guy at the Chest."

"What?"

"This is us, trusting you, yeah?" Jericho says.

"This is it? I thought—"

"You thought what?"

"You said it was something about the Chest. Something about the location."

"Yeah. It's a CCTV blind spot, the space at the back. It's good for moving things, exchanging. But you don't have to go there tonight. Ipswich, yeah?" Jericho slaps his back.

52

The smell does not wake him.

It is the ringing that breaks his sleep: his mobile jangling from the mess of his desk. Rupert sits up and curses. It is three forty-eight in the morning.

The taste of the air is sooty and hot as he fumbles through unopened letters and leaflets and vouchers. He follows the smell into the hallway. Down the steps, turning lights on. The house blazes with light but there is no sign of smoke. Yet the smell scours his throat and bitterness coats his mouth. He opens a window. The smell of burning is coming from outside.

Somewhere distant, sirens wail.

From upstairs, his mobile is still ringing. He starts up the stairs but then the doorbell joins in, chiming. Someone is pounding on his front door. The din is overwhelming. He freezes, then chooses the phone and retreats into his room.

"Rupert here."

"Rupert," Elaine breathes. "Thank God. Are you home?" A siren is wailing close behind her, and the sound is piercing his eardrum.

"I'm home, yes," he says. "I'm all right."

The doorbell rings again. More pounding. Fists beating his door.

"Is it a full moon? What's all this noise?"

She tells him the Chest is burning.

★

After a sunrise that is foggy and bleak, there is still no clarity. Rupert adds his own theories to the speculations of Elaine and her family, of passersby too, who stop to take pictures or to simply stare.

Could have been kids. Gangs. A fight in the unit next door. An accident, most people agree. A faulty socket perhaps, or candles left burning below.

"I said it. I said call the police. That boy. The Black boy who was always hanging around," Elaine says. "Always at night. I'm not the only one who saw. A few people saw him around. Trouble."

He walks along the back wall. All is blackened and acrid.

Elaine follows. With both hands buried in her coat pockets, and with her shoulders hunched, she seems like a scavenging bird. Nothing remains to save. He has moved the paintings they could salvage to the corner by the door. He has the little drawing, still in its modest wooden frame, the drawing that started all of this madness, in his hands.

"The one thing the council won't talk about," comes Elaine's voice from behind him. "People who move here but don't drink in our pubs, so now our pubs have closed. They can't control their kids, yet they have so many, schools are full of them. And they won't give to our charities, they don't pop in to say hi. They send all their money to their own countries." Her tongue pokes out and licks the corners of her lips. "They're always on the phone on the bus, always shouting in their languages, speaking to people all over the world. Anywhere but here."

He steps back. Pulls his coat tighter.

"It's got arson written all over it." Elaine inclines her head.

He steadies himself against the wall. A kind of peace is settling between them, a new clarity. Everything about this space feels repulsive, even the air that scours his throat.

"Where are you going?" Elaine asks, as he turns away.

"I'm going to catch up on sleep." He can't stand to share this space, this moment, with her any longer. "Please don't call me or bother me, all right?"

53

Dawn. The fire trucks have gone. He counted three earlier and the third one just rolled past. They were all around the Chest when he got off the night bus, alongside police cars that choked the street. For all the firemen and police officers on the corner, the shopkeeper was nowhere in sight. Kwasi hurried past the chaos, the taste of soot coating his mouth, all the way to the shopkeeper's house. The smell of burning followed him. In the quiet on the man's front step, he knocked and knocked and knocked. Footsteps sounded from inside, and lights clicked on somewhere, but the man didn't open up.

He has been in this alleyway since, unable to stand and walk away, watching to see when the police cars go. Perhaps it serves him right: it was probably Jericho and his friends who set the Chest on fire. He missed the ten-thirty to Ipswich. The Tube betrayed him. After holding him in a tunnel moments away from Liverpool Street Station for a painful twenty minutes (during which his phone's remaining battery life halved, for no reason), it released him into chaos. The platforms were dense walls of commuters, all of them queuing in crowds.

Kwasi imagined himself as a robot, a machine built to board that train. He made himself narrow as a knife and cut ahead in quick steps. He watched the floor stream about his trainers, from gray to off-white tiles to steps up and up and up into the glare of the station.

A cathedral of a station with time ticking everywhere: there on the row of black noticeboards suspended from on high, in fiery orange digits, and every digit was made of tiny dots. He thought of the book Kumar lent him, about Seurat and pointillism. How alive a scene could become, composed of so many brightly colored nodes. How each image defied replication. He remembers thinking then, it might be the only way to honestly depict the movement of water.

A sob squeezed up his throat, beneath the boards in the middle of the station, as flickering digits blurred, and the sob soured to anger.

He missed the train, of course, but got the next one and was only half an hour late, and he gave the men what they needed. Five of them, wearing coats inside a draughty husk of a house, and they gave him cash in return. The night had a hollowed-out feeling, and it was in their gaunt faces too. When he said he was going back that night they laughed.

"On what train?"

They advised him to chill, that there was no rush. Insisted he stay to charge his mobile. While it was charging, more people arrived. Girls too. He shrank under their rising voices. A girl said she'd drive him back, that she had to be in Brighton for the morning anyway. She didn't look old enough to be driving. Her car smelled of hazelnut and nail polish remover. On the drive she played songs he wished he didn't know, that had slipped under his skin in easier times. There were shadows in these songs that revealed themselves tonight. He pretended to be asleep. He got back in the small hours of the morning and gave the money to Selim's brother. Selim said he should stay. Jericho was snoring on the sofa, and Wade was there too, eating Hula Hoops.

"Why would you go home now?" Selim asked. "Your aunties will beat you on sight. Just go back later. You told them it's a sleepover, right?"

But still he left. He left with two hundred pounds zipped in his jacket. For a precious few steps, the night belonged to him. The street stretched like a red carpet. But then he saw the flames.

The last lights on the black stretch of the high street: orange-white-orange licking the Chest away.

All is quiet, now the police and firemen have gone, but ringing echoes in his ears, the day's noise thinned to a keening. He pushes himself up. Soaked, shivering. His legs are knotted with cramps. His throat is sandpaper. He walks away from town.

It takes twenty minutes to reach the brook from here, following the path that runs up from the park. Here, the underground river gushes. It is not green, as he drew it years ago. Neither is it blue and white, as it was when he visited it in his mind. It is deep brown and smells ruined. There are no ducks or fish or frogs. Concrete steps lead up from its banks. Rushes thin to weeds, which turn into pavement, which hardens into road. He follows the bus route toward the roundabout. The warehouses and not-quite-parks where he first glimpsed a gun.

Waits at the crossing for the green man to appear.

★

Home: Auntie Aha's embrace. The smell of onions and ginger.

Squid gathers them both in her massive arms. Holds his face and looks at him.

"Kwasi." Her eyes are red and puffy. "Did he hurt you?"

He thinks of the men, their big house in Ipswich. The smell of meat grilling, a cacophony of barking from the back room and icy air spreading through gaping windows.

"Kwasi."

"Oh, he is so cold."

"Kwasi. That man at the shop. Did he? That man. He is troubled."

"Did he hurt you?"

"How long have you been going there?"

"Did he?"

"Let him rest. Come."

"Kwasi, did that shopkeeper hurt you?"

Kwasi shakes his head.

Squid holds him tight. Her body shivers around him. She is not so big as she seems; she is not nearly so big.

★

Shouts wake him, voices from downstairs. He sits up. Women's voices. He pads across his room, before going out onto the landing. He peers between the banisters.

The front door is open. The old woman who some-times helped at the Chest stands waving her arms, her face flushed red, in the doorway.

"... burned the Chest. I just wanted to make sure you people know. Poor man's in hospital, he's in intensive care.

337

That's his whole life's work. Before you moved here, he ran it with his wife, the loveliest woman you could meet. And the Chest was all he had. All he was living for. So now your boy's a murderer. That's all I wanted to say. Well. Have a lovely day."

54

Jada.
 Here.
 In the hospital. Jadainthehospital.
 That they would keep her alive, slowly poisoning her,
and of course he took her, stole her away, and in the shop
they bathed in decades of music and
 filled themselves with tea. Her last days
 were
 bliss.

55

Voices at the door:

"Absolutely. I understand. It's just that we have had a number of reports that he was seen walking down the high street at night. We have footage of him taking the Underground. Do you know where he might have gone that night?"

Ma shakes her head.

The police officer leans into view, the top of his black helmet.

"We're going to need you to come to the station with us."

"Listen. I know my son. He wouldn't do anything like that."

"We just need to have a chat and work out what's happened."

Kwasi goes back up to his room. He puts his palms over his ears.

56

How a home is made:

From old sofas rescued from the skip, cheap beanbags and cushions. Sketches, collages, doodles, and paintings on old bedsheets, boards of flame-licked smoke-shaded wood, on lengths of ruined linen (which will be taped up as curtains), affirmations and words of hope and healing painted under the black night sky, taped to temporary walls of wood fences and one portable loo. Music: *Sgt. Pepper's Lonely Hearts Club Band. Artpop* and *Dookie*. All of it at once, from speakers great and small.

The Tin Shack arrives with ceremony on the second day (loaded on a huge rusty yellow lorry that gets stuck at the top of the street and reverses, beeping, and backs up traffic to the roundabout). The Tin Shack is a shipping container, which its owner, one digital nomad named Milshek, purchased with the intention of turning it into a tiny house. He comes, with his documentary film crew, to help them kit it out. They set it amid the ruins of the Chest and stretch a tarp canopy from its rear.

Friends of friends bring cushions and rugs and cover the

Tin Shack's floor until layers of fabric soften everything. When a Beatles song comes on, everyone sings.

Police arrive, of course. Phones are raised, as officers approach. Helmeted officers looking for a tussle, light glancing off their visors and the assorted accessories that stud their uniforms and belts. Seven, nine, thirteen officers coming like a swarm of ants.

"What's up?" Lake calls, hanging out of the Shack's doorway.

The police stop and squint up at him.

Lake is a photogenic saint, especially now his beard is back, and here is his close-up. The scene is live-streamed on twenty-eight Facebook accounts. An excerpt makes the evening news.

"We have every right to stay," Tulip calls. "We entered the Chest with the owner's permission. I've known Rupert for like ten years. It's a space for community, for sharing. The council, which is supposed to serve the community, wants us out. But then again, it seems like councils want to kick out ordinary people everywhere." She smiles. "We've also attracted tourists. You are most welcome, councillors."

The boy arrives two days in, beneath a huge black umbrella. He brings a backpack rammed with books and papers and crayons, pencils, Biros and felt tips. Tulip draws him into the Shack and holds him tight. They are shaking, her or him or both. Neither laughing nor sobbing.

"You're okay," she says.

"I didn't do it."

"What?"

"The fire."

Lake joins them, and explains what he can't say, that the

police took him to the station. That he came here as soon as he could.

Her arms tighten around him.

"I didn't start the fire," he says into her sweater.

"No one sane believes you did."

★

How a home is built:

Scrap materials secured and delivered through crowd-funding and Gumtree and Twitter. Cement and a mixer, bricks and plywood. Volunteers.

They build together. Press their hands into drying cement.

Journalists come. Following Lake's lead, the volunteers answer questions as one. Their drawings are auctioned each day at six online. He wasn't sure at first, but Lake said they have a moment, and the money they make can help them keep this going.

"It's the spirit of our high streets we need to fight for. It's not just about buying things, yeah? It's about community. About people being able to connect, find inspiration, and express themselves."

New ideas come every hour, from conversations around him, the buzz around them all; it feels as though everything he sees and draws becomes part of a stream, and a flood is surely coming. Somewhere, people understand. Or, Lake says, want to be seen as people who understand.

"We should defo prioritize giving to charities," Tulip says, "do as much good as we can. That's what this place is about, right?"

"What about the actual Chest?" Kwasi asks her. "How are we supposed to fix this place?" Another question remains too, one that twists his stomach, of what will remain when this is over. Everything is moving too fast: an unraveling, and it is not clear what will be left, of the money, of what he has drawn, separate from everyone else's work, of how much of the money can be traced back to his hands.

"Don't stress about it," Tulip says. "We have a special moment here. The more we show people what we're about, the more they will support us." Perhaps she senses the question shame won't let him ask, because she adds, "And your art is amazing. You'll get everything you put in back, and more. Exposure is everything."

Miri has taped a list of charities and causes to support by the Shack's door. The list is longer each time he looks. People keep adding to it, lots of the charities are related to the refugee crisis. Miri says what's happening in Syria is Britain's fault. "These are innocent people who just want to get on with their lives," she says.

They give to art collectives, too. Still, some disagree with this focus on giving; there is talk, at the start of each day, as smells of porridge and coffee fill the Shack, of investing.

"We should buy up some units. Should we try to talk to the landlord? We basically own next door too, might as well make it official."

They could definitely use more space. They have turned no one away. Some have parked vans in the car park behind, and others are putting up tents. They take turns and hotspot, sharing internet from their phones. Tweets of support inundate their accounts. From across London, France, Greece, Brazil, Portugal, Trinidad, Spain. They stream music, trade photos from around the world.

Despite all that is generous and hopeful here, sometimes Tulip gets this look, like she is at war with everything. It makes him wonder, if every battle leads to a bigger war, as rivers pour into the sea, as that list of causes grows, how much of this gnawing worry belongs to him and how much is from elsewhere. Whether he always wanted to draw like this or if something bigger is working through him. Whether he is here only to draw, like the journalists who come and film, each from a different angle, or to recolor something, to distort.

He wants to look up some of the causes on that list, to read more online, but it's best to not look at his phone; best not to see the messages where his aunties' questions await, where Jericho may or may not have left further instructions.

On day something or other, Councillor Obi walks up the high street, flanked by two other men—Tulip says they are from the council. They have come for him.

"Relax, it's all good," Lake says. "If they try to come in, you and I hop in the car and take a trip. Unless you *want* to go back. You want to go back?"

"Not a bit."

"My guy."

Councillors only stand outside, thankfully, talking to camera people from the press vans. Darkness is falling when Councillor Obi turns to address the Shack.

He raises a megaphone and says they are causing a public nuisance. "If you come out, we can talk through this and make sure everyone gets home safe."

"We're talking now," Tulip shouts back. "We want to build, not destroy. It's your council that wants to tear down our high street and turn it into a commuter resort. When

Rupert came to you for funding, you turned him away. You basically told him his business was worthless."

As the councillors go, everyone cheers.

"Hey, K. I'm doing another run to the shops," Lake says. "You want to come help?"

"Where will you go?"

"Anywhere. I'm taking the car. Going to see my sister and I'll be back tomorrow."

"There is somewhere . . ." he says. "It's not far away."

"Yeah?" Lake says, smiling. "Miri," he calls as he goes. "Are you coming?"

57

This time he awakens all at once. Tipped complete from sleep, he stretches his legs under the blanket. Movement sets off throbbing in all the places where his bones meet.

"Rupert." Councillor Obi is perched on a chair beside the bed.

He closes his eyes and tries to sink back into sleep.

"I'm not leaving, Rupert. Not today. Not without a conversation."

He grips the edges of his mattress and pushes himself up. The ward is dazzling, and light punches the backs of his eyes.

"How are you feeling?"

"Brilliant. Yourself?"

Councillor Obi's hands splay over his knees. "I've spent all day trying to sort out the Chest. People keep coming. It's something of a squat. Some internet celebrities have taken Tulip's side. They like the cartoons. The sketches and comics those 'kids' draw."

Laughter warms Rupert's chest. "Really."

"There's not much funny about it. It is unsafe. With your substances in there, and so many young people—"

347

"Harmless," Rupert says. "It's harmless stuff in there."

"I don't think you are in a position to call anything harmless. If not for Elaine, you could have been in serious trouble."

"Thank heavens for Elaine. Can we all go home now?"

Councillor Obi bows his head.

"Councillor. As soon as they let me out, I'm done."

Councillor Obi straightens up. "What's this?"

"I've done my time. Tell the landlord you want to buy it. Have him sell to developers if you want. I can go up there myself and ask the kids to clear out. Should have left years ago."

Obi shifts on his chair. He sits forward, bowing his head, as though leaning into a prayer. "You have to understand, Rupert," he says, "that I would never try to disrespect that space, as some people are suggesting."

"I suppose you have bigger plans for it. I know you like to be in everyone's business, but maybe you ought to pay more attention to what's going on in your own home."

"What do you mean by that?"

He is thinking of Jada, how determined she was to fight the council to get a license to serve drinks. She said they would make it their mission, that she had friends in California who were campaigning to educate, to decriminalize and destigmatize. She said they would be part of a movement, a global awakening. Sickness stopped her before she began, and he has made a mess of it now, has completely failed to take any of what she started forward.

"Really, Rupert. What do you mean?" the councillor asks again.

He lets his eyelids rest. "I have seen your boy hanging

around the old Barclays at night. Seen him messing about in the park with his friends and all, and I'm not the only one."

Councillor Obi stands. "It's good to see you're recovering. Please. Get some sleep."

58

Five days after becoming the Shack, the Chest transforms once more. This transformation, which will be far from its last, is an unmaking, a scattering of all who made it home. It starts and ends like this: the shopkeeper returns. He stands out on the pavement where for years boxes of donated goods were piled, where locals slowed to appreciate one-of-a-kind window displays. Today, the shopkeeper taps his stick on the pavement and shouts to those inside:

"Everybody out. House rules. Whatever your issue is, whether it's with your parents, your universities, bosses, exes, your government, races, genders, go on and settle it over tea. In your own kitchens, or bedrooms, or your fancy cafés. My stash did not grow on trees. I worked for it. Earn your tea. Share it, by all means, but earn it first."

"Rupert." Tulip, wearing Miri's purple lipstick, steps out of what appears to be a shipping container. "Are you okay?"

"I'm well." He opens his arms and catches her in an embrace. She smells terrible. "Will be even better ..." He stands back and looks at her. This is important, he really shouldn't smile. "... once you all clear out."

350

"We're not using your herbs. That's not what this is about."

"Whatever it's about, it's not my problem."

Her face falls.

But.

She is not his. None of them are.

Not even the boy, Kwasi, who peers from the container's doorway now.

Not even the Chest.

"What's wrong?" asks the lad with the dreadlocks—River or Rain—as he comes out. "What's up?"

"Your time, is what's up," Rupert says. "I want you all out."

★

The sign at the bus stop says no buses will stop here; all services have been diverted.

"Will you tell me what happened?" Tulip asks. "Here." She passes him a paper cup. "It's just water. They wouldn't tell us anything. I went to Elaine's, and her husband said you overdosed."

He sits beside her on the bus stop bench. She is wearing flip-flops with fluffy pink socks. "I went a little too far. I think we all have, at this point. Tulip, it pains me to be harsh, but I have seen what people are saying. The Chest was never about this. Jada was no communist. She took pride in earning her way, we both did. We wanted a delightful shop, to serve and watch people. To do our business freely."

"But come on." Her voice is small, tremulous. "We're close. We're creating something."

There is a point in the road before which vehicles falter. Some sort of elongated pothole, a great rupture in the

351

street. Overly cautious drivers brake early and slow the vehicles queuing behind. What a curious sight. Inexplicable
regret envelops him, an appreciation of loss, for he never
noticed this pattern before. His vision grows foggy; brake
lights shimmer.

Tulip is sitting so close he can hear her halting breaths.

"The Chest is—was—a business. That's what the high
street is. Politics happens in the town hall. Jada and I wanted
the Chest to do good, but that was our choice because it
is our business."

"You don't think work should be about doing good?"

"Work is about meeting needs. Being useful to others
means meeting your own needs. Same for every generation. All that changes is what people need."

She seems unable to blink. Her eyes are shot with red,
and shadowed. At last, she lowers her gaze. "Isn't it funny,
how just when we were getting somewhere, the Chest
mysteriously burned? Councillor Obi must be—"

"Obi did not burn this place. Neither did his son. Maybe
it was a terrible accident. Perhaps, this time, I lit too many
candles."

Tulip frowns. "Wait," she says. "After I went home, what
exactly happened? You said you were going to finish your
tea, and then? Did you turn everything off? Blow the
candles out?"

"Whatever happened already happened. Something was
bound to go wrong. What a state it was. Jada would have
sorted out the wiring, would have raised it with the landlord earlier. I didn't want him down there."

Traffic washes up and down the street.

"So," Tulip says, "what now?"

"I have a box of paradises. Places I might retire to. I'll

go home and look through them. Perhaps I'll flip a coin." He permits himself a smile. "Now I have some coins to flip."

"So. Everything we talked about. That's all just over?"

"These things come and go. It's a vast world out there, and a big country too. You don't need to pull stunts like these. Just listen, for a moment. There are proper channels for changing things, if that's really what you want. You have half an art degree. You're smart. You'll figure out how to get to where you want to be. Anyway." He rolls his shoulders slowly until he hears the muted click. "I had better head off. I wish you luck with it. All of it. I know you'll do all right."

"Will you come in for just a second? Kwasi would love to see you again. He's been through hell because of this, but he stayed."

A cruel card to play. He feels heavy, like he might sink through the asphalt.

"You have to say goodbye, if you're serious about leaving."

"I can't. But would you do something for me?" He reaches inside his pack. Takes out the little photo frame. "Please see that this is returned to its creator."

"How did you—"

"Just make sure the boy gets it."

She places the frame on her lap. "Please come in. For two minutes. The kid has a surprise for you."

"Surprises," he says. "I've endured more than my fair share. Go on and enjoy your surprises and let me get home."

"Wait here," she says.

He watches until she vanishes down the alleyway, and then, leaning against the bench for support, rises.

One last time down the high street. The smells: sweat, pizza, tobacco. The sounds: a faint melody (surely not the Beatles), wheezing traffic, the *thud-thud* of steps behind. The yapping of a very excited dog. And a voice shouting Rupert, wait.

59

He always ruins it. Whenever things are going okay, he ends up breaking his own rules. Forbidden places are magnetic and he is all paper clips tonight.

Something drastic must have happened, for Rupert to come back and yell at them the way he did.

On his phone, Kwasi searches for Councillor Obi. Sure enough, there are recent interviews, saying the council has worked closely with all local businesses, how it's mostly people who don't live locally here, how it's all performative. He goes back to the search page and reads far down the list of links. Stroking his screen with numb fingers, he reads of King Obi's career. A human rights lawyer. It says that he campaigns for kinder asylum pathways, for priority housing for refugees, for student exchange programs. "People move in order to improve their lives and to share their skills with new communities," he is quoted saying in one article. "They should be empowered to do so."

Kwasi reads down the search results, back through several years, wondering if there is anything on here about his other jobs, the ones he and Jericho are not allowed to talk about. He looks around, and it's a sickening feeling, the knowledge that he could possibly find some dirt on Councillor Obi that might give Tulip's friends something to negotiate with. Now his skin simmers with it, that there might be a trace of Da's work on here too.

Miri arrives with pizzas. He feeds half of his—the chorizo and chicken pieces and some of the crust too—to the dog.

"Are they still at the bus stop?" he asks.

Lake nods. "Don't worry about them. Rupert's well."

Something serious must have happened. He thinks of Selim's brother. The guys in puffy jackets, in the house in Ipswich. The girl who drove him back. The pizza is coming to life in his stomach.

"You good?" Lake asks. "Want to take Wander for a walk around the car park?"

"You take him," Kwasi says, crossing his arms.

"All right. There's more pizza if you want."

When they go, Kwasi lies on his back and looks at his phone. Searches Councillor Obi and Africa to Europe. No one seems to have made the connection online; none of the search results are relevant. Probably King Obi did all his work with Da under some other name. He must have been super smart about it.

Now he can't stop thinking of Auntie Baby. That enough searches might bring up a connection to her, that enough time spent looking could surely return everyone, every auntie who moved through his house.

From there, it is a downhill rush, into the swell of messages waiting to be read. One message leads to another, notifications draw him in without mercy. Messages from Jericho, which say they are in fact Uncle Obi, and *can we have a chat?* He wants to talk about Kwasi's art. *You don't need to be involved with people like this, Kwasi.* More messages, from Ma, Squid and Auntie Aha.

. . .

Come home.
Come home.
Kwasi, please.
Please, we don't want to get the police to look for you. Come home.
Your dadda is here.

Kwasi gets up. Steps carefully around Tulip's dozing friends. Climbs out into the night.

Tulip is up ahead, running down the alleyway.

And now he can't move. Rupert is not even with her, though she said he would be. "Hey," she calls. "Where are you going?"

It's silly to feel bad. He has already helped a lot. "I have to. Sorry."

"Just a second. Wait." She hands him a framed drawing. His drawing from years ago. It feels tiny in his hands.

And now here comes the man, the oldest shopkeeper in town. Limping, moving as fast as he can. Wander scurries at Kwasi's side, running around him and ahead, stopping and waiting for him to catch up.

They have never hugged. He doesn't know what to do with his arms. Wander jumps up at him and so he kneels on the wet concrete and ruffles his fur.

The man leans against the wall by the overflowing bin.

"You're better," Kwasi says.

"So I've been told." The man is watching the ground. His face is in shadow.

"Where will you go?"

"I'm not sure, really."

"Are you going to just take a train and see where you end up? I used to do that, on the Underground."

"There's an idea."

"You guys should come inside. There's loads left," Tulip calls. She's back, holding a pizza box. Wander trots over to her, yapping.

"We're okay," Kwasi shouts back.

"You've really made this place something," Rupert says, looking toward the squat.

"It was cool before. The way you made it."

"It was."

"What do you think will happen to it?"

"I think . . ." The man glances down toward the road. It's dead quiet since the bus got diverted. "I think that might be up to you. I've worried about that long enough."

The man looks up to the empty sky. How small and thin he is, under the darkness of the universe.

Kwasi offers him the drawing. "Keep it."

"I couldn't."

"Remember our deal? That you could keep my drawings if I drew more stuff. And I did. I want you to keep this one."

"Really, I—"

"Don't go and just forget this place. Sometimes it's like you pretend you don't care, and you forget stuff if it doesn't go how you wanted it to. But you should remember. Seriously." He looks back toward the Shack, which hums faintly with music and echoes of laughter. The basement is still there below, charred and silent and ruined. Nothing remains of all that was exchanged, of all that was created. Nothing but themselves, for as long as they remember. "It was good. The best."

60

All the ways he pictured meeting Da again, sometimes in Ghana, sometimes here, sometimes at school, or at swimming, at Councillor Obi's house, in the sea of faces at carnival, quietly, here at home, he never imagined that Da himself would change, that time could have reduced him.

Da has become old. It hurts to look at him. His hair is sparse and graying. How shrunken he seems, back in his armchair at last. New glasses, square ones that look incorrect, make his eyes small and scared.

The sitting room is too tidy and clean. Quiet, in a ruffled sort of way; like several arguments have worked themselves out here.

"Drink up," Auntie Aha says.

He lifts the cup and sips. Water never tasted so rich. He drinks it in four gulps.

"So. Tell us. This Rupert," Da asks. "How many times did you visit him?"

"Oh," Ma says, and gives Da a look. "Obi said the man has left. He left and his lawyer is handling business there. Can we please leave it?"

Da does not move.

"You can go and take your bath," Squid tells Kwasi. "And sleep. Early start tomorrow."

It is crawling up his back, the certainty that more chaos is coming. "Why? Where are we going?"

Da sighs.

"We are going home," Ma says. "We're going back." She throws Squid a wicked glare and walks out toward the kitchen.

"What. Are we moving back to South London?"

"To Ghana," Da says. "The house is ready. A very big house. Just for Mama and our sisters, and you and me. I will send someone else to watch this house. You will like it in Ghana. We all deserve a break."

He's already shaking his head.

"Kwasi."

He puts his empty cup on the floor. "I like it here."

"Here does not like you."

Auntie Aha sucks her teeth.

"We will pack up tomorrow and go and stay with Uncle James in Luton. As soon as we have tickets, we go."

"I don't want to."

"How much will you take from them before you understand? This is not our place."

"It is my place. You have to try, to make it your place."

"I didn't try?" Da sits forward. "Do you know about trying? How we tried? I worked very, very hard for Obi, to find people for his restaurants, people for his barbershops and hairdressers and cleaning company. Even *escort* businesses. All of them, across Europe. Do you know how much we have given?"

"Don't make me go."

"Kwasi. In this life, we must do many things that we

would rather not. Do you think I wanted to return to Ghana and leave you here? Do you think I wanted to *leave* Ghana in the first place? These people will never—"

"They like my drawings. They pay for them. That's how much they like them."

"Oh. They find you amusing for now. Okay. These same people accusing you of arson, of carrying drugs? Let me tell you this. The only time some people like to hear about men so black as you and I is when we are dying. That's when they become interested—when they know we are going to die. At school they say you are a problem, they want to give you medicines to change the way you think. Do you think they like you?" Da says something very fast in Ga.

Kwasi shrivels inside.

"They do like me," he says. "Maybe some people don't, but lots of people do. I've had video calls with people in Greece and Spain and other places in Europe who believe in my work. In my art. They want me to make a graphic novel. They'll help me to do it."

"You are a boy, you can only see things from your height. You don't see how the world is turning, how this place is becoming more hostile."

He explains it then, how all of this started, with his drawing from years ago. That more of his work is selling, even as they speak. "Look on the website," he says, and from his phone sends the link to one of the earliest articles to Da's number. "I wanted you to see it in real life. I had all my drawings in frames, in the shop. That's why I kept going there. Lots got damaged in the fire, but I kept making more."

"This one is your painting?" Da asks. He looks crushed.

His hand is on his cheek, as he looks through the website on his phone. "So it is true? This is your own drawing? Yours alone?"

"Yes," Kwasi says.

"They won't give you anything," Squid says. "Have they given you your money?"

"I gave those pictures to the Chest. To the shop, I mean. I wanted to help save it, so it wouldn't have to close."

"But it's closed. So what, will they give you your money?"

He looks up at the opposite wall. It is a blur in his head.

"Did they talk about money?" Da asks again. "Or did you just trust them, and let them tell you anything?" Da rests his chin on his cupped hand, like his head is too heavy for his neck. And the light in his eyes is wrong somehow, it's like he is looking beyond this moment, seeing more than Kwasi. "At some point, you have to be practical. Otherwise people will treat you anyhow."

Annoyance bristles inside him, scratching against his collarbone. "It's not just about money," Kwasi says. "I have more drawings anyway. And even more I need to work on. I need to stay here. There is heaps more to do. And Uncle Obi said he can help. He said we should talk about it together."

Da is silent for a long time. And then at last he says, "Take your time and think about how you would like to proceed. Obi will help you if you want to stay here, maybe if you stay with him. But think very carefully on it."

A NEW START

Spring 2016

61

There is a boy in the town on the bridge. He sits in the sunshine in the new gallery, the one on the corner, a stone's throw from the bus stop. He watches through the glass and draws. People. Trees. Rivers. Shops. Things that no longer exist and things that might never be fully realized. He draws visitors, who come in to look around, or to buy coffee at the kiosk.

Some days it feels clearer, what exactly he is trying to draw, in so many separate pieces. He is trying to draw a kind of home, a scattered kind of place, glimpses of which appear in unexpected spaces, in moments that call him back. It comes with a certain aroma, a mix of lavender and coffee, of shoe polish and ginger and rain. It manifests in lulls, when quiet falls. A new sense of home develops too, every time Ma videocalls him. It is in the glare of daylight behind her, and the shine on her earrings. It is in the steady hush of the ceiling fan. Ma smiles more over videocall, she says sunshine is their inheritance, that she forgot how gently time can move, and how patient time can be. "Everything happens well in God's timing," she often says. "It's not our place to worry." And then she seems apologetic, like she has remembered everything too late. "Don't let worry become your master," she says. "Remember whose child you are. God is always surprising us, isn't He? Look at what He has done."

Sometimes he wishes she would see how much of this grew from *his* plan, and most of what has happened was because of his work and King Obi's help, but mostly he just agrees. She tells stories, about what the aunties are doing, about his cousins at the new house. He misses her sometimes, but missing her feels cozy. He never really missed Ma ever before. It must be a good sign. It means more happiness is in that house waiting, and soon he'll visit that place too.

King Obi says he should shout anytime he wants to visit Ghana. "I've only been there once before," he said, "in my student days, to the castle at Elmina. About time Jericho got to see it." And then King Obi lowered his voice. "Of course, if you want to go just to see your family without us behaving like tourists, that's fine as well."

King Obi is really not as bad as Jericho said. Maybe someday Jericho will agree. Jericho reminds him of Da lately, the way he keeps coming up with new ideas, playing with them for a while, and then moving on to something new. Jericho loves to take credit for things too, but it was fun working together, to make the second guest room Kwasi's bedroom. Even when they argue he learns something. Like the other day Jericho revealed he has a girlfriend.

"That's the only reason I'm not going out that much. She's got me listening to all this old jazz. Proper old hip-hop too. There's so much of it."

He hears Jericho talking on videocall late some nights, although Kwasi has yet to see or hear who is on the other end.

When he asks if Jericho is going to invite her over, Jericho turns the conversation on him. "Gemma is asking about you," he'll say. Or "There's this new girl at school, she's so weird, I reckon you'd get on. I can invite her over for you if you want?"

"It's okay," Kwasi says. "Maybe another time. I have loads to do."

Here is a boy who will not be moved, not until he has finished. Though his new friends in Spain keep pestering him to come visit. Especially now everyone is working themselves up about the referendum.

"But if people vote yes," Marco says on the video chat now, "imagine. *Guau*. I mean. You guys are just going to be trapped on that puny island."

Kwasi grins at the screen, where Marco is sculpting wet globules of clay in his studio on the outskirts of Barcelona.

"Give me a second," Marco says. "I need to turn on the fan."

Kwasi looks over the vast windows. King Obi let the Collective build the maker's gallery on the condition that they have big clear windows at the front, that they remain open, that nothing murky goes on inside, with or without tea. Which is fine, because a clear window, and all this daylight, helps Kwasi to see, and the better he sees, the better he draws.

King Obi likes to see everything he draws, and to discuss what he wants to make next while they eat dinner.

The King also insists on hearing about all the people he meets online, whether they are members of the Collective or not. Sometimes King Obi has good ideas for people he should talk to next. That's how he got talking to Candace in Jamaica, and the kids she teaches to paint there. He also talks to school kids in Accra, who share ideas of what to draw, ask advice for how to showcase their work, and when he will visit. Home is in these moments of connection too, of seeing people who get it, who are moving toward this same space that calls him too. And this corner here is the center of it all, the place everything begins from and returns to.

Da asks about math now and again, says it's good to have a backup plan, alongside his art, but now he is homeschooled, by a tutor Kumar's mum recommended, it is hard to measure how well he is doing. Although he's started toward the GCSE, lessons are moving at an excruciatingly slow pace. It is fine, he reminds himself. There is time.

"If they vote to leave," Marco says, "honestly, we might never meet. Without, I don't know, applying for a visa or something. I mean, if you guys leave the EU, will you even have internet?"

They laugh. Kwasi is mostly laughing at the way Marco's microphone, internet connection, electricity, distance from Britain, and his own speakers, laptop, electricity, and internet connection make garbled crackles of their giggles.

"I can't believe you guys are seriously going to vote on this. If they vote yes, Kwasi, you had better get on a plane soon; this might be your last chance to see our paradise."

Kwasi smiles and says, "If."

He will need a better reason to move. All the world is here. He could live years and years in this same chair. Yes, he could happily remain always, in this space he has made.

ACKNOWLEDGMENTS

I am thankful to my wonderful and legendary agent, Juliet Mushens, for believing in this story from the start, and for her advice, enthusiasm, and encouragement throughout this journey so far. To my fantastic editors, Francesca Main and Katherine Nintzel, for seeing the heart of this story, and for their brilliance, creativity, tenacity, and support.

To workshop friends and tutors I met at the UEA, who shared feedback and wisdom with kindness and care. To the Turn Up Squad, who gave me indescribable happiness on nights out in Norwich—and so much more besides. To the Kowitz Foundation for their generous support. To *Lolwe*, for publishing my first short story, and for the beautiful space it's opening. To Ink.Academy, for providing thorough and incisive feedback on earlier projects, and for many joyous evenings spent (happily) lost around Covent Garden.

To former colleagues and fellow volunteers who cheered me on and inspired me.

To Ms. Parfitt, for telling me to keep writing.

To friends and relatives who told me stories before I could read, who indulged my curiosity, joined in with my imaginings, who kept asking, "What happens next?," who accompanied me to talks, exhibitions, cinema trips in Wood Green, and on long walks around Brighton, who called me out of solitude and insisted I read to them, who walked me to East Barnet Library, enriched my life with music, laughter, cups of coffee and tea, love, and so much more.

ABOUT THE AUTHOR

SUSSIE ANIE is a British Ghanaian writer, born in London in 1994. Her writing has been published in Lolwe and was shortlisted for the 2020 White Review Short Story Prize. She has an MA in creative writing from the University of East Anglia, where she was the recipient of the 2018–19 Kowitz Scholarship. *To Fill a Yellow House* is her debut novel.